To Lillian Emma

BLEEDER

Prologomena

There are some who presume so far on their wits that they think themselves capable of measuring the whole nature of things by their intellect, in that they esteem all things true which they see, and false which they see not. Accordingly, in order that man's mind might be freed from this presumption, and seek the truth humbly, it was necessary that certain things far surpassing his intellect should be proposed to man by God.

— St. Thomas Aquinas

We must begin with what is known.

— Aristotle

CHAPTER 1

My Volvo's windshield wipers slapped away spots of mid-March drizzle, chanting *shouldn't, shouldn't, shouldn't.* The traffic thinned, the road narrowed to two lanes, the sky turned gun-metal gray, and the Chicago music stations crackled away into static.

The patchwork fields of rural Illinois rolled away from the ditches in soft waves, with snow lying in stripes across the rows of cornstalk stubble, like a lathered but unshaven face. The rusted road signs became harder to read through the chilly mist. When I saw more cows than cars, I wondered if I'd taken a wrong turn. *To err is human, to forgive bovine,* I told myself, checking the cell phone. Was the signal too weak to reach anyplace civilized? Even if it could, I'd wait a long time for Triple-A to show up out here in the boonies if I had any trouble.

I imagined the operator saying, *We need a street address, sir.* There isn't one, I tell you; I'm in the middle of nowhere. *What is the nearest address, sir?* I'm near a barn with a faded Mail Pouch Chewing Tobacco ad. Community-college teachers can't afford a new car with a global positioning system or the monthly fee to have the service on a cell phone. *Even I have that, sir.* That's great; maybe it can tell you where I am. *Very funny, sir. The truck will still need a number.*

I glanced at the torn Triple-A map, draped on the passenger seat. The blue capillaries of county roads spidered out from the state roads' red arteries. The towns pimpled the white page like blackheads on a freshman's face. A muscular pickup truck hissed past, spitting into my windshield. *Gun control means using both hands,* snickered the bumper sticker. Distracted, I ran over a dead raccoon, and the thump of it turned my stomach.

That's when a familiar heat arose in my chest and my breastbone pressed into my heart, crushing it. The double yellow lines in the road writhed like serpents. I slipped my foot off the gas, angled the wheel, and rolled to a stop in the gravel shoulder. Breathe in, breathe out. In, out. Focus on something. That sign up ahead — the one with the big red star.

It's not uncommon for gunshot victims, the doctor told me. *Anxiety attacks can be a response to a stressful event: an act of violence, a job change, the loss of a spouse by divorce or death.* Lucky me: I had all three. I was shot. I was on a Leave Of Absence from the college. And Peggy died when the leukemia came out of remission two years ago.

Breathe in, two, three. Breathe out, two, three. *Wait quietly. It will pass. You are not going to get lost. You are not going to die in this lonely place.*

The sky lightened. My breastbone released its grip. A pickup with a horse trailer whooshed by, and the Volvo shuddered. My heartbeat returned to a trot from a gallop. *You are going to be OK. Keep going. The roadkill and that bumper sticker set you off.*

Gun control means using both hands.

Indeed.

The sign ahead was for Red Star Gas, and I decided to swallow my city pride and ask for directions. The concrete was veined with cracks, and the weeds reached up from them like the hands of buried men clawing their way out. One pump, shrouded in silvery spider webs, was *out of service*. Discolored paint flaked off the building like scabs. A man with high Indian cheekbones and black hair spraying from a White Sox cap reached my window before I gathered the nerve to unbuckle my seatbelt and get out.

"Hey, meester?" He knocked at the window with a gold ring. *Tik tik.* "You want fill 'er up?"

His corn-colored teeth spread in a two-octave grin, and the dark eyebrows undulated like caterpillars. I checked the gauge, nodded and popped the gas-cap lock.

While he circled to the back, I shouldered open the door and swung my cane into position. The film instructor gave it to me in the hospital, and we joked that it should be called Citizen Cane. I dug the rubber tip into the cement, gripped the brass head, and rehearsed how to get out. For six weeks after the hip surgery, my physical therapist Paula taught me in the transfer training how to sit up, how not to twist or cross my leg, since the pin was screwed in, not cemented. She said I'd be OK to drive after two months, provided I kept up with the treadmill, the isokinetic leg presses with ankle weights, and the balancing exercise where I walked through the rungs of a ladder laid on the floor. I'd been good about it all, so that I could retreat to my brother Dan's hunting cabin by mid-March and get started on the book I'd always wanted to write on Aristotle in peace and quiet. I just expected to do it during a sabbatical leave. Not like this.

The ideal man bears the accidents of life with dignity and grace, making the best of circumstances, Aristotle reminded me.

I levered out.

"You Chicago, eh?" the leathery attendant called.

He aimed the gas pump at me like a pistol.

"Yes," I replied.

"All the way out here?"

"Visiting relatives."

"Yeah, sure." He lowered the nozzle, pumped gas and pointed at Citizen Cane. "What's wrong with the leg, *señor?*"

"I was shot. In December."

The eyebrows turned into Mexican jumping beans. "*Ay, caramba,*" he said with a whistle. "An accident, no?"

"A college girl with a touchy 9 millimeter in her purse. She pulled it on a rival in a hallway catfight over a boy. I broke it up and —"

When the first bullet hit my chest, I thought of Peggy. Is this what it feels like to die, not in pain, really — the shock prevented that — but in wide-eyed surprise, that it should come so soon and so stupidly? Once the second shot shattered the head of my right femur where it forms step in the acetabular groove of the pelvis and I dropped to the tiles with my blood fanning across the floor, I wished Peggy could have gone like this, not by having her blood poisoned by leukemia, draining her life away.

"*¿Señor?* Then wha' happen?"

"Well, I got in the way, that's all," I concluded.

"Anyone else hurt?"

I shrugged. "Just me. Some guys have all the luck."

"So you are here to see the healer, eh?"

I squinted at him. "The what?"

"The healer in River Falls? You know, for the leg."

"I'm going to River Falls," I conceded. "But I'm not going to see any —"

"Ees OK," the man said with a cackle. "I talk to a dozen people like you today who are lost. The only reason people from Chicago are on this road is to find him. I hope, *señor,* you have made your motel reservations."

"I'm staying in my brother's hunting cabin in Tall Pines Park."

"That is good, very good," the man said with a wag of his head, "for there are no rooms for twenty miles around."

The Tall Pines Park sign, peppered with buckshot, appeared three miles from the town turn-off, just as the gas-station man had told me. The cartoon raccoon on the park billboard told me the fire danger was LOW today. It did not say the danger was high for raccoons.

I decided to find Dan's cabin first, and then check in with the resident managers. The car crunched on the sand-and-cinder road past their permanent trailer, its aluminum awning festooned with red and green plastic lanterns. A golden light glowed inside. A country-craft sign out front with crossed fishing poles bid "Welcome. Beth and Hadley Berger." White wooden arrows nailed to a post directed "Cabins left, camping right." I found the cul-de-sac for the three-season cabins and rolled to a stop at #3, the farthest one. The others looked vacant, as one might expect.

No one will be there 'til Memorial Day, Reed, Dan had assured me. *You can write and do your exercises without no one botherin' ya. Just what you need.*

"I dunno, Danny," I had hesitated. "It's the middle of nowhere and —"

C'mon, you crybaby, he said, whacking my head lightly with a rolled-up newspaper. *It's downstate Illinois, not Africa. What are you afraid of?*

Fear is pain arising from the anticipation of evil, Aristotle whispered.

I shoved open the car door, grasped Citizen Cane, and swung out my legs with help from my cupped hand. The bracing air sent a shiver through me, but it felt good after the nervous drive. I pressed out with my elbows on the doorframe. The goose-down vest rustled on the steel. Once upright, I held my breath. No pain. If it ached, I could take some aspirin without any bad interaction with the anxiety meds.

I dug in my vest pocket for the skeleton key with Dan's Mack Truck bulldog key chain. Just as Dan said, I faced only a single step up to the porch and front door. The therapist told me stairs would be tricky for a long time. I chipped away some ice-crystals from the lock and then fit the key inside. It clicked. The door creaked open. Too easily, I thought. There'll be a draft.

The musty cabin looked spare but suitable, decorated in Early St. Vincent DePaul. A rocker with alligatored black paint flanked a stone fireplace. Freshly chopped wood filled a metal bucket beside it. Bless Dan's heart. And it was all one floor; no loft, second floor, or basement to think about, and I'd obviously never need to visit the insulated crawl space. The dread of descending even a few steps sent me into a spin. I still couldn't "find my leg" as the therapist put it. And when the meds made me drowsy, the balance problem worsened.

I elbowed the door shut against the moaning wind. The calico window curtains fluttered. The plank floor squeaked. I checked the narrow kitchen — tested the light switch, the sink, the stove. All on, just as Dan promised he'd do when he passed through on the way to Iowa in his 18-wheeler.

When the second-hand Frigidaire hummed into life, I remembered how Dan said everything would be stocked and ready: cold dark beer, brie, dill pickles and sauerkraut, chocolates and red wine. What a kidder. He knew that anything fermented or pickled, anything with tyramine — and it was a long list — could react with the MAO Inhibitors and burst a blood vessel in my brain. It was the main reason most people stayed away from MAOIs when choosing anxiety meds. They preferred the mild dizziness or diarrhea of SSIs like Prozac or Zoloft to the extremely vigilant diet of MAOIs. No one wanted to die from eating a chocolate bon-bon or black out from drinking a glass of Beaujolais.

Most people can't handle MAOIs, the doctor said. *They can cause more problems than they solve.*

They worked a miracle for me.

I opened the fridge — bottled water, white bread, deli chicken slices, tuna and a brand-name baloney. Dan figured either the chicken, fish, or the baloney would be safe. Processed meats were iffy; I'd have to consult my list of forbidden foods before I made a sandwich. The cabinets were full of chicken soup — no doubt Dan had seen it served to me in the hospital. In the lower cabinets, I recognized the pots and frying pans from our Boy Scout days together, the kind that fit inside each other and the frying pan handle screwed down to hold the kit together. *So this is where they went. I thought we'd lost them.*

I shuffled to the small bedroom, where I tested the rail Dan nailed to the bed frame. The yard-sale dresser drawers stuck a little. I picked up the Princess phone. Dead. Guess he figured I had the cell, so why bother getting it reconnected.

Back in the parlor, I noticed the cherry desk — or was it a sewing table? It was chipped and speckled with white paint, as though it had spent time in a rural garage as a workbench. It still had the price on one of its graceful legs, marked with felt pen on yellow masking tape. Dan got a good deal. I brushed away some dust and cobwebs, set up the laptop, and loaded a CD of Strauss's "Waltz in C Major" for a serene background. I certainly wasn't going to dance to it.

It was while using the facilities that I first heard it — a scraping noise in the walls. At first I thought it might be a tree branch rubbing the cabin in the wind, or a squirrel at the window. The scratching and shuffle moved across the wall behind the pine paneling. Bits of wood and plaster crumbled behind it. Silence. I listened. The scratching started again, little claws on drywall, crawling. My flesh crawled with it. I hadn't noticed any droppings in the kitchen, but I figured the cabin had chipmunks, shrews, mice — or worse, bats — living in the wall. I tapped it with the cane. Crumbs of plaster tumbled, and the scratching stopped. Something would have to be done about this. I'd have to keep the kitchen extra clean. *Ye gods, did they come out from the walls at night?* I could set up traps around the bed and try not to step on one in the morning.

I pulled on my Chicago Cubs ear-band and gloves, checked for the key in my vest, seized Citizen Cane, and scuffed outside. I'd already had one anxiety episode today; no need to dwell on the image of little blood-sucker vampires in the walls and have another attack so soon.

The walk to the manager's trailer in the cold air did me some good. I took my time, nose down to watch for ruts and the potholes where thin ice glittered like cellophane. The burr oaks raised their gnarly arms to the slate sky. Soaring honey locust trees swayed, the Norway spruces swished. Patches of snow hid in hollows from the oncoming Spring. A tang of applewood smoke incensed the air, the managers' woodstove, I presumed. I looked forward to sitting by a blazing fireplace myself. I might have to ask for some matches. I had quit smoking my pipe when Peggy was first diagnosed with the cancer.

An RV the size of a small bus entered the park and rumbled down the right fork toward the camping area. The silver-haired driver waved.

I stopped and saluted with the cane. Through my polite smile I thought: who in their right mind goes camping in a drippy and cold northern Illinois March? It can't just be the swell off-season rates. Of course, they were probably wondering the same thing: *Doris, lookie there — what's a crip doing out here in the middle of March? Homer, honey, be nice: he's here to see that healer the Mexican gas-station man done told us about.*

Shrugging off the thought, I tugged my collar up against the sharp wind. Hot soup, a snapping fire. That would fill the rest of the evening. I'd plan out the week. I'd write —

"Watch out, mister!"

I skipped aside by instinct. My hip flared. I sucked in my breath. Two bikes clattered by, with boys dressed in parkas and ski caps. They spun through the loose sand and pumped for the campground.

"Sorry, mister!" one called over his shoulder.

I gritted my teeth. I steadied myself and eyed the two boys pull wheelies and drop out of sight. Facing that way, I realized the smoke was coming from the campsites. And that smell: was someone grilling meat outdoors? In March? Odd. Must be a burger joint nearby, I guessed.

Just before I reached the worn path to the manager's trailer, the front door swung open. A portly woman in a puffy coat backed out the storm door, a large board under one arm, bending for the inner door to pull it shut. I offered to help.

"Oh dearie, you startled me," she said, clutching the board. She smiled warmly, but instantly her eyes creased in worry. "You here for a campsite?"

"No, ma'am," I replied. "I'm Reed Stubblefield — Dan's brother?"

"Oh, sure," she said, eyebrows lifted with relief. She tucked some frosty hair back into her beret. "Danny told me all about you. The college teacher. Exceptin' he didn't say you were such a nice-looking man."

"It's the cold," I said. "It tightens my skin."

She laughed. "But it don't stop you from blushin'."

"Say," I returned, trying to ignore the warmth in my cheeks, "do I need to register or something?"

"Nah," she shooed with a flick of the wrist. "Just so's I know you're here. Sign out when you leave for good, that's all. How's the leg? Or the hip? Was it the hip?"

"The hip. Getting better. Should heal up fine, now that I'm here."

"Oh, sure, dearie," she said. "You come to the right place for that." Her face pinked in the cold. "You need anything, you just holler. I got lots of wood, all cut up. Already put some inside for ya."

"I saw it. Thanks so much."

"Danny keeps the matches on the mantle," she said. "There's old newspapers and kindling behind that rocker. Oh! I'm Beth Berger. The manager here. Shoulda said so."

"I figured."

"Hadley's gone to town to the Value Mart for a few things. They close at nine o'clock. Ya got time, too, if ya need something — milk or bread or cold beer or whatever."

"I'm all right for now."

"Suit yourself." She shook off a chill. "Flurries, they say. Gonna be cold in the tents tonight. Too bad they can't go to the motels — they're all full. You stay warm, OK?" She shifted the board to the other arm and marched away toward the park entrance.

The sign said *Sorry — Camp Full.*

CHAPTER 2

River Falls (pop. 800) welcomes visitors with a totem pole of signs for the Lions and Kiwanis and local churches. Once across the Sinnissippi River Bridge, one meets the only stop light. River Street, the scenic tourist route, features two gas stations, a diner, a '50s-style drive-in (closed for the season), Ace Used Cars, and a Town and Country Insurance office. My company. I made a mental note to check on my disability insurance. When was the first check supposed to arrive? After sixty days? Was it ninety? What was the agent's name on the sign? Something de la Cruz. Sally Ann? Selena? *Should be in the phone book*, I thought. *I'll call later.*

The "business district," one block further on Main, looked a little like an abandoned Wild West movie set without the hitching posts. The angled parking was full of Chevy Silverados and Ford F-150 pickups and RVs with "disabled" plates. A tavern on every corner, with "Karaoke every Friday" signs and NASCAR banners advertising cheap domestics on tap. One had a faded "Welcome Hunters" banner that had never been removed. The bank looked updated with a single-lane drive-through. A Fix-It Hardware, a video rental place, a craft store, and Value Mart, alongside some boarded-up shops.

The Mart was a hybrid of pharmacy and Five-and-Dime, with bargain bins by the entry, and steel shelves stocked with housewares, home remedies, greeting cards, gifts, and cosmetics. A "sportsmen's corner" featured a rack of fishing poles and a locked glass case of lures and ammo. I noted the office-supplies aisle: notebook paper, index cards, pens. You could spend a little more here, but save a trip to Sterling or Freeport.

I noticed the camping gear on my way to the glass-paneled pharmacy counter in the back, passing a family of Hispanics. Farm workers, I supposed, given the straw Western hats, denim jackets, and rough hands. A gaunt Anglo man leaning on a walker dropped two propane bottles into his basket. There weren't many bottles left on the shelf. I almost bumped into an old woman in a wheelchair rounding a corner. "Pardon me," I said. She adjusted the nose-tubes connected to the mounted oxygen tank and straightened the stems in her lap. A man on crutches passed me and said good morning.

I was third in line and should have brought a book. I usually do. I might have taken one from the table there, but they were all romances and westerns — prescription fiction. The magazines were all about cars and outdoor sports. No *Harpers* or *New Yorkers* here. Not even a *National Geographic*.

The pharmacist worked alone. Looking over his glasses, he explained the dosage and cautions to the first customer, a gouty woman in her forties, with braces on her thick, blotchy legs. A diabetic, perhaps. The next customer, a rail-thin man with a nervous squint, had a problem with his insurance card. The pharmacist — Cliff Barnes, by the framed license — pecked at his computer and told the man to check back later. The man grumped.

I clutched. I thought I'd cleared this, but what if he wouldn't take it after all? I should have used the mail service, but —

"Yes, next?" the blue-frocked druggist called.

I hobbled forward, gave my name. "I called about the Nardil."

"Oh, yes," Barnes replied. He ran his fingers through his salt-and-pepper hair, just beginning to recede. "I don't get much call for MAOIs any more."

Did he have to say it aloud? He fished through a basket labeled "call orders." The basket was full. "Simpson, Stowe — here." Several brochures were stapled to the bag.

"Now, you know about these, right?" he said, pulling a pencil from behind his ear and tapping the brochures with the eraser end. "This can make you feel sluggish, especially in the morning when your blood pressure is low. Wiggle your feet and move a little before you get up. Here's a list of foods high in tyramine you can't have or you'll get 'The Cheese Reaction,' a spike in your blood pressure. Very high, very fast. Very bad. You know all this already, right?"

I'd been nodding the whole time. "Yes, I've been careful."

"A baloney sandwich won't kill you, but you'll get a headache you won't forget."

Good thing I passed on Dan's lunch in the fridge.

"The ProCardin is in here, too. That's the antidote in case someone slips some Chianti in the spaghetti sauce or soy sauce in the burger for flavor and you didn't know. You have to take it within five minutes of symptoms. Massive headache in the frontal lobes, sore neck, rapid breathing, chest pain, the sweats, fainting — you know you ate something you shouldn't have."

"I'm on bread and water," I assured him.

"As long as it isn't banana bread or raisin bread," he retorted, all business. "And if you catch a cold, given the season, stay away from antihistamines or cough suppressants that have dextromethorphan — you know, Tussins and anything with 'DM' on it. Those are the main things; there's more. It's all explained in here. Any questions?"

"I think I've got chipmunks in my cabin walls," I said. *Or rats. Or bats.* "Do you have something here to get rid of them?"

He peered at me over the glasses. "Chipmunks? Hmm. Could be mice, maybe shrews," he said. "Been a problem lately with so much corn in the elevators going for ethanol production. Try the honey-flavored rat poison in aisle 2. Comes in soft blocks you break off and put along the walls. Oh — any pets, kids?"

"No."

"It's strong stuff. Wear rubber gloves. Anything else?"

"Rubber gloves."

"Aisle 4, housewares." He handed me the bag. "Pay up front. And go easy on that. If you take more than the label says, you'll hallucinate. God knows we have enough visions of the Virgin Mary around here."

"Pardon me?"

"Aren't you here to see him, too, like everyone else? I mean, you being an out-of-towner, with the cane and all?"

"See who?"

"Father Ray. The Bleeder. Well, the healer. You know — the priest with the stigmata."

CHAPTER 3

Dr. Rashidi's clinic receptionist called to move up my appointment due to a cancellation.

"Someone get healed?" I asked her flippantly.

"Excuse me?"

"See you at three. Thanks." I pressed "end call" on the cell.

The office, in a landmark Victorian home with a wrap-around porch and a new handicap ramp, was mostly deserted. The few waiting patients, bundled in winter wear, hunched when I hobbled in. A blast of cold air followed me. A wrinkled man coughed, and I thought of the druggist's warning about catching a cold.

The gum-snapping receptionist, a Latina with a page-boy haircut and too many silver rings, gave me forms on a clipboard to fill out. She drew a plastic pen from a mug and handed it to me, but I produced my own Cross chrome pen. I noticed they didn't keep the BicStiks in an alcohol jar, like they used to do with thermometers. Who knows how many rhinoviruses swarmed on it?

"Remember to tell us who your new doctor will be so we can forward your records," the girl said, bright-eyed. She pointed behind her to the bilingual notice on the wall: *The River Falls Clinic closes June 1. Sinnissippi Health Systems regrets the inconvenience.*

"Not enough patients," she said, anticipating my question.

I lowered myself delicately into an orange vinyl seat and rested Citizen Cane on one knee and the clipboard on the other. I glanced up at the wall sign and noticed the receptionist staring at me, her mouth open. When I smiled at her, she averted her sienna eyes and blushed. Maybe she wasn't used to seeing a white guy in the clinic. After all, everyone else in the room had dark hair, dark eyes, swarthy skin, and second-hand clothes. Medicaid cases, quite likely — no wonder the clinic had financial problems. It might not have struck me in the big city. But somehow I expected this part of rural Illinois to be, well, north European: German farmers, Swiss dairymen, Swedes who stopped on the way to Minnesota, maybe a few French descended from the fur-trading voyageurs of Joliet's days.

I smiled at a Mestizo mother who held a baby to her high cinnamon cheekbone. Were they legals? Undocumented? Was it my business? No. I pulled out a book, a new translation of Aristotle's *Poetics*. I remembered to bring something to read this time. Besides, the research had to start sometime. Aristotle was a physician. Did he ever have a problem with *"Not enough patients"*? Maybe the healing priest was taking a bite out of the business.

I just reached the part where Aristotle begins his history of art when I felt that familiar whoozy whirl of dread, that lightheaded and illogical gathering of mist that blurred the words on the page and quickened my breath. What if I stopped breathing altogether? What happens then? No one knows. Not even Aristotle. We live between two darknesses.

I clapped the book shut. I needed some air, something to focus on at a slight distance. But I dared not rise too fast and risk a twinge in the hip, a fall, or a dead faint. *God, not here.* That's when the office door mercifully squeaked open, and a rush of cold air washed over me. The room stopped spinning just long enough for me to hear my name called.

"Stubblefield?"

I was saved.

The nurse held the door while I tottered into the hallway, stepped on the scale, and then proceeded to the exam room, where I dropped into a chair. She took my temp with a gun in my ear, made a face, and then checked my blood pressure.

"Temp's a little high," she said. "So's the blood pressure. Nervous?"

I looked away from the plastic pistol she'd put to my head. "Sometimes."

"I mean now."

"A little, I guess."

She rolled up the armband. "That's kinda normal when you're seeing a new doctor for the first time," she said. "We'll try another reading before you leave. So relax. He'll be right with you." She scribbled something on a clipboard. *Skittish around guns,* no doubt. "Just relax," she repeated, and left.

I did not relax at all; I rubbed away goose bumps. I hoped the doc wouldn't make me get up on the exam table. It was a little high, with one narrow step. I always felt like a kid on a school bus when I sat on one, heels dangling above the floor. Maybe they are meant to make you feel that way. As if one didn't feel vulnerable and helpless in a doctor's office already.

"Mr. Stubblefield, the allogeneic bone-marrow transplant for Peggy shows signs of GVHD disease and internal bleeding because of the intra-thecal chemotherapy meant to bypass the blood-brain barrier."

"Or it might be the interleukins and colony-stimulating factors from the clinical trial."

"It hasn't been tried much with the acute myeloid conditions your wife has. Do you understand, Mr. Stubblefield?"

"Mr. Stubblefield?"

Dr. Rashidi strode in. He stuck out a cacao hand and shook mine perfunctorily, once. I felt blinded by the white coat, like an angelic apparition. "How are we feeling?" he asked in a monotone. There was a hint of a refined British accent, any Indian or Pakistani flavor long trained out of his clipped speech.

He scanned my records, the thin lips parted slightly to show his pearly teeth, glittering in contrast to his dark complexion. The thick, black brows moved with a life of their own, reacting to my history. "Any trouble with breathing?"

"No; back to normal."

He checked with a stethoscope, asking for a few deep breaths.

"Good. Problems with the hip?"

"No. Tender sometimes, when it's cold."

"Pain? Throbbing?"

"No. A little sore after my therapy exercises."

"Trouble sitting? Walking? Using stairs?"

"Stairs are hard."

"Normal anxiety. Getting in and out of bed?"

"No. Well, I have to take it easy."

"Could be the Nardil, too. Any dizziness?"

"Just first thing in the morning," I said. "And people say I look a little dazed if I take any meds during the day."

"That's a problem with those Monoamine Oxidase Inhibitors."

He checked my eyes and ears and probed my nose. "So Prozac and Zoloft and Paxil didn't help? More complications? Sexual side-effects?"

"I'm a widower."

"So sorry."

"They made me so dizzy I'd vomit," I said.

"How about Effexor?"

"Raised my blood pressure. Made me irritable and weepy."

"That's too bad," the doctor said. "The newer drugs are so much better for most people even if they lead to weight gain. I call MAOIs the St. Jude drug — a last resort, and you have to give up so much, like a good Catholic."

"I'm Presbyterian — sort of," I offered.

He ignored the comment. "Taking any herbal supplements? Drink herb teas?"

"Nothing."

"Good. Lemon grass is fine. Some others may interact badly. And how are we doing with the dietary restrictions?"

"I had to miss some good wine and cheese socials at the faculty meetings," I said lightly, "and dark German beer and pepperoni pizza with my students."

He wasn't amused. He looked down my throat with a tongue depressor in place as though to make sure I hadn't eaten any such things. "Any episodes lately?"

"A couple."

"You're making another change, coming out here to the hinter-lands. Not unexpected. Moving for good? Or just visiting?"

"Visiting. Just needed some time away."

"Don't take a vacation from your exercises," he said. "Take aspirin if the hip is uncomfortable from strain. As for the anxiety, do not exceed 60 milligrams per day of your current medication. If you feel faint, drink fluids and take the doses after meals. Since you have felt some chest pains, do not begin any exercise program other than the physical therapy without checking with me first. And I'll renew your prescription. Now, let's have a look at you."

He inspected my hip injury and measured my range of motion. He quizzed me about a number of medical conditions to be sure the MAO Inhibitors wouldn't kill me.

"It looks good," he said while I zipped my slacks. "Stay with the strict tyramine-free diet. Even small amounts add up. You can have a little yogurt, but don't have smoked fish on sauerkraut with sour cream followed by a dessert of raspberries and chocolates with coffee."

"There goes dinner," I said dryly.

He didn't smile. "Some people resent the diet so much they blame the doctor and refuse to cooperate."

Some patients listen attentively to their doctors but do none of the things they are ordered to do, Aristotle the physician agreed.

Rashidi scratched out the prescription, tore it from the pad, and gave it to me. "They end up dead from a brain hemorrhage."

"OK," I said meekly.

"And stay away from sick people," he added. "It's flu season, and you don't need a respiratory problem. Cold remedies will provoke a hypertensive reaction, like the so-called 'cheese reaction.' The most dangerous are the over-the-counter medications with decongestants like pseudoephedrine, anything with dextromethorphan, you know — anything with 'DM' in the name."

"The pharmacist already warned me."

"I'm sure. If you catch a cold, stick to chicken soup."

"Or I could go see this Father Ray that everyone is so excited about," I quipped.

A shadow passed over Rashidi's face. "I am a scientist," he said coldly. "I do not believe in weeping statues." He tugged his coat tight and headed for the door. Before he left the room, he pivoted, apologetic. He shook my hand again. "Of course, you may see for yourself. My patients have been talking about him for weeks. He has a service two Saturdays a month, and one is tomorrow. I concede there could be a placebo effect. Good thing you're not Catholic."

"Why's that?"

"You can't take Communion. The red wine would give you a headache for days."

CHAPTER 4

Warning: Poison. Harmful to children, domestic pets, and wildlife. Follow all directions. Causes internal bleeding.

"But, mousies, it tastes so good," I called out loud. "Come and get it."

I snapped on the rubber gloves and opened the rodenticide package. I shook out the little green bricks wrapped in cellophane. They were scored for breaking into smaller pieces. I peeled away the plastic, broke off the little blocks, and set them strategically behind the fridge, near the stove, by the cabinets, and along the wall. After a few days, as soon as the rodents began to complain of swelling and dizziness, I'd know it was working. Well, I just wouldn't hear the scratching and crawling any more. It was worse at night, of course. It took a while even for the MAOIs to knock me out. In the meantime, I set a circle of traps baited with peanut butter around the bed and hoped I would, in my morning stupor, remember they were there.

In the morning, while waiting for my blood pressure to rise enough to stand, I listened for the scratching. Nothing. Maybe word had gotten out, and the rodents had all moved to the campsites, where there was plenty of food and trash to be taken from the tents and trailers. I listened to cars come and go, marveling anew how odd this was, in the muddy frost of March, to have the tourist parks and local motels flashing their "No Vacancy" signs, their parking lots full of the elderly, the infirm, and the inquisitive, looking for a miracle. How could anyone believe that nonsense?

Men are swayed more by fear than by reverence, Aristotle suggested.

I hazily recalled that crowds pressed upon Jesus himself, grasping for his robe, hoping for a fleeting touch, even for his shadow to pass over them. To be sure, there was no shame in simply wanting to be healed, when nothing else helped. I knew that as well as anybody.

Still, none of the blow-dried healers I ever saw while flipping television channels were like Jesus:

I have a word of knowledge about a woman with a post-nasal drip. The Lord is drying that up now. Thank you, Lord. Someone broke a tooth, but the Lord is replacing it with a straight one, hallelujah. And there is a man with money problems, a big debt — oh, at least ten thousand dollars. It's not your fault. Your need will be met in three days. Amen. Now, if you've been touched today and would like to say thank you with a gift, here's the number to call . . ."

I had little use for healers, either the miraculous kind or the medical kind. They both took your money and ran. But I wouldn't pass judgment on desperate people who had bad luck with doctors. Wasn't there once a woman with a chronic bleeding problem who saw many doctors and spent all her savings, who, beyond all other hope, came to Jesus and tugged on his robe?

I tugged at the sheets and remembered Peggy lying in that hospital bed. She bruised easily, and bled from her gums. Her skin was pale but peppered with tiny red spots the doctors called petechiae. When she was coherent, she joked about becoming polka-dotted.

"You never liked polka-dots," I said.

"I can live with them."

She did, for a while. A catheter delivered one kind of chemo, another kind was injected into the spine. Treatment, recovery, treatment, recovery. Some recover from leukemia for good. She never did.

Not even Aristotle, a wise physician, could have saved her. Of course, he would have made her worse, seeking to restore her humors to balance through bloodletting. Somehow, it made logical sense to the Father of Logic: out with the excess bad humors, problem solved. But what was the logic behind a bleeding priest? He bleeds on behalf of others? It couldn't be that.

Your faith has made you well. Yes, that's what Jesus told the bleeding woman. Mind over body, that's all.

I opened my laptop, launched the Bach "Sonata for Two Flutes in G Major," and started my exercises.

After making some lemon-grass tea and toast, I checked the baseboard rodent bait. Sure enough, there were nibbles and crumbs. *Bon appetit, mousies.*

It reminded me that I needed groceries; Dan's stash would run out soon. The camp manager could direct me to the nearest supermarket. After that, I'd take my first pill for the day, set up a little office area while it kicked in, and take a long nap.

When Beth Berger answered the door, she took a look at Citizen Cane and shook her head. "Nothin' happened?"

"Pardon me?"

"At the service? The anointin' of the sick?"

"I don't know. I didn't go."

"People are shy at first. I understand."

"Maybe next time." I almost said *Mumbo Jumbo* instead.

"That's the spirit," she said. "Now, what can I do for ya?"

I told her, and she gave me directions to the River Falls Country Market. She was telling me about their great cinnamon buns when a Winnebago camper crunched to a stop at the trailer's driveway. Two bicycles rattled on a rack mounted on the back. A side door banged open, and a boy with a Cubs baseball cap bounced out. It was the boy who almost ran me over with one of those bikes.

"It's gone, Missus Berger, it's gone," he spouted.

"What's gone, Tommy?"

"My bump, Missus Berger. I can't feel it no more. Look!"

He pulled open his Chicago Bears coat and yanked up his t-shirt. His ribs stuck out, as though he hadn't eaten for weeks. The camp manager put her hand in his side.

"By gum, you're right," she said, ruffling his head. "Wonderful!"

The cap nearly slipped off his bald head.

A thirty-ish woman stepped up behind the boy. She adjusted his cap. Her blotchy face was streaked with silver tears. "Well, we do have to get it checked by the oncologist," she said thinly, "after we see Dr. Rashidi first."

"He don't believe in such."

"Good," the woman replied. "Then we'll be sure."

"Oh, I'm sure," Berger said. "Checking out, then?"

The woman dabbed at her eye. "Yes. There are more coming behind us."

"You see, dearie?" Berger said to me with a reassuring nudge. "Your time will come, too."

Whether my goose bumps came from the wind or the willies, I couldn't tell. With the groceries put away, I started the fire before the Nardil settled in like a Lake Michigan fog. Bending down to arrange the wood was a little tricky. I took some old newspapers from behind the rocker for kindling. *The Sinnissippi County Weekly Observer* on top, dated September 1, featured an Ag Show story, a church spaghetti-dinner notice, and an update on a murder trial for a Mexican cannery worker. In the shaded side column was a story headlined *St. Mary parish welcomes associate pastor.*

So this is the guy, I thought, unfolding the yellowed paper. The photo was fuzzy, but he seemed to be in his mid-thirties, thin and a bit stooped, with a close-cropped beard shading his narrow face. No halo.

The story said:

St. Mary's Parish of River Falls will welcome its new associate pastor, Fr. Raymond Boudreau, with a pasta dinner hosted by the church's Women's Association on Friday, September 5, at 6 p.m. in Rosario's Restaurant.

A brief program and an address by Rev. Boudreau will follow the dinner.

A graduate of Loras College in Dubuque, Father Boudreau studied philosophy at the Pontifical Faculty of the Dominican House of Studies in River Forest, Ill., where he completed a Master's degree and took his vows. Following further study at the Pontifical University of St. Thomas Aquinas (Angelicum) in Rome, Father Boudreau began his pastoral ministry at

Blessed Sacrament Parish in Madison, Wis. He returned to
Dubuque for a second Master's degree from The Aquinas In-
stitute of Theology, and has traveled widely as a lecturer for
The Thomist Association, a study program for the laity.

Father Boudreau comes to River Falls after serving several
parishes throughout Illinois and southern Wisconsin.

"Once everyone gets healed in one place, I move on to the
next," Boudreau said.

No, it didn't say that. But outside, more RVs, vans, and pop-up
campers were pulling out. "Nah," I said aloud. I balled up the news-
print, tucked it in place, and lit it. I angled my aching hip to the fire.
The heat washed over me soothingly; I'd obviously overdone it today.
I closed my eyes and reviewed the scene with the boy.

I honestly hoped that boy was healed. But I had no way of knowing. Had the tumor been so small that it was hard to feel? Berger was
no doctor. Besides, she wouldn't break their hearts — Oh, wait,
Tommy, here it is, big as a plum. Too bad, dearie. Maybe next time.

Then again, maybe it really happened. Did it? There are more
things in heaven and earth, Horatio, than are dreamt of in your
philosophy.

In all things of nature there is something of the marvelous, Aristotle
agreed.

Still, the only way to know the truth about this alleged marvel was
to ask Dr. Rashidi. And the patient-physician privilege wouldn't permit him to tell me anything. So I'd never know.

*A likely impossibility is always preferable to an unconvincing possibil-
ity*, Aristotle teased.

CHAPTER 5

A chirping startled me awake. The bats in the walls? Bird stuck in the chimney? Smoke alarm with a low battery?

I dared not sit up too quickly or I'd faint, or worse, fall.

Cheep cheep cheep.

Finches at the feeders? No, I hadn't filled them. It wasn't my cell with the Beethoven's Fifth tone. It was the bedside Princess phone. Probably Dan calling to check whether the service had been reconnected.

Cheep cheep cheep.

I fumbled for the phone on the bed stand. It kept chirping like a cardinal spotting a cat. When I picked up the handset, the number buttons lit up.

"Hello?" a male voice said. "I'm looking for Mr. Reed Stubblefield, please."

"You got him," I said drowsily.

"Mr. Stubblefield, this is Father Ray Boudreau, at St. Mary's Church in River Falls."

I think I used the Lord's name in vain in reply.

"I'm sorry, did I wake you? Is there a better time to talk?"

I sputtered something profane.

"Oh, forgive me, you must be wondering how I know you, and this number."

It must be a miracle, I almost told him.

"Your brother Dan told me you'd be at his cabin about this time. He said you might be able to use my help."

Oh, did he indeed? I said to myself. "I'm fine, pastor. Really. I got my prescription filled, and saw the local doctor."

"Oh, not that," he said with a warm laugh. "Dan says you're writing a book about Aristotle while you're here."

My focus improved. "Well, yes — well, not exactly. Not yet."

"I'm a big fan of Thomas Aquinas. Did my graduate work on him. As you might guess, I've collected quite a few books on Aquinas and Aristotle along the way. Thought you'd like a look. The town's library collection is — well, somewhat spare on the classics and the scholastics, let's say."

"I don't know, I —"

"It can get lonely in the sticks in March, besides chilly. Come over for some hot coffee and see if there's anything you could use."

"I can't have coffee, pastor, my medications react to it so I'll just —"

"Herbal tea, then. I have several kinds. How about that? My place, the rectory at the church? How about Monday? Sundays are full for me. Go fig." He laughed again.

I shook my head, both to clear it and to emphasize my reply. "I don't think so. I'm quite busy. Thanks anyway."

"You're certain? I can come to your place."

"No," I said. Too sharply. I repented. "No, really, you're trying to be kind, I know, but I can't. I just can't."

I hung up.

Some nerve.

I shook my head to full alertness. *Well, I'll be damned*, I said to the walls, reconsidering. Somehow Dan knew this guy. Sure, Danny became a Catholic convert when he married Loretta, but he never seemed very serious about it. And he hadn't gone to church since the divorce. Maybe he's starting to go again, I thought. That's how he met this cleric. One thing looked certain: Danny planned for us to get together all along. The sly devil. Just trying to help in his own way — like those blind dates with his girlfriends' younger sisters. Good ol' Dan. Always looking out for his little brother. And he put that *County Weekly Observer* on the top of the newspaper pile for me to notice, too, didn't he? Pretty sneaky of him.

What else did Dan say to this priest about me? *He won't come to no church service, Father, so you'll have to invite him over personally to zap his hip.*

Dan didn't mean any harm by it. But I wouldn't be pushed. Not by Dan. And certainly not by a faith healer calling out of the blue.

I eyed the phone. So it was reconnected. Dan thought of everything. Guess it just took a little longer out in the country. I picked it up again.

No dial tone. I tapped the hook.

No light.

It was dead.

CHAPTER 6

"Can I, like, take the final exam early? My grandmother just died and —"

"Didn't she die in March, Miss Hernandez? Just before Spring Break, as I recall. That's why you took the midterm early, remember?"

"Like, that was my other grandmother."

"Tough year."

"Yeah."

"The funeral was in Cancun?"

"Say what?"

"Your T-shirt? *Spring Break Cancun*, with this year's dates on the back?"

"Oh, yeah, that."

"Take the final at the scheduled time, please."

Beth Williams, bug-eyed and white as a ghost, elbows the girl aside. Here come the excuses. *Omigod I overslept! Can I please please hand my paper in Monday?*

"There's a fight in the hall," she gasps. "You better come right now, Mr. Stubblefield! Mr. Stubblefield!"

Two shots. Bang. Bang.

Warm blood running down my leg.

"Mr. Stubblefield?"

I awakened with a sharp intake of air.

Bang. Bang. A woman's voice. "Mr. Stubblefield, are you all right?"

Beth Berger rapped the door twice again.

I mopped my brow, then felt my wet pants. Oh, Christ. At least this time I didn't wet myself much. Did I shout in my sleep too, as at the hospital?

"Hello?"

"I'm all right," I called, heart knocking against my ribs. "Hold on. Coming." I couldn't arise too quickly, or I'd pass out. *Make an excuse.* "I've — I've got to find my glasses, Mrs. Berger. Be right there."

I adjusted my glasses. They were already on my nose — I'd fallen asleep with them on again. I gripped Citizen Cane, pulled on a robe to cover my dampness, and hobbled to the door looking as rumpled as Edgar Allen Poe after a binge. Did I smell bad? I sniffed. No, I was OK. When I threw the latch and opened the door, winter light howled into the room.

Beth, in silhouette, eyed me up and down. "Sorry to bother you while you're writin' and all."

"It's fine. I was at a good stopping place. Really, I was."

She peered past my shoulder, no doubt noticing that the laptop was closed, the lights out. She cradled a shopping bag in her arms. "Had a potluck after church today," she said. "Thought you'd like some of Betsy Hansen's tuna casserole for lunch. There was plenty of it."

Was it Sunday already?

"It's OK for your diet and all, I hope. If not, it's OK, I'll just —"

"I'm sure it's fine," I said, accepting it. The paper was warm. "Thank you."

"You know, if you're lookin' for somethin' to do or you need a break, there's a new bookstore down in Sterling Falls. Just opened. Used books, old magazines. Some records. Hadley got some bound volumes of *National Geographics* from the '50s yesterday. I says to him, I says, where we gonna put them? But we love the car ads. Brings back memories. Nice little café, too. I told Hadley you're the kind of person who likes stores like that, I betcha. They're open Sundays 'til 5. Ya got time. Easy to find."

She gave me written directions with a penciled sketch and left with a finger-wiggling wave. I blinked away the blaring white sky, as blank as page one of my manuscript.

What the hell, I thought. I decided to go.

After all, I had plenty of time to kill.

Books and Brews turned out to be a paperback exchange, with a large romance section in bins and folding-tables piled with trade-paper remainders. Piled in cardboard boxes on the floor, however, lay some Loeb Classical Library volumes — Claudian, Lucian, Virgil. In very good condition. An extraordinary find. My stomach leaped the same way my brother's probably did whenever he spotted and bagged a pheasant. I scooped them up, hugged them to my chest, and planted myself at a wobbly bistro table to examine my treasures.

Three women behind me chattered over hot chai tea and steaming bodice rippers. At the other table, a bearded middle-aged man hiked a tartan scarf higher against the draft and scribbled on a legal pad. He gripped his pencil in fingerless wool gloves. The store's clerk dropped a napkin on my table and asked what I was having.

"You have green tea?" I asked.

"Sure. Anything else? I got a cranberry scone left. Raisin-bran muffins."

Off my diet. "Just the tea, please."

She drummed her pencil on my books. "Say, those just came in," she said. "That's my fastest turnaround ever. In fact, that's the fellow who brought them."

The man, overhearing, nodded cordially in my direction. He returned to writing. Beside his pad lay a paperback copy of Hesiod's *Theogony* with *Works and Days*, a book he decided to keep at the last moment, I presumed. He opened it, checked a reference, traced the pencil tip through the footnotes, and looked up.

"Pardon me," he said, "if you don't mind my asking — could I have a look at my — I mean your — *Aeneid* for a moment?"

"Oh, sure," I said, a bit embarrassed to be caught staring at him — and to be in possession of his book. Maybe he repented and wanted it back. "No trouble at all."

"Please join me," he invited. "Perhaps you could help me."

"In what way?"

"I'm trying to confirm the story where Apollo defeats Python. You look like the sort who might know where to find it."

I shrugged a modest *maybe* and crossed gingerly to his table. Once settled, I said, "Could I ask first why you're getting rid of these Loeb editions? They're hard to find."

"They're just exam copies," he replied. "I have others at home."

"So you're a teacher?"

"Oh, just a part-time adjunct at Sinnissippi Community College. In their literacy program for Spanish-speaking immigrants. And you?"

"Stateline Community College," I said. "Classics — well, mostly rhetoric and freshman comp. I'm on leave for —" I coughed the words back. "For this semester."

"On medical leave?"

"How'd you know?"

"The cane," he said. "It looks new." He grinned and continued, "I knew you were the right one to talk to, although I don't want to put you on the spot."

"That's fine. Apollo and Python, you said? My guess is you'd find the story in Homer or Aeschylus, not Virgil. As a Roman, Virgil would have no interest in the outcome of the struggle. Apollo, as the son of Zeus, took over Python's control of the Delphic Oracle, which would give the Greeks guidance concerning the war with Troy. From that point on, Apollo becomes the patron of seers."

"You're right. Must be the *Iliad*, or the *Orestaia*, then."

The tea arrived.

"Put that on my ticket, please," the man said.

I raised a palm. "That won't be necessary."

"My way to say thank you," he told me. "You saved me a lot of time."

"This is research for something?"

"A poem," he said, lifting the legal pad's edge. "I dabble. I wouldn't ask you to read it, though."

"Why not?"

"It's an early draft," he said, tearing it off the pad. "And it requires that one know a little about Greek mythology, which I know you do, but I wouldn't impose on a stranger."

"A stranger might be the best one to read it," I said. "It could be more awkward with a friend, don't you think? So many feelings to hurt."

"Well, if you wouldn't mind?"

"Not at all." I snatched the page and read:

At Table

Dionysus brought the wine.
Demeter brought the bread.
(*Athena* would have dined
but she was still in *Zeus's* head).

Apollo lit a candle
with his finger and he said:
"At first I did not recognize
You, risen from the dead."

The Host smiles warmly, takes the cup,
and lifts it overhead.
"The Hebrews had their prophets
and you had yourselves, instead.

"When *Hercules*, for love,
went down to *Hades* for his bride,
or you, a son of god,
defeated *Python* in his pride,

"These were but shadows on the wall
of *Plato's* cave, so cast
by higher, firm realities
though dimly seen at first.

> *"Isaiah* uttered oracles,
> and *David* sang withal,
> but you had stories, pointing to
> the truest tale of all."

"As I said, a first draft," he said humbly, eyes downcast.

"No, this is clever," I said, shifting in my seat. End-rhyme was out of fashion, and iambic tetrameter was sing-songy, but that's not what troubled me. "You were right about the mythic allusions."

"Too obscure?"

"Not too much. The religious ones, however —"

"Too obvious?"

I shifted in my seat again. No, *squirmed.* "Do you truly think they would have recognized him?"

"The idea isn't original with me," he admitted shyly. "J.R.R. Tolkien once said that all ancient myths are dim foreshadowings of the Gospels. For instance, take the story of Hercules: the son of a divine father and human mother gives up his divine rights and sacrifices himself in order to rescue his beloved from the clutches of Hades."

"Mythologists call it the monomyth of the hero," I instructed him. "Every culture has a story with a similar motif."

"Exactly," he said, brightening. "No culture is left without a witness. That way, when the gospel comes to them, they recognize it."

"You're kidding." *Great, a religious fanatic.* And I had hardly begun drinking the tea.

"Why else did the Irish poets and warriors lay down their harps and silks so readily when Patrick arrived?" he said, enthused. "It's because they already had the story of Cuchulain, the divine son of the High God who was betrayed by a close friend, lashed to a post, made to wear a hawthorn crown, and wounded with a spear thrust in his side while the druids mocked him. Sound familiar? That's why, when the real story came, they recognized it."

"The parallels are superficial."

"Are they? The apostle Paul said the Greek philosophers are like schoolmasters who lead their students to Christ. It makes you wonder whether Aristotle would have recognized him, doesn't it?"

My defenses arose like the walls of Troy. "I don't know. I doubt it."

As Homer said, Aristotle butted in, *"He did not seem to be the child of a mortal man, but as One who came from God's seed."*

He was speaking of Priam, not Christ, I corrected him.

"Pardon me?" the man said.

"It's very interesting, to say the least," I said, gathering my things. "And thank you for the tea. But I've got to be going."

"But you haven't finished."

"I have. I mean, I have something to get to," I rebounded. "It was a pleasure to meet you, Mr. —?"

"Boudreau," he said. "Ray Boudreau."

"Wait a minute. You're the — what do you call it — the —"

Bleeder.

"Pastor at St. Mary's Church, yes. That's me. Well, part-time. We spoke briefly on the phone."

"This is quite a coincidence," I said, suspicious.

He laughed. "There are no coincidences, Mr. Stubblefield. Coincidences are just God's way of remaining anonymous."

"Beth Berger told you I was coming here, didn't she? She sent me here to meet you."

"No, she didn't send you."

Go on, say it: God did.

He didn't say it.

"Anyway, thanks for the books," I said, rising. My temperature rose, too. Someone set me up. "Good day."

I snatched Claudian and Virgil's *Aeneid*, stormed to the door, and then limped like Haephestus the Healer to my car with a stinging westerly wind slapping my hot face.

As soon as I had cooled off, reached the cabin, and picked up the books from the car seat, my stomach squeezed. In my hasty escape, I hadn't paid for them. Worse, the yellow page of the priest's poem was stuck between the books. Not only did he pay for the tea I didn't drink, but he probably also had to pay for the books he himself had brought to the store to be sold. And I had his only draft of a work-in-progress. I moaned with mixed disgust and guilt, resolving to mail him the poem and a check. I could get the address from a phone book, but I didn't have one. Or I could ask the Bergers, although I'd have to make a trip into town to buy envelopes at Value Mart and find the Post Office, but the clerk will wonder *why not just take it down the street and drop it off at the church office,* and I'd lie about my inability to walk, given the cane and — I yanked out my cell phone and called Information at 411. When I punched the church office number, a secretary answered.

I identified myself and asked her if I could drop off something belonging to Father Boudreau and what hours —

"He's right here. Hold on."

I breathed an imprecation.

"Hello, Mr. Stubblefield? Good of you to call. Thanks again for the help on my poem."

"I didn't help at all. In fact, I —"

"I know. You didn't get to finish your tea. I'll brew some fresh here at my place, and we can talk about your writing for a change. I'm so sorry; it was rude of me not to ask about it at the bookshop. How about it?"

I found myself making an appointment for my penance. I was the one who needed to apologize for being rude, not him.

When I pocketed my cell phone, I paused. Did I mention anything about writing a book? How did he know about that? Oh, yes, Dan told him. But how did he recognize me at the café? Are healers mind-readers as well? Was someone playing a trick on me?

The gods, too, are fond of a joke, Aristotle chuckled.

CHAPTER 7

How do you shake hands with a stigmatic? Clasp but don't squeeze? Is the hole in the hand or the wrist? Do they close up between episodes? *Let him make the first move.*

When I pulled Ollie Volvo into the church's parking lot, I expected to see a queue of people winding through rope barriers and following ushers' instructions shouted through bullhorns. Instead, a single, rusted Ford Escort wagon faced a screen storm door, like the last penitent of the day at the confessional. The blinds were shut and the lights turned on. A yellow bug light illuminated a little sign, "Rectory." My watch blinked "4:30" as the dull-white disc of the sun, like a Host, dipped into the wine-dark clouds. The moon wore a halo; rain was threatening again.

I knocked with my left hand, my right fist gripping Citizen Cane. With my right hand occupied, he probably wouldn't ask to shake my hand.

The reverend opened the door. "Mr. Stubblefield, good of you to come. Watch the step." He held the door with one hand, wiping his nose with the other using a bandana. "Sorry if I don't shake hands, but I seem to have another cold coming on."

"Sorry to hear that," I said, and meant it. I refused to get sick.

"Something I probably picked up at Mass, during the passing of the peace," he said with a smile. "I call it the passing of the germs. Like doctors say: it'd be a great job if it wasn't for all the sick people."

He indicated a coat-rack for my slicker and said something about the weather. I nearly knocked my elbow into the holy-water font mounted beside the door jamb, and when I caught sight of the silver crucifix, framed photo of the Pope, and a gilded icon of the Madonna with Child on the walls, I knew for sure I had stepped into an alien world.

"Thanks for bringing the poem," the cleric said. "I wondered where it had got to. Just put it there on the end-table, won't you?" He crossed to the divan without a hobble. His boot-cut black jeans were pulled over '70s-style zip-up boots — providing support for wounded ankles, I imagined.

"I brought a check for the books, too, pastor," I said, contrite. "I'm really sorry about not —"

"Aw, don't worry about it, you're forgiven. Hey, that's my job, right?" he said, with a little wave of his hand. He wore fingerless gloves here, too, although these looked to be Spandex, not wool. "Here, have a seat. I've got the kettle on, and we've got some finger sandwiches left over from a weekend funeral." His eyes creased. "Oh, maybe I shouldn't have said where they were from. I sure hope you don't mind."

As long as the deceased person doesn't, I nearly said as I lowered myself into a wing-backed chair. "Not at all, thanks. I just have to know what's in them. I have a long list of diet restrictions."

"I understand. I've a few myself."

He looked well enough for a man who gets crucified now and then, although his ruddy face looked a little overheated. A slight fever from his cold, I surmised. It was, indeed, warm in the room. But his flush darkened in spots at the temples and above one eyebrow in what looked like small bruises.

"I got a list of forbidden fruits from your brother," Ray said. "I sorted out the cheese and salami ones, and anything with olives or sour cream. The rest should be fine." He pointed to Citizen Cane. "Sorry to hear about your accident."

"It was no accident," I said. "That girl meant to hurt somebody. I just got in the way, and I don't know why it had to be me. I really don't like to talk about it, Father Boudreau."

"Ray. Call me Ray."

"OK." *And please don't try to counsel me.*

He grinned puckishly. "As for the 'why me' part, there's a saying in my line of work: 'It's a mystery.' We'll leave it at that."

I was starting to like him. "Maybe you can solve another little mystery for me, Ray," I said. "Just how is it that you know my brother Dan?"

"Ever since his breakdown."

"Pardon me?"

"His truck. He looked like he was in trouble, pulled over with the hood up. I happened to be out on a call. I gave him a lift to the garage. We got talking."

"When was that?"

"Last fall, when I first arrived. We kept in touch. When he's in town, he comes to Mass. After your — incident, he said to expect you."

So I was right. Dan planned to fix us up all along. Just like with Suzie Plotnick for the junior prom. No wonder he was so eager about my coming here. "Well, he's quite a guy."

"Yes. He really cares about you."

"He told you a lot about me, did he?"

"More than he should, maybe. But don't hold it against him. It's just that he admires you so."

The tea-kettle trilled.

"I'll get it," came a gravelly voice from the kitchen.

"Thank you, Father," Ray called over his shoulder. He cupped his mouth conspiratorially and leaned toward me. "That's Father Brian, the rector here. Been here for years. Came in a canoe with Père Marquette, they say." The eyes twinkled. But what I noticed was that the elastic wrist wraps extended up his arms. Could be a sprain, I thought.

Carpel tunnel.

Circulatory problems.

Nail holes.

I tried not to stare.

"So, how's the cabin working out for you?" Ray asked.

"Fine. Just what I needed. Some peace and quiet."

"And how's the book coming? Tell me about it."

There wasn't much to tell, but I said something pompous, the way academics do when measuring each other up, dropping names, seeing who can pee higher on the wall. He listened patiently, nodding at the right points to wordlessly communicate: "I understand that" or "I've read his work."

As soon as I'd exhausted my bellows, he said, "There was a fine piece along those lines in last quarter's *Context* — or was it *Rhetorica*?" Ray stroked his chin, unmindful of the Spandex across his palm. "I forget. They all run together. Let's have a look after tea, and I can photocopy it for you in the church chancellery. Oh, that's our fancy Catholic word for office. Our secretary, Lois, is already gone for the day."

Father Brian shuffled through the archway pushing a wheeled cart. Two porcelain cups on saucers with spoons chattered beside a steaming pot and a bowl of various teabags. Small biscuits and preserves sat in a basket. The old priest's jowled face turned down in a scowl, and the small, stern mouth looked like a Christmas nutcracker's. He was *Going My Way*'s straitlaced Father Fitzgibbon to Bing Crosby's breezy Father Chuck O'Malley.

"Thank you, Father," Ray said. "Stay and join us?"

"I've got things to do," he said woodenly. "Will you be long, Mr. —?"

"Stubblefield," I said, warm in the neck. "I just came to drop off something."

"And maybe pick up a few books," Ray said.

"Be sure that's all you pick up," Father Brian said, his eyes narrowed.

"It's a particularly nasty cold going around," Ray explained. "Father's just getting over it." He turned to the rector. "I told you my decongestant would work. Isn't that right?"

Father Brian sniffed, disdainful. "Just be careful, Mr. Stubblefield. Good evening." He left, checking his watch. Timing my stay, perhaps.

Ray chose a biscuit and apricot spread. "Try this," he suggested. "Father Brian makes the preserves himself. A family farm recipe."

"Not keen on visitors, is he?" I commented.

"Just a bit tired of them," Ray replied. "There haven't been this many people coming here for a long time."

"But since you came —"

"A deluge." He poured the water. "From thirty families to near three hundred. And visitors galore. And do you know why?"

Because you're a stigmatic and heal people? I nearly blurted.

"Consolidation. We're the only Catholic church serving a fifty-five-mile radius. And I'm part-time, if you can believe it."

That wasn't what I had a hard time believing.

"I'm also with the diocesan healthcare and bioethics commission. That chews up a lot of time, if you think about all the hospitals and nursing homes the Church operates."

Sounded logical to me. Maybe he took his healing show on the road.

"But our growth is mainly due to the growing Latino community: Mexicans, Salvadorans, some Guatemalans. Immigrants looking for work. I'm part Hispanic, you know. Mexican grandmother. I never learned the language. But the seasonal workers, the cannery men — they hear there's a *padre* who speaks to their issues, respects their ways — they come with their families. I started Guadalupe services in December and went bilingual for some Masses. Spanish — not French, as the name Boudreau might suggest." He smiled winsomely. "At first, Father Brian wasn't too happy about it."

"Why not? He would be glad, I'd think."

"He's a dear man, accustomed to his privacy, a tad old-fashioned and, shall we say, a bit on the clericalist side." He caught himself using a technical term. "I mean, the sound of a guitar at Mass still makes him squint. But I tell you, the Latinos have brought new life to the church, new life for a town that was hemorrhaging young people. I'm sure you saw all the Spanish businesses in town, just on the drive over here?"

"Yes, I saw some," I answered, thinking of *Angelo's Auto Repair, Laredo Liquors, Taco Grande, Casa Musica.* The Town and Country

Insurance office — which I needed to visit later to check on my disability insurance — had a neon *Se Habla Español* sign flashing in its window. I also thought of the trailer parks full of loitering coffee-colored men and rusted muscle cars.

"Not all the businesses are good, mind you," he said. "Take those check-cashing shops promising *rapido* service, for example. They advance cash to customers at a 20-percent interest rate for a two-week loan. If the debt can't be repaid, they will gladly roll it over for another 20 percent. In Illinois, the average customer has ten renewals. Can you believe it?"

I did the math in my head — not an easy task for me. Peggy always paid the bills. "That means in just a few months they'll owe more than they borrowed."

"Twice as much, in interest alone," he specified. "A field worker or meat packer making minimum wage, whose dormitory-housing costs are deducted from their wages, can't make it."

"So what do they do?"

"Some sell drugs — meth labs are all over, the ingredients easily available from farm operations. Some come to the church for help. Not for money, mind you. They are proud people. They want a voice, someone to speak up for them, to speak up for their rights and dignity. So I do. I've made a few enemies that way."

"Like who?"

"Owners of the large businesses who employ illegals. I guess I threaten their supply of cheap labor. The slaughterhouse, for example. I should be careful, don't you think? They're accustomed to killing." He waved his wounded hand at the basket. "Oh, forgive me. I prattle on so. Please, take any tea you like. There's green tea. That's what you had before, right? I like this Red Zinger, myself."

I chose the green. "What about all the old folks I see everywhere in town?" I ventured. "They're not Latino."

"Ask Father Brian — he's better with the senior set, since he's getting ready to retire, too." He set down the tea gently with both hands, as though the cup had become heavy. "But I think I know what you're getting at. I'll put it this way: You didn't want to talk about your condition, and I feel the same way about mine. I'm sure you, more than others, will understand. Besides, in the words of our mutual friend Aristotle, 'It will contribute toward one's object, who wishes to acquire a facility in the gaining of knowledge, to doubt judiciously.' "

"I'm already good at doubting," I said, impressed by his fluency in Aristotle.

"Good," Ray said. "It will keep you open-minded. But uncertainty is no virtue in itself. Humility of the intellect is. As Aquinas says, 'He who has never doubted has never truly believed.' "

"Undoubtedly."

He grinned. "Tell you what," he said. "Come to the Friday Fish Fry. We run it all through Lent in cooperation with the county Food Pantry. I could use some more help, even though I've got a regular crew of college kids. You'll like them. Father Brian calls them my groupies. Ha! Anyway, you'll get a home-cooked meal and meet a bunch of people who live out Aristotle's principles practically because they know that you are what you do by habit."

"You've read *Nichomachean Ethics?*"

"Religiously."

We shared a laugh, compared more notes on the *Ethics*, and drained the tea. We repaired to his first-floor office after we both struggled a little to get up from our seats. We had that in common, too, it seemed. Once he clicked on the brass lamp, I saw that the collection was, indeed, rather good. I recognized many of the titles printed on the spines, and should not have been surprised that many had Greek and Latin lettering. *Try this one*, he said. *And this. How about this one?* He plucked them without pain from between two bronze bookends, one a model of the Parthenon and one a basilica, lamenting about the small book allowance he had in such a small parish.

In the Volvo, after waving farewell — I still didn't want to shake those elastic-wrapped hands — I forgave Dan for trying to hook me up with a healer. *He'll be good for me, although I'll remain lame,* I told myself. One doesn't often find someone conversant in Aristotle, in the boonies or anywhere else.

Wishing to be friends is quick work, but friendship is a slow ripening fruit, Aristotle reminded me as I pulled away, adjusting the mirror.

The blinds snapped shut.

Father Brian was making sure I was gone.

CHAPTER 8

On the way back to the cabin, I stopped at the Value Mart for some facial tissues and cough drops. I didn't reach First Class in Scouting for nothing. *Be prepared.*

To exit the store, I cut through a snaking line of muscular men with tattoos and olive-skinned women hugging fussy babies, all awaiting a turn at the Western Union machine. A teenaged girl thumbed through a plastic rosary, reciting under her breath *Padre nuestro, que estas en los cielos, santificado sea el tu nombre.* It was pay-day somewhere, and money — along with a prayer or two — was being sent back home to families south of the border in Mexico, Panama, and elsewhere. I supposed the Value Mart owner took a profitable cut, but would prefer that the money be spent in the store itself on hardware, household items, and overpriced convenience foods.

A light sleet needled the windshield. A city sander sprayed salt that clicked in my wheel wells. At least I wouldn't fishtail into the river tonight. I imagined getting back to the cabin safely only to slip on the glazed porch step, my leg pretzeled under me, with Citizen Cane spinning away in the dark like a hockey stick after a hard check. I ached for the fire where I might unknot my knuckles, now locked on the steering wheel. Thank the gods I had nowhere else to go to-night. Maybe I'd play Terrego's "Recuerdos de la Alhambra in A Minor" before nodding off with the priest's copy of Nussbaum and Rorty's *Essays on Aristotle's de Anima.*

Tucking that title in my coat pocket, I left the others on the passenger seat. No need to try a balancing act. Good thing — I needed the spare hand to pluck a note tacked to my cabin door: *Young gal came to see you. Said its urgent. See me. Beth.*

She was watching out for me and dropped in. That saved a treacherous walk across the drive.

"How young, Beth?" I asked after I closed the door behind her. "Kid from the campground?"

"Oh, no, dearie," she said, flashing a flirty smile. "She's a sweet twenty-something. Well, she's closer to thirty by now, I think. Maybe the other side of thirty. Hoo-boy, the years fly by, don't they? She turned into a looker, too. She used to be a skinny thing. Big eyes, the color of peanut-butter fudge. Got married too young, went away a while, it didn't work out, came back to town. Oh, she gave me her card."

It identified Casey Malone, a reporter for the *Sinnissippi County Weekly Observer*.

"That's our weekly shopper," Beth explained. "Says what the Kiwanis and 4-H are up to, church suppers, farm auctions. And the police blotter, everyone reads that so's to see whose kids got in trouble for squealing tires and — well, other things."

"Sounds like you know her."

"Oh, sure. She's a local girl. Married a Malone. Common name here. They come in the 1850s with The Homestead Act and their farm is still out by The Four Corners, you know where the big blasted oak is? No? I forget you're not from around here. Lots of settlers come then by mule train from out East and up the river from St. Loo. The farms have passed through the families for generations, but now young ones are movin' away. Some come back home, like her. They get homesick, and then they —"

"Did she say what she wanted?"

"Nope. She just said she wanted to talk to you."

Just ducky, I thought. The city reporters hounded me after the school shooting and even out here they just can't leave me alone. "Talk about what?"

"Didn't say. Your book, maybe?"

"You know about that?"

"Danny told us."

I flipped the card. "Did you read the back?"

Beth blushed. "Can't be helped. She wrote it while I was standin' there. Sounds like she wants to see you bad."

Can you meet me at The Firehouse? it said in loopy script. *See you their tonite?* I'd seen such writing dozens of times in student papers, with the mixed homonyms *there/their* and alternate spellings. It often turned out to be the kind of student who used "like," "I mean," and "you know" as punctuation in speech.

"What's the Firehouse?" I asked.

"That's a new bar and grill downtown," Beth said. "Some retired firemen bought the old fire station and fixed it up like a firehouse. Brass pole in the middle. Coats and helmets on the walls. Model firetrucks all about. I hear the reubens are real good."

Sauerkraut was bad for me, but I didn't say so. I now recalled the place: cheap domestic lagers on tap. Not really worth driving in slippery winter weather — especially to talk to a young reporter about something I was trying to forget. "Maybe I'll call tomorrow," I said.

"She's got dimples to die for, and she's still single," Beth said with a wink.

Was she deliberately trying to hook us up? Before I could ask her if she arranged my meeting with Ray at the café, she stepped off the porch, held up her palm to the sky and announced: "Rain stopped. Guess things are warmin' up."

They certainly were.

CHAPTER 9

A serpentine haze coiled among the spotlights in the smoky Firehouse. The new Illinois laws banning cigarettes in restaurants were cheerfully ignored. A Shania Twain tune wrapped itself around the firehouse brass pole in the middle. At the bar and the tables, men in flannel shirts and John Deere caps watched the Bulls game on TVs or played euchre between tumblers of pale blonde beer. Along the far wall, at a booth beneath a fire hose, a waitress cleared dishes from the place of a young honey-haired woman in a navy-blue blazer. When the woman saw me, she beckoned with a blood-red fingernail and her glossy lips mouthed, *Stubblefield?*

I introduced myself. "You must be Miss Malone?"

She glanced around me. "Were you followed?"

"Sorry?"

"Did you notice anyone following you in a car?"

"I don't think I understand."

"No, I guess you don't. Have a seat. Do you need a hand, Mr. Stubblefield?"

"I'm OK," I said, holding in a grunt. Citizen Cane banged on the wood bench and dropped to the floor. She retrieved it for me. So much for impressing an attractive young woman. I took the cane, leaned it against the wall and suddenly I wished I'd shaven. *Ye gods, I must look like a homeless vet under a bridge.* I folded my hands and said, "Now, why don't you tell me what this is all about, Miss Malone?"

"Call me Casey. Say, can I buy you dinner? The chicken parmesan is on special, and it's good here. I just finished mine, but —"

"No, that's OK." The cheese and tomato sauce would make me faint. Very bad form.

"A drink, then? The house merlot isn't bad. Better than what you find in a campus bar, anyway."

"Thanks, but —" I couldn't have red wine, either. I decided not to explain. "I'll have a light beer."

She ordered it.

"What's this about being followed?" I asked.

"Have you spoken to anyone else about your time with Father Ray?"

"How would you know about that? And what business is it of yours?"

"I'm a reporter. *The County Observer*? I'm after the facts."

An eager beaver. What was this, a school project? "Facts about what?"

"About Father Ray. You're his friend, right?"

"If I were his friend, I wouldn't tell you anything."

The beer arrived. I took a deep swig from the tall frosted mug and swallowed my ego. As much as I didn't want to meet with a reporter, suddenly I resented not being the real subject of the interview. I felt silly for thinking so.

"Well, I just assumed that since you spent so much time with him since you arrived —"

"How would you know about that?"

"There are three parts to a news story," she said, tucking a tendril of hair behind an elfin ear. "Observation, interview, and background. I was observing."

"You mean you were staking out the church?"

"Just driving by. I noticed your car."

"How did you know it was my car?"

"From the description I got from the bookstore."

"And how'd you know where to find me?"

"Campground sticker in the windshield when you parked at the church."

"So you're a detective, too."

"Reporters have to be sometimes."

"And you've been following me."

She stroked the stem of her wine glass and licked her lower lip deliciously. "Look, I don't mean to offend you. It's just that this could be my first big story. It could be my big break. Nothing like this has ever happened in this town before."

"Nothing like what?" It couldn't be my visit, for sure.

"Nothing like Ray."

"I see. You're hoping for an exclusive interview with an insider. Is that why you're wondering if I've spoken to anyone else?"

She glanced up. Beth was right about the eyes. "Yeah." She smiled. Beth was right about the dimples, too. I took another swallow to cool off.

"Ever since the feast of Lourdes in February," she said, "there have been more people coming, and a few out-of-town reporters, too. I figure the hometown girl deserves the inside story, an exclusive."

"I can't really help you," I said. "I just met this fellow, and I know the least of anybody, I'm sure. Why don't you interview him directly?"

"I've spoken with him. At some length, actually. We were volunteers together in the literacy program at the community college for a while in the Fall. But he never talked about his — you know — condition."

"Well, then, I'll tell you all I know," I teased a little. "He's an Aquinas scholar. He's been here about seven months. He likes Red Zinger tea, and he knows a little about Greek mythology. He has a nice library, and he writes passable poetry. Your turn."

"A notable Aquinas scholar stuck in a backwater like this?" she pressed.

"So he's humble. And he's from this area. I saw that in your newspaper."

"I wrote the story," she said. "Did you meet Father Brian?"

"Yes."

"He's been here for decades. Actually, he baptized me. It's not really common for priests to be at one place for a long time, you know. The Church moves priests around a lot, every seven years or so. But the Church hierarchy seems to shuffle Father Ray from parish to parish much more often than others. They're pretty hush-hush about why."

"Like the way they used to move around pedophile priests?" I asked. "Is that what you suspect?"

"Nothing sexual like that," she said, combing her hair back behind the other ear. A pearl winked from the lobe. "Although he seems to be sick a lot, with frequent flu-like symptoms, and he has bruises like someone with AIDS."

"So you think he's gay and has AIDS?" I laughed.

She laughed in reply, and the dimples deepened. "No, nothing like that. It's all the commotion he stirs up from — you know. Want another beer?"

I saw the creamy froth slide down the glass. Had I finished it already? "Sure," I said absently. She signaled the server.

"Church records are closed to public scrutiny," she said. "But my check of diocesan newspapers shows he's been shunted around, like, a lot. Fire and police records show his churches have had a number of ambulance calls — but there aren't any more after he leaves."

"So you think more people are getting hurt and not healed, and he's a charlatan? Is that your story?"

"No, not at all. The ambulance calls are all for him."

The server swiped my glass and set down a full one.

"So he has health problems," I said. I knew all about that. "He's entitled to some privacy about it."

"I understand where you're coming from," she said, with a nod at Citizen Cane. "But a public figure has fewer rights."

"He's not Bing Crosby," I said. "He's just a priest."

"Not if he has The Gift."

"The what?"

"You know — the stigmata. The wounds of Christ in his hands or wrists, his feet or ankles, and maybe even his side and brow."

"I don't know anything about that."

"They say St. Francis had it first. And there were several reports of the phenomenon in the late nineteenth century, early twentieth. The bleeding comes at times of spiritual intensity, especially around Holy Week. It's usually accompanied by the ability to heal others. The latest one was Padre Pio in the 1990s, and he was made a saint. They exhumed him a while ago and put him on display in a glass case. He had hardly decayed."

"Very good. I see you've done your homework," the teacher in me said.

"It's possible Father Ray is someone like that, too."

"It's a mystery," I said with a devilish grin, "and you won't find out the answers from me." Maybe I liked the attention of a nice-looking young woman who wasn't there to draw blood or exercise my leg. It had been a long time.

"Was he wearing his bandages or braces when you saw him last, Reed?"

Reed? Who gave her permission to be familiar? Still, I liked it. I saw no harm in being honest, and the beer was loosening my tongue. "Sort of. Fingerless gloves and a Spandex-type wrapping. Like the kind typists with tendon problems have. Lots of secretaries in my college wear elastic braces like it, for carpel tunnel. He's an academic. He types a lot."

"Anything else?"

"He had a rather bad cold, and he's taking decongestants or anti-histamines — I forget which."

"They say he absorbs the illnesses of others, and that's how they get well, and that's why he's always sick. *Surely he hath borne their sicknesses and carried their sorrows*, like Christ, so they say."

"Who says?"

"His fan club."

"You're kidding."

"They find out where he's been moved and follow. They put out a newsletter, post information on their website, and hire chartered buses for the sick."

"Maybe that's exactly why he moves around," I suggested. "To get away from them."

"Or to avoid being exposed as a fake."

"Maybe the real scandal is in the fan club charging an arm and a leg for the trip." I regretted the idiom, but she took it in good humor with a laugh. The dimples killed me.

"They're convinced he's a living saint. They say they document the healings so they can make a case to raise him to the altar someday after he dies."

"Raise him where?"

"To the altar. It means to declare him a saint."

"So you don't believe it?"

She pursed her wet lips. "A reporter has to remain objective. Skeptical. I just want to know if he's for real. Don't you? Isn't that why you're here in this godforsaken town?" She nodded toward my cane.

"I came to recover from a work-related injury in some peace and quiet, that's all." I took a swig of beer. "And to write a book."

"So how'd you connect with Father Ray?"

No need to mention Dan's set-up. "We share an interest in Aristotle. That's what my book is about."

She wasn't interested. "Did you notice his needle marks?"

"Hmm?" I said with my nose in my mug.

"Some think he has a drug problem, and he wears the bandages to cover his tracks. That might explain the fits of illness and the bruising. Or he's into self-mutilation like cutting for — you know — mortification."

I drained the glass. "I didn't see any marks. I don't know what causes the bruises, but they looked awful —"

I felt a hand on my shoulder. "I think you've had enough, sir."

The server, a girl with the nametag *Bianca* on her apron, lifted away my glass and slapped the bill on the table. "Juan will take that up front, miss."

"Now wait a minute," I objected.

"It's OK, Reed. We're done here."

Casey helped me out of the booth. The hip didn't hurt, but it would in the morning. "I'd better pass on the beer at the Fish Fry," I muttered.

"Oh, are you going to that?" Casey said. "I've been going, too. I guess I'll see you there."

"Good," I said, my tongue thick. I steadied myself with Citizen Cane. A little wobbly. "You know, that server had some nerve hustling us out."

"She's one of them, Reed," Casey said, a finger to her lip.

"One of who?"

"The fans. I wasn't sure at first. She looked unhappy when she realized what we were talking about."

"Why unhappy?"

"They don't want any skeptics getting in the way of their cause. They might keep an eye on you from now on."

The server was whispering something to the cashier. A cluster of Mexican men, the busboys and cooks, gathered at the bar's cash register, arms folded, glancing in our direction.

"I'll take care of the tab," Casey said close to my ear. The fruity smell of merlot on her breath was intoxicating. "Thanks for talking to me. See you Friday. Can I pick you up?"

"Yeah, sure."

"About 5:30? They serve at six."

"OK."

I hoped by then the hangover would be over.

CHAPTER 10

Casey picked me up in her crimson Grand Am at 5:30 sharp. Beth Berger waved through her window as we left the campground. An old matchmaker from way back, I laughed to myself, maybe a believer in the "second younger wife" school of thought that some of my divorced contemporaries followed.

On the road, Casey filled me in on the Helping Hands Food Pantry. It borrowed space from St. Mary's Church, a 1960s brick facility built beside the original that had been erected in the early 1800s by pioneer settlers and the Sinnissippi Indian tribe using riverbank rocks. The nonprofit pantry packed and distributed food twice a month to families falling within a monthly income range. Most of the immigrant families qualified. The Fish Fry, though, was open to anyone.

"So who comes to this?" I asked.

"The Mexican families who use the pantry, mostly. Some of the old members. A few drifters. It's a social event, and a way to observe Lent. You Catholic?"

"No," I said. "My brother is. By marriage. So, is that why you go?"

"Not really," she replied. "It's to see Ray."

I arched an eyebrow.

"The background part of my story," she said. "C'mon. You don't think I'd hit on a priest?"

"He's about your age," I said.

"I like older men," she said, a tempting smile playing at the corner of her mouth.

She parked on the street behind the church. The main parking lot out front was full of pickup trucks and Latin rhythms. Inside a garage with lawn-care equipment, two men in white aprons and blue

Knights of Columbus caps worked the fryers. One man with oven mitts carried a large pot indoors. We held the doors for him.

Inside, two college-aged boys — one in a flowered beach shirt and the other sporting a World Youth Day commemorative tee — played guitars softly as I'd seen in campus cafés. Once the doors opened, the tables filled with short women gabbing in Spanish, dark-haired kids, weathered men in straw hats, blue-haired parishioners. Some college students took donations at the door. Father Brian greeted guests by name, bending his ear to a woman in a wheelchair, holding her knotty hand.

Ray met us in the kitchen, where a few other students were already working the stoves. He wore rubber gloves up to his elbows. "Hey, Reed, you're just in time," he said. "I need a dishwasher. How about it?"

"Sure," I agreed. No walking involved.

"I'll serve the corn like last week," Casey said.

"Sure," Ray said, watching the crowd gather. "Sure, if you want."

"Can I bring your plate to you?" she asked.

"You don't have to."

"I will."

"You really shouldn't," he said.

"No problem," she said. "I insist."

Father Brian rang a hand-bell, and Ray excused himself hastily for the blessing. We bowed heads for grace, in English, then in Spanish. I discreetly scratched my eyebrows. After the Sign of the Cross, the music and chatter resumed.

I donned an apron while Casey left for the serving tables in the dining room. I ran water in the deep aluminum sinks. It felt like scout camp. Scrape here, wash here, and bleach rinse here. The pots, fryers, and such wouldn't show up for a while. The rest was paper and plastic. I examined the kitchen to see where things went. In the walk-in storage closet, little green bricks lined the baseboard. So I wasn't the only one with a rodent problem.

"Help you find something?" twittered a cheery voice.

It was one of the students, a pencil-thin girl with black bangs and a shock of blue dye. The silver piercings in her eyebrows glittered in the fluorescents, and the layered pinks and limes — not to mention the red Converse high-tops — shouted "artsy."

"Bleach?" I said.

"Under the sink," she replied, leaning back a little with her oversize fawn eyes fixed on me. A painter, for sure. "You're new here."

"Yes," I said. "I met Ray this week and he —"

"Oh, like, isn't he GREAT?" she squealed, hands clasped to her chest. A medal hung there. "He, like, saved my LIFE."

"How so?"

"I write poetry, OK?"

Quelle surprise.

"And I, like, gave up on it when all my professors said it sucked, but Brad — that's him over here — said he knew a cool priest who wrote poetry too and I should show my work to him and I never thought a priest could be cool but if he wrote poetry how cool is that? So I showed him my stuff, and he said once you find meaning in your life, Ashleigh — that's my name, Ashleigh and it's spelled funny but anyways — once you find meaning in your life, he said, your poems will find meaning on their own. And I was, like, wow! I never thought of it like that. And he wrote me a poem on the spot that I still carry around — here, look."

She plunged her blue fingernails into a fringed leather purse attached to her belt and pulled out a wadded sheet of yellow legal-pad paper — just as Ray used in the bookstore. She unfolded it reverently and handed it to me. The blue pen script was Ray's all right. The centered title read, "Penelope at Easter":

> Odysseus strips off his rags and bends the bow,
> And all the mean suitors for my soul
> Gasp
> When he who they thought was dead
> First folds his headcloth in the corner

And shows himself alive,
Having gone through Hades to reclaim me as his right —
Home.

"So that's what I did," she said.

"Did what?" I inquired.

"I came home, too," she said.

"This is your hometown?"

"Home to the Church," she giggled.

"Need a little *help* here, Ashleigh?" It was Brad, the fellow she pointed out, juggling a stack of dirty serving pans. "Where do you want these, sir?"

I indicated the far sink with the disposal unit.

"Brad, what'd he tell you?" Ashleigh asked, grabbing a spatula. "C'mon, don't make me wait."

"I gotta think about this," he said.

She spanked his shoulder with the spatula. "Tell me, Bozo."

"He didn't think it was right for me. He said I was overreacting." He wiped his palms on the apron and then smoothed his golden hair back with both hands while looking at his reflection on a shiny saucepan.

"Brad just converted," Ashleigh explained. "Thought he should leave school for seminary or something."

"The fraternity wasn't happy about it," Brad said.

"Well, neither is Father," Ashleigh said. "You heard what he said: first the blade, then the ear, then the full grain in the ear."

"What's he mean?"

"You got corn in your ears or what? It means it's a process and you need time to grow."

"You're making me hungry." Brad reached for one of the dessert cakes.

"Hey!" Casey said, bustling in and rapping him on the knuckles. "The help gets to eat after the guests. I put some aside for us. I gave Ray his already and he's having it now."

66

"So, do we eat before or after the acrobats and musicians?" I asked.

She wrinkled her nose at me and left with the dessert tray.

Beth never mentioned the cute nose wrinkling.

"Isn't she great?" said Ashleigh. "I mean, like, after that jerk dumped her and she got all depressed and got hooked on those pain pills? And then she met Father Ray and that all stopped."

"That's when he started to — sir, you know, right?" Brad asked.

"Bleed?" I said.

"At this parish, anyway," Ashleigh said. "He's a victim soul. He's offering up his suffering for someone's sins."

"For Casey," Brad said. "It's gotta be."

"He's, like, a saint," Ashleigh breathed.

Through the serving-window, I saw the alleged saint seated at one of the tables, finishing his meal. A knot of people tightened around him, chatting. No one fell into a seizure, and no demons screamed out.

Except one.

"C'mon, sweetface. Just one kiss for dessert!"

"No, thanks, Kenny."

"One! That's all I'm askin'!"

"Keep moving, Kenny."

It was Casey's voice. I took Citizen Cane and shambled to the doorway for a better look. A dark man with a wooly beard bent over the bean-bowl, smacking his lips.

"Put 'er there, sweetie face," he rasped, tapping his pruny mouth.

"Forget it, Kenny," the server next to Casey said.

"Shut up," the man snarled. He grabbed Casey's apron top. "C'mere!" He pulled.

I was there by now. "That's enough, bud," I said, poking him in the chest with the cane. "Sit down."

He released Casey and huffed at me. He stank of gin. "*You* sit down, altar boy." He grabbed the cane and shoved it. I stumbled backwards and fell into the serving table with a clatter.

From behind, Ray touched the man's shoulder. "Kenny, come out with me."

Kenny cringed as though he'd been burned. "You freak!" He raised his metal tray and smashed it down on Ray. In reflex, Ray lifted his arms. The tray smashed into his wrists and the priest crumpled to his knees.

Women shrieked. Brad and another male student tackled Kenny. Food spilled. Kenny howled and kicked. Babies cried. Someone shouted *"Ambulancia!"* and when a few men parted, I saw why.

Bloody rivulets ran down Ray's arms from the wrists, soaking his wraps. A few people crossed themselves, and one man stripped off a shirt to apply pressure to the wounds.

"That won't help," I heard Ray groan. "Get me to the clinic — now."

Kenny thrashed free, strong as a dozen men, and cannoned out the door drunkenly, knocking over chairs and children. They bawled.

Phones beeped.

"¡Llame el dispensario!"

"¡Un doctor!"

"¡Policia!"

Brad pulled the priest up by the armpits, but he couldn't stand on his own feet. Ray broke out in a sweat and wiped his brow, smearing it with blood. The two students carried him to the door, where a truck waited, engine running. Once he was outside, several people prayed aloud: *"Ave Maria, repleto de la gracia —"*

Casey recovered my cane and wiped corn kernels off my face with her apron. "Are you OK?" she asked.

"I think so, I just bumped —"

One woman began to pray louder than the others, then even louder. Shouting, almost. She walked tenderly, shuffling by inches, and clapped her hands. Tears glistened in her eyes. The room fell silent. Behind her was an empty wheelchair.

Hers.

"I can walk!" she cried, arms outstretched for balance. "I can walk!"

CHAPTER 11

In investigating the cause of each thing, it is also necessary to be precise, Aristotle prompted me. *Every effect has a particular cause.*

So what caused the wheelchair woman to walk? What caused the campground boy's tumor to disappear? Aristotle allowed that "the doctor is the cause of health" in a similar way that the sculptor was the "cause" of a statue. But was Ray — or some power in him — the "cause" of these healings? And were they "healings" at all, rather than euphoric, temporary remissions based on an intense emotional experience? Perhaps the "effect" was in question as much as the "cause." Hope and hormones can do powerful things. I'd seen remarkable things happen in hospitals where Peggy stayed. One thing for sure: Ray's reputation was causing the campground to fill again.

I tried calling Ray after my exercises to check on his condition. All I got was the answering machine — as the day before, and the day before that. Father Brian was screening the calls, I guessed, and dumping mine. I said something polite about returning Ray's books, but still heard nothing back. I wondered if he'd been hustled away again by his superiors, or removed to the county hospital. I called there to ask for the visiting hours and a room number. *We have no one here listed by that name, sir.* Then he's been released already? *There's no record of anyone by that name here.*

That evening, in the middle of my leg exercises, a car purred to the cabin. By the time I stood and steadied myself, the visitor was at the door, rapping. *Maybe it was Ray, coming out of hiding, asking for refuge,* I joked with myself.

It was Casey. She wore a chocolate sweater, and her butterscotch hair poured around the vanilla blouse collar gracefully.

"Glad I found you in," she said, glancing around. "Nice little place. Am I disturbing anything?"

"Not at all," I said, my neck hot. "Come in."

"No, that's OK. I was passing by and thought I'd say hello."

"Just hello?"

"I wanted to tell you that I saw Ray at the rectory. I didn't have your phone number, so —"

"Where's he been?"

"There the whole time, I think. Just lying low."

"How'd he look?"

"The usual. A little hunched over, a bit slow — like he was really tired. I don't think he'll do the Friday Fish Fry this week. But the anointing of the sick is still scheduled for Saturday. Care to go?"

Not exactly dinner and a movie. I hadn't darkened a church door since Peggy's funeral, and didn't care to do it now. The smell of gladiolas and roses still sent me into a spin, and who knows how I'd react to old ladies' perfumes or the spikenard of a censer? But if I said no, then she'd —

"Reed? What do you think?"

"Yeah. Yeah, OK. Great." A date is a date.

"Good," she said with an adventurous toss of her tawny mane. "Meet me at the church's back door at about six?"

I agreed. She touched her fingers to her lips and blew a kiss carelessly as she backed down the porch and slid into the Grand Am. Her goodbye wave stirred a quiver in my gut. What was I thinking? There was nothing going on here. She was just a little older than my students, for heaven's sakes.

The body is most fully developed at thirty, and the mind at about forty-nine, Aristotle said.

If Dan finds out about this, I mused, he'd needle me about going to church and getting religion. But more than that, he'll either kid me about seeing a younger woman or scold me for forgetting about Peggy.

It was everything I feared it would be.

First, the buses. Four chartered coaches in convoy, marked "special," with tinted windows like state-trooper sunglasses, belched into town and lined up in single file in the church lot. When the bus doors hissed open, the faithful flowed out like tourists on a spiritual package tour, camcorders humming. Walkers popped open like umbrellas; canes unfolded and snapped straight.

RVs and vans with motorized lifts lined the streets. Two television vans with antennae and satellite dishes on their roofs had found spots on someone's front lawn. I had to park the Volvo several blocks away. I passed vendors in hooded sweatshirts, seated at card tables covered with medals, plaster statues, and bottled holy water from the Jordan River. I once heard that sellers near medieval shrines hawked vials of the Virgin's tears, splinters of the True Cross, John the Baptist's teeth, Gabriel's wing feathers. But thank heaven, there was none of that here. Still, I was embarrassed by my own spiritual voyeurism, the same ambivalence one feels at a carnival when the barker urges customers to see the three-legged lady for a nickel. There is revulsion and morbid curiosity together when he calls, "Step right up," and you do, on a dare.

The pilgrims herded quietly to the church, rosaries clicking. Some glanced upward to an April sky blue as the Virgin's veil, half-expecting a spinning sun as at Fatima. Two squad cars blocked the street at both ends, their blue and red lights flashing like votives. I hoped they wouldn't throw anyone into a seizure.

Casey waited at the back door. "It's locked," she said. "We'll have to go in the front like everyone else."

"I don't know about this."

"Don't worry. You fit right in."

She was right. I felt old.

Women in wimples and veils steered wheelchairs bumper-to-bumper up the handicap access ramp, as crowded as the on-ramp to the Eisenhower Expressway on a Friday afternoon. A gabble of Mexicans, some of whom I recognized from the Fish Fry, pressed inside. The town's policemen, greatly outnumbered, directed traffic as best they could at the intersections, waving vehicles through with glowing batons. A scuffle erupted across the street — someone objected to having a picture taken. A flash, a shout, a shove. Two cops shouldered their way into the melee. They hauled out a lanky man with spaghetti hair and three cameras swinging from his long neck.

"Freedom of the press!" he croaked, his upper arms secured in the officers' grip. His alligator boots carved two furrows in the muddy lawn of the corner lot. "First Amendment! I have rights!"

More cameras emerged from jackets and purses — single-use Fujis, a few digitals — to record the event. Snap snap. Snap.

"Someone you know?" I asked Casey.

"One of those out-of-town reporters I told you about," she said with a sour look. "Let's keep moving."

No sense in staring, I agreed. I felt as much an intruder as the photographer. I wondered if my skepticism would deny these sincere people their sought-for succor. After all, didn't the Gospels record somewhere that "he could do no mighty work there, because of their unbelief"? I resolved to look it up later, appalled by my ignorance. I could cite the Greeks but not the texts that divided history in half. All those Gideon Bibles gone unread in hotel drawers during academic conferences. At some meetings, they had served as thick coasters for cocktails while we argued over a "modes" approach to composition versus an epistemic approach and the politics of grading black dialect.

Once inside, I made my first mistake by missing the holy-water font. When I slipped into a rear pew, I saw Casey dip her knee behind me and realized I'd made my second mistake — I'd failed to genuflect before entering the row. Then I kicked the kneeler. A few accusing eyes turned to me, as though I were a stray dog.

The church looked plainer than I'd envisioned. No Baroque columns, Michelangelo statues, or Sistine ceiling. Remodeled in the space-age '60s, the sanctuary's focus was a sleek altar-table on a dais, standing in relief from a brick backdrop and a soaring abstract stained-glass window with thick pieces in stone frames. Silver-bowl chandeliers, like flying saucers, hovered beneath the plank ceiling. If I'd stood on my head, it might look like the hull of a ship. The word *nave*, after all, employed the same root as *navy*, as though the church were the Ark of God in the tossing sea of the world.

I fumbled with a missal from the pew rack as the people stood. The seats creaked; the ship was being launched. A reedy organ led the entrance song. I didn't know the words, of course, but it didn't seem to matter much. Few men around me were singing, anyway. When Casey turned to face the rear narthex entryway, I pressed myself up to watch the procession.

Two altar attendants, both girls in ponytails and dressed in alban surplices, led the way. One bore a high cross like a standard into battle. A layman in a rumpled suit followed with a gilded, oversize book raised to his chest — probably the scripture readings for the day. Ray followed in whispering vestments. He limped. Wheelchairs and walkers squeaked as supplicants turned for a better look. No one fawned or fainted or stretched out to feel him. Ray passed behind the altar, kissed the lacy linen, and hobbled to a chair on the side.

I recognized that halting gait, that gritty look, that grip of the hands. It was the mien of a man in pain. When the song wheezed to an end, the assembly remained standing for the opening. Gesturing a Sign of the Cross, Ray extended his hands:

"The grace of the Lord Jesus Christ and the love of God and the fellowship of the Holy Spirit be with you all."

"And also with you," the people chorused. Some held up medals and beads.

Ray wore his fingerless gloves and long sleeves. His face was shaded a sickly green and purple from the reflected sheen of his vestments.

After Ray announced the saint's day and guided a corporate prayer of confession followed by a sung *Gloria*, the Liturgy of the Word proceeded. The layman read the passages blankly, tripping over words as though he'd never seen them before. But when Ray read from the Gospel, the candles shuddered whenever he waved those wounded hands for emphasis.

I missed the well-practiced responses. I managed to sit without a grunt after the Gospel reading from Luke — a physician, I later learned, although I shouldn't have been surprised that a Greek doctor took interest in the healings of Jesus. I wondered if Aristotle — also a physician — would have. I also wondered how Ray managed to remain standing at the Plexiglas lectern. After all, if he was "stigmatic," would the feet be horribly wounded as well? Or did the wounds come and go?

He sniffled, his narrow nose rubbed raw. The cropped hair poked this way and that as though he'd just been awakened and could not find a comb in time. He steadied himself, lips taut, working them into a reassuring smile. I must have looked like that during the walk-the-ladder exercises with the therapist watching.

"In the name of the Father and of the Son and of the Holy Spirit," he said.

Hands flew. I missed the cue again.

"Friends," he began, "the word *salvation* in English has as its root the word *salve,* that is, 'to comfort with ointment,' 'to soothe a wound.' Next to it in the dictionary you'll find the word *salvage.* To *salvage* something means to rescue and reclaim what is yours by right, to raise it up from ruin and restore it to its original condition and to usefulness. Think of a long-lost ship raised from the bottom of the sea by its owner, and made to sail again. Or some of you know how to rescue an old muscle car from someone's backyard, put a new engine in it, grind off the rust and repaint it, to make it look like new."

Several of the Mexican men buzzed at this. They should have — it was a clever etymological argument.

"This is what God does with us in Christ Jesus. He came to rescue us from the depths of our own helplessness, when it looked, for a while, as though we were lost for good, crusted with the rust of our sinfulness and self-centeredness."

Was it the heat? Was it the homily? All the carbon dioxide in the room? My head had that floating feeling.

"So it is no accident that the Greek word 'to save' — *sozo* — is the same word as 'to heal.' We may not be sick because we have sinned, as some religious people suppose. But I tell you, until we are sick of our sins and unhealthy habits and forsake them, we will never be truly well."

It's the candles, I thought. They're burning up all the oxygen in here, replacing it with fumes. My lungs labored.

"Are you all right?" Casey whispered.

"Just a little warm," I lied. I felt like I'd swallowed a huge stone and it sat where my heart was. What kind of idea was this, to confine myself in a walled space with all these sick people? Who knew what was in the air? Didn't entire churches die off from tuberculosis and influenza in the last century because infected members sang hymns and sprayed the air with germs?

With the homily over and the creed recited, a lector rose for a call-and-response prayer litany:

"To the Lord of love and life, let us pray. For all in need of healing."

"Hear our prayer."

"For all disabled by injury or illness."

"Hear our prayer."

"For all who cannot sleep . . ."

Ye gods, they were all praying for me. It was hard to hear the rest with the throbbing in my ears.

"Come unto me, all you who are burdened and heavy laden, and I will give you rest, the Lord says." With this invitation, the lector took Ray's elbow at the top step. He helped the priest to descend delicately to the prie-dieu rail. Ray walked as though he'd stepped on a nail.

"Showtime," Casey said in my ear.

The pews emptied front to back in the center aisle like oil poured from a vial. Crutches clicked; wheelchairs creaked.

Panic seized my reins, and I gripped Citizen Cane. *Don't expect me to go forward,* I said under my breath.

While supplicants knelt and wheelchairs rolled into place, Ray dabbed oil with his thumb upon each person's forehead. "May the Lord who frees you from sin save you and raise you up."

No one screamed, or sang, or swooned.

Except me.

The ship of the sanctuary spun in a whirlpool, and my head with it. The floor pitched and rolled as on an unsettled sea. "I — I gotta go," I groaned. I slid out; I lurched for the back door, green in the gills. My hip felt like a rusted winch in need of oil.

The frosty air bit my face. I pushed through a knot of bystanders and dropped to one knee on the sidewalk, head bowed to restore the flow of blood, one hand to my hot forehead, one on the cane.

"Reed? Reed, for God's sake, what happened?" Casey asked, following me.

"I just — I just get this way sometimes," I managed. I still saw spots before my eyes — no, they were flashes. The *paparazzi* photographer was at it again.

"I don't know who the hell you are," I said through gritted teeth, "but without a release form, you'll be in for a lawsuit."

"Ah, we pulled in a lawyer this time." The stringy-haired shooter whirled his hand beside his Nikon and pulled it up as though fly-casting. "But not a very good one. Not intrusion. Not false light. Public event. City sidewalk. You'd lose."

"Get the hell away from us," Casey said. "The story's inside."

"Says you," the man said. "Didn't get healed, did we? O ye of little faith. Care to talk about it?"

I tried to stand with Casey helping. "See here, mister —"

"Boyle," he said. "Lance Boyle. *The Weekly Beacon.*" He flashed a smile and a business card. The gold tooth caught me short. He noticed.

"Oh, the tooth," he said. "Red Fox Reservation toxic waste dump. The guard had brass knuckles."

"I have nothing to say. Come on, Casey." I pivoted away.

"Oh, we don't, Mr. Stubblefield?"

I froze. "How'd you know my name?"

"Psychic." He laughed, a donkey's bray. "Well, to be truthful, as a journalist must be, you looked familiar. I ran your plates."

"Excuse me?"

"Motor Vehicle Bureau. Easy to hack if you pose as an insurance rep. Then I checked the news archives from the *Chicago Trib*. There you were, mug shot and all."

"You've got a lot of nerve," Casey said.

"That's how to succeed in this business, Malone," he said with a triumphant smirk. "Maybe if you hadn't flunked out of college and gotten a divorce and a drug habit then —"

"Shut up," she said.

"You know him?" I asked.

"We've met," she answered with a squeezed face.

"So, did you see the bandages? Or did he have the bike racing gloves today?" Boyle asked me.

"Pardon me?"

"The wraps on his hands and wrists? Like Padre Pio. He wore half-mittens, you know. For the bleeding."

"I don't know what you're talking about."

"Sure you do. The last known stigmatic, Padre Pio. Pope John Paul Two made him a saint, not long ago. Not a good Catholic, are you?"

"Not one at all, Mister —" It hit me. "Lance Boyle? Are you kidding?"

"A pen name. I expose frauds. Poke 'em and watch 'em burst. UFOs, weeping icons, photos of heaven's door. They're selling them right over there. Funny how it's the same shape as a Polaroid aperture. I could make a fortune."

"Christ, a tabloid writer."

"Oh, puh-leeze," he grimaced. "Investigative reporter. No 'Turtle with Man's Face' and 'Bird Boy Flies from Cops' for me. That's harmless fun." He tilted his head toward the church. "But this stuff hurts people."

"That is enough, Mr. Boyle. You are the one hurting the people."

It was a short woman, with midnight-black hair, crescent-moon eyes, and a high, gibbous forehead. She wore an aqua raincoat and a stern look. She marched up to Boyle and poked him in the chest. "You stay away from him."

"It's OK, lady," I said with a wave, "we were just leaving —"

"It ees not ho-K," she huffed, Spanish flavoring her vowels. "Look at you. The presence of his scornful spirit is a hinder to the work of God. That is just what you want to have happen, is it not, Meester Boyle? You want for to make Father Ray out to be the fake."

"Because he is one."

"How dare you."

"Hold that pose, Estrella," Boyle said, raising his camera.

She swatted at it, knocking it aside.

"I'll have you arrested for assault," he sneered. "How'd that look on the front page?"

Other women joined Estrella's side, jostling Boyle away from me. Voices were raised. A policeman approached, tapping his baton in his glove. Casey took me by the elbow, and we turned to go.

"Sir?" the policeman called. "That man bothering you?"

"Not anymore," I said with a backward glance.

But Boyle had already slithered away from the clucking women. I turned to Casey. "Who was that woman?"

"I call her The Fan," Casey said. "Estrella Esperanza. She's the postulator."

"The what?"

"Advocate for Ray's cause. The head of the group that wants Ray sainted."

"Wait a minute," I said. "Doesn't he have to die first?"

"Yes, he does. She'll probably see to that, too."

CHAPTER 12

"I'm really sorry 'bout that, Reed — well, sort of sorry."

"You oughta be, Danny-boy," I half-scolded him into the cell phone. I still wasn't sure whether to be mad or amused. "You set me up so I'd get healed by this guy — or worse, converted. Isn't that right?"

Dan coughed and the phone crackled. "Well, OK, I confess." He laughed. "Y'know, I've had a lot to confess lately."

"What do you mean by that?"

"Look, you know I did this Catholic thing because of Loretta, but I gotta tell ya, on my hauls I've been listening to these guys on the radio, and they make a lot of sense. One of them is even a former Presbyterian pastor who — well, you should hear this guy, Reed. I got some of his tapes."

"Keep 'em, Danny," I said.

"And then I met this guy Ray and we got to talkin' and he's just — I dunno — he's so different."

"Tell me about it."

"Not just like *that*. Hey, he reminds me of you."

"Really?"

"All them books. Look, bonehead, you said you were gonna write a book. I figured you'd like someone to talk to who understands your big words. And I thought, geez, as long as you're there, maybe he can help you with the hip, too, and maybe you'd even go to the anointing of the sick. So give it a try. What the hell ya got to lose?"

"My pride?"

"Not a bad thing to lose."

"Truth is," I admitted, "I went last Saturday."

"Ya did?"

An attractive young woman with caramel eyes asked me to go, and how could I say no to her? "Yeah, me. Just curious."

"What happened? Wait — are you calling to say your leg is all right now?"

"No. I got sick. Almost passed out in the middle of the service."

He chortled. "Only you, Reed."

"I didn't take my meds so I could drive there without feeling woozy, OK? Then I got to feeling closed in. It was crowded."

"You're OK now, though?"

"Sure."

"Good — 'cause I thought I'd swing by for a little visit."

"When?"

"Wednesday. It's Easter weekend, so I'll take a couple — three days off. That OK with you?"

I balked. I might not get to see Casey then. I was beginning to like her company and attention. If Dan teased me about seeing a much younger woman, or disapproved, especially in Casey's presence, then she might not —

"Reed? You still there?"

"It's your cabin."

"Gimme a list of things to bring. Tell Father Ray I'm coming if you see him. It'd be good to have lunch or somethin' like that."

"That'll be hard," I said. "I can't get through to him on the phone."

"Busy time for him, no probability," Dan said, "with Easter and all that."

I didn't mention the fish-fry incident.

"Try this number; it's his pager," Dan said. "Ray gave it to me in case I had another engine problem. He'll answer a page." He recited the number.

"Speaking of phones," I said, "did you have the cabin phone reconnected?"

"Why should I? You have the cell. Or did you change your mind about having an Internet connection?"

"No," I said. "Don't bother. Never mind."

The Princess phone rang.

I stared at it. It had to be Ray. Or Dan asked the phone company to connect it right after our conversation. So fast?

"Reed? Father Ray here. Got the page. Dan give you the number? How is he?"

"Fine," I said, trembling.

"Look, I know I've been hard to get hold of. I've been lying low, fighting a fever. I wanted to be ready for Masses and services this weekend. Coming to any of them?"

"I don't know," I said. "Maybe."

"I thought I saw you at the Saturday service," Ray said. "I looked for you afterward."

"I left early," I said. "I wasn't — feeling well."

"Is that why you called? Something you want to talk about?" He sounded stuffed up.

"Dan's coming Wednesday, to visit for Easter," I said. "He thought we could have lunch sometime."

"Big weekend for me," he said. I heard him flipping through a calendar. "Wednesday's best, before everything gets going. Brunch, 10:30? That would work. He can come directly here, park the rig at the edge of the lot and leave it there." He coughed. He wasn't 100 percent. Not even 75 percent. "And if you're done with the books, you can pick up some more."

I agreed to arrange it and hung up. I didn't bother to test the phone. I kicked it under the bed, out of sight.

The chaplain at Rush Presbyterian Hospital who came to Peggy's room looked like a seminary student doing his internship. Gaunt and sallow, he needed a square meal and three days of uninterrupted sleep, I thought. The tight collar seemed to squeeze his voice.

"We have a service in the chapel on Sunday morning at nine o'clock," he said. "A volunteer can bring you."

Peggy struggled to open her eyes. "What time?" she whispered.
"Nine. After rounds."

"That's OK, Reverend," I said with an indifferent shrug. "I think we'll pass."

"It's an interfaith service," he said, as though that might sell me.

"Maybe next week," I said. If Peggy survives.

"Is there anything I can do for you?"

Sure, kid. You can explain to me why your God is allowing my Peggy to be poisoned by her own blood, offering a lollipop of hope now and then, only to jerk it away. I've read the book of Job, and I don't know what to do with a Deity who lets the Satan character have his way with a good man just to settle a bet. We didn't do anything to deserve this, and unlike Job, I have no faith to test. None. Nada.

"No. Nothing."

"Would you like me to pray with you, or for you?"

Oh, sure: *Our Father, who art in hiding, though hollered be thy name.*

"You can, if you want," I snapped.

He got the hint. He handed me a card. "Call me if you need something." On the way out, he noted the name on the door and scribbled it on a spiral pad.

"It wouldn't have hurt, you know," Peggy said, squeezing my hand.

I wasn't so sure. Doctors and clerics make all kinds of promises they cannot possibly keep.

I was perched in the fake leather chair sipping hot lemon water when Ray came in looking like hell.

"Sorry I'm running late," he apologized, wiping his nose. Blood dotted the handkerchief and crusted his nostril. His face looked flushed, as though he'd just stepped from a sauna. "Lots of details," he said, "not the least of which is making sure we have enough wine ready for Masses tonight and tomorrow. Of course, you can't have any, my friend."

He patted my shoulder going by and I felt a jolt. Static electricity, I guessed, with the heat on all the time and the air so dry. Maybe I was just surprised.

He eased into the divan. "Been on my feet all morning," he said with a wan smile. "Good to get off them for a while."

"Look, if this is not a good time for you anymore, I'll understand."

"No, no, it's fine. 10:45 already? Please, help yourself to the muffins. I'm glad Father Brian could set them out before he had to rush off."

"I wonder what's keeping Dan?" I said.

"Holiday traffic, I guess. Small towns, big families, you know? Relatives come to visit. Do you two get together every Easter?"

"No, he just happened to be in the neighborhood."

"It's good of him to come by. Holidays can be difficult for you, I'd imagine."

"How so?"

"Well, we miss loved ones the most at those milestones. It gets lonely. There are memories. Traditions."

"If you mean Peggy and me, we didn't do any of that. And we didn't have children."

"No egg baskets? Jelly beans? Chocolate bunnies?" He took a muffin and broke it.

"Just the newspaper. Like any other Sunday. Nothing else."

I regretted sounding terse. Ray just smiled.

"It was about this time of year, too," I added. "April. Just as Spring was starting."

"It's difficult."

"Death is the most terrible of things, for it is the end."

"That's from Aristotle, I presume?"

I nodded. "And Aquinas would disagree, I presume?"

"Not entirely," Ray said. "He'd say, 'Death is terrible, but if there's no Easter, what's the point?' Shorter Summa, chapter 151. I paraphrase, of course."

"Never read it, I'm afraid."

"You'd like him. He knew Aristotle as well as you do. Oh, one more thing, if you'll permit a fellow teacher?"

"Scratch a professor, get a lecture."

"Just a three-sentence one," he assured me. "We believe in something called 'the Communion of Saints' — heard of it?"

"Presbyterians recite it in the creed."

"I know, and I'm glad. It's something you can hold on to, believing that our loved ones who leave us in Christ's friendship are in his presence and praying for us. Peggy's probably praying for you right now."

"That was four sentences," I said.

"The last one was a footnote," he said with a laugh.

The pager beeped. Ray checked the message. He excused himself and labored to reach the phone. He punched a speed-dial button and listened. "Yes, right away," he said. He rang off and gathered his thoughts.

"You need to go?" I asked.

"There's been an accident," he said, suddenly somber.

"Father Brian left with your car," I said. "Need a ride?"

"I do." He lowered his voice. "Reed, I think it's Dan."

That was Dan's Mitsubishi Fuso truck in the ditch, all right, the flat-front cab crushed into a burr oak, a guardrail twisted to the side, the trailer section listing on the shoulder. A policeman waved us through the traffic when he recognized Ray. A rescue truck and fire engine were on the scene, lights blazing. A couple of paramedics knelt over a body on a stretcher near the truck cab, a third man holding defibrillator paddles. With my halting breath and galloping heart, I thought I'd need the CPR.

The air stank of burning rubber and diesel; a firefighter sprayed foam on the hissing engine. A Chevy Cavalier with a smashed side and spidery windshield lay on the banking, the hood yawning open as though the car needed to vomit. A shrieking ambulance rushed past us in the opposite direction. Why was it leaving without Dan?

Ray limped down the embankment, and I followed, trying not to trip on the debris — boxes, tangled air-brake hose, bits of glass and chrome, Dan's boots. The EMTs brushed themselves off and stood. A dark pool of blood soaked the gravel. The men dropped polystyrene catheters, bloody gauze, and empty liter-bags into a bio-waste bin while the third man rose, checked his watch, and turned to me. It was Dr. Rashidi. He had a word with Ray, and then approached me. Ray genuflected by the stretcher. He crossed himself and touched Dan's forehead with his thumb.

"I'm sorry, Mr. Stubblefield," Rashidi said. "We did all we could."

"All you could? What are you talking about?"

"Once we knew the neck wasn't broken, we intubated him and —"

"What?"

"We used a tracheal tube with an Ambu bag to ventilate the collapsed lungs — to force air into them by hand. We infused him with plasmatein and dextran, but his blood pressure went into a free-fall. I injected high-dose epinephrine and tried a defibrillator to get the heart going instead of pumping the chest, since I suspected fractured ribs."

"I saw the ambulance leave," I said breathlessly, hardly paying attention. "Why isn't he in it?"

"He won't need it," Rashidi said. "He's gone. I'm sorry."

"Maybe in the emergency room —"

"We worked on him for a half-hour. There's nothing to be done."

My head spun. "Don't you have a helicopter or something?"

"I've already pronounced him dead at the scene. I'm calling the coroner and signing the certificate as soon as you identify him for certain so we can begin testing."

"Testing?"

"For alcohol and drugs. It's the law."

"No," I said. "No."

"I'm sorry," Rashidi repeated.

A rasping cough ripped the air. Ray clutched at his chest with one hand while the other hand gripped Dan's bloody shirt.

Another cough, a wet, rattling hack, came from Dan. Bloody foam gushed from his mouth. Ray let go of the shirt and fell back with a gasp. Dan kicked once and the cyanotic blue drained from his lips.

"Holy Christ!" an EMT bellowed. "Call a code!"

The second man shouted into his shoulder mike. "Code 99, shock trauma! Code 99! We got the other one coming in!"

"It can't be," Rashidi muttered, his lips taut as a tourniquet. "It just can't be."

He sprinted back, leaving the death certificate a crushed ball on the grass.

CHAPTER 13

They let me see Dan late that night. I was busy in the meantime with the trucking company, the tow truck, the police report, hospital admissions, insurance. By the time I got to his room, I probably looked as bad as he did.

The EKG monitor chirped like a nervous sparrow. Liter bags piggybacked on an IV pole dripped into his arms, and an oxygen tube whispered at his nose. They said he'd had a transfusion for the shock and hemorrhaging, and he still had test results coming for kidney, liver, and spleen functions, since organs fail in a vicious sequence from blood loss, and these three lay near the cracked ribs.

I wondered what to say when he woke up. Something funny to deal with the fear? *All we could save was your brain, Dan. It's now in the body of your ex-wife. You always said Loretta had no brains. Now she has one.*

The internist had told me some questions to ask. "We don't know how much he'll remember," he had said.

"Of the accident?"

"Of anything."

A tap at the door turned my head.

"Hello, Reed," Casey said softly. "Can I come in? Don't bother getting up."

She dragged a chair next to mine. "How is he?"

"Out cold for now. Demerol. They removed the respirator in recovery. Say, how'd they let you up here?"

"It helps to be a reporter in a small town sometimes," she said with that disarming smile. "How is he?"

"Touch and go."

"And you?" She pressed her hand on my knee, and I put mine atop hers with a grateful squeeze.

"They said only two percent of people who code in the ER survive," I said, tears hot in my eyes. "Jesus."

"Where's Ray?"

"Treated and released."

"How about the other driver?"

"Down the hall, just broken bones. You'd think the guy driving the truck would do better. But since Dan went down the banking, he — say, how'd you find out about what happened?"

"Police scanner in the newsroom. I called the EMTs; they talked to me. They usually don't, to respect people's privacy. But they're really spooked about what happened. One of them wants to speak with you."

"Me? Why me?"

"He didn't say. To get some answers about what happened, I guess. Dr. Rashidi isn't answering calls. Guess he's shook up, too. What'd you see?"

"I'm not sure," I said. I described our arrival on the scene, and how Ray clutched his own chest when Dan coughed into consciousness.

"Was he bleeding? Ray, I mean."

"There was blood all over his arm. Must have been Dan's, since he was laying hands on him." I removed my hand from hers. "Say, you're not putting all this in a news story, are you?"

"It'll be a standard accident story," she assured me. "I'll play it straight. But the word on the street is that Ray absorbed the injuries and that's what brought your brother back to life. There's a small crowd outside right now holding a candlelight vigil."

"Whatever for?"

"They want to see Lazarus — the man raised from the dead."

"I can't believe it," I sputtered. "It's not logical."

"If it's not logical, and not a miracle, what is it?"

"It's — it's a mystery," I said.

A nurse bustled in to check the monitors. "We're going to try to wake him soon and ask him to cough," she said. She eyed Casey narrowly. "You family?"

"Visiting."

"She can stay," I said.

"Family only," the burly nurse said, crossing her arms.

Casey pecked me on the cheek and rose. "I'd better be going, then. When you leave, Reed, go out through the hospital laundry. Otherwise, those people outside might hound you."

"Why me?"

"You're Lazarus's brother," she said with a wink, and slipped out.

I said goodbye, and then watched the measured rise and fall of Dan's sheets. They were tucked into his sides like Lazarus' winding-cloths. I wondered whether he would recognize me, and then wondered if, in death — that greatest of mysteries — he had seen and recognized Peggy.

Peggy wore the Macy's silk kimono I bought her for our twentieth anniversary. The cotton hospital gown wouldn't do, I said. The lingerie matched the red bandana she wore for the hair loss, and the wine-colored bruises on her arms hardly showed. The doctor allowed us to toast the occasion with sparkling grape juice.

She raised the hand without the IV. "To another year," she said.

Of course, it's all we could hope for. We clicked the plastic Dixie cups. I'd forgotten to bring the stemware. "To another year," I said. Another year of life, not just marriage. We sipped. It tasted like the sweet cherry wine from our Door County, Wisconsin, honeymoon.

"Are you sorry you married me?" she asked.

"What kind of a question is that?"

"I don't know," she said, swirling the ruby-red juice. "It's what you ask at times like this."

"Anniversaries?"

She put the cup down. "There won't be another one, Reed, will there?"

"Don't say that."

"Every day I wake up, I'm thankful for you. Every day I wake up. Wake up. Wake up."

"Wake up, Mr. Stubblefield," the internist repeated, jostling my shoulder. "Your brother is coming out of it."

"That you, Reed?"

Dan mouthed the words with a dry croak, but it was music to my ears.

"I'm right here," I said, patting his hand.

"Go ahead, ask him," the internist said to me.

"Do you know your name?" I said, enunciating.

"D-Dan," he said, the eyes pinched and the throat struggling. "Stubble—"

Good enough for me. "Dan, where do you live?"

"Forest Par— Park. Illinois."

"How old are you?"

"Fifty-one."

"Dan, do you know what happened to you?"

"A crash," he managed. "Car ran a stop sign." He tensed. "He OK?"

"The other driver? He's fine. You glanced him, and he spun out. You went down the banking."

"Chest. Hurts."

"You cracked a rib. Collapsed a lung. Went into shock. You were —" *You were dead.* "You were in a bad way for a while, Danny-boy. But you're going to be all right."

"Where?" the tight, flaky lips moved.

"Sinnissippi County Hospital," I said. "You've been here for about two days."

The internist stepped forward and introduced himself. "Mr. Stubblefield, I'm going to take a look at you now and ask you a few questions. We'll not make you talk; that throat must be sore. Then I'm going to ask you to try to cough to keep the lungs clear. It will be uncomfortable but you must try."

He checked Dan's heartbeat, probed here and there with a flashlight and a tongue depressor, moved his finger in front of Dan's eyes,

90

asked yes/no questions. The cough, when it came, was weak and wincing.

"We'll let you rest now, Mr. Stubblefield," the internist said, popping the stethoscope out from his ears. "Someone will be checking on you every twenty minutes or so. Your throat is going to be sore, and inhaling won't be easy, but it's better than the alternative." He smiled at his own joke, and tapped the IV drip. "Besides, we have you on some good stuff to help you feel more comfortable. Oh yes — and Dr. Rashidi from the town clinic will come by to visit later. I think you remember him? He says you might. He's taken a special interest in your case. Lucky for you that he was training with the EMTs when the call came in."

The doctor discreetly motioned for me to leave with him.

"See you later, Dan," I said, touching his arm gently. "I took care of the truck and everything, so don't even think about it."

"Ray," he breathed.

"Yes?" I leaned closer to him. "What about him?"

"He was there."

"Yes."

"He OK?"

"Sure," I replied. "He's back on the job, saying Masses for Holy Week. Want me to tell him something, like, 'Sorry I missed brunch'?"

"He's in danger," Dan said, and passed out.

The intern walked me down the hall. "You all right?"

I must have looked ashen. "Sure," I said, unconvincingly.

"I understand," the intern said, although he didn't. "Family members feel the trauma, too. But just by being here, you're bringing him strength to recover. I hope you are staying in the area?"

I nodded. Would I leave now, considering Dan's whispered warning? I didn't dare mention it to the medical professional — too metaphysical.

"That's good. He's going to be here a while until we're sure what happened to him. We'll run a series of MRIs when he's stable to check for brain injuries. We'll also —"

He listed a number of other tests to be run, but I'd stopped listening. Doctors, like other high priests, speak an ancient and cryptic tongue.

Once he patted me on the back perfunctorily and disappeared in an elevator, I paused at the water font to regain some composure. What could Dan have possibly meant by saying *Ray is in danger?* Was Dan suddenly prescient? Impossible. I splashed water into my face, on my neck.

"Sir? Sir?"

A male voice called to me. It was one of the EMTs, in fresh blue coveralls, approaching from Dan's room. "A word? Please? Do you have a moment?"

"Sure." I dried my face with my sleeve. I remembered Casey saying one of them wanted to see me.

He trotted through the hallway traffic double-time. A dark toothbrush mustache underlined his hatchet-shaped Latin American nose, his coal-black hair cropped in a military crew, the shoes spit-polished. He carried his cap in his hand. The bouncing nametag around his neck said, "GARCIA."

"Is he all right, sir?" he asked genuinely.

"Yeah. Well, he's alive. Thanks to you."

"No, no," he said. "Thanks to Father Ray."

"If you say so."

He glanced over his shoulder, stepped closer to me, spoke under his breath. "There is something you do not know about Father Ray."

Oh, please don't tell me he abused you as an altar boy —

"I know where he gets his healing power." He let a group of nurses pass, nodding hello, before speaking again. "I'm on break. Let me get you a cup of coffee or soda or something, OK? Let me explain. There's a lounge right over here."

"Fine," I said, my mouth suddenly dry again.

We stepped inside. He fed quarters into a vending machine and we sat at a round table among several patients, a daytime drama babbling on the wall-mounted television.

"What's this about, Mr. Garcia?"

"Manny. Call me Manny." He popped open his soda. "That's what they called me in the army. I was a medic. Served in the Gulf, Iraq. Saw death close up. Too much of it. I knew I wanted to stay in healthcare when I got out. But I wanted something more. I wanted to know about saving life, sure, but also about the *purpose* of life — and death."

"So you found it in the church with Father Ray. Is that where this is going?"

"No. Not at all. I found the power that Father Ray uses, and that Jesus Himself used, to heal the sick and raise the dead."

"Is that so?" I said, cocking my head. "Where did you find it?"

"In the Ascension."

"What's that?"

"It's a group at church — well, the hospital, too. We do alternative medicine. You know — wholeness practices." He sat up higher.

I knew a little about alternative practice. Peggy tried a few things for pain management. "You mean herbs? Acupuncture?"

He shook his head and lowered his voice. "It's all about energy. We listen to the powers of light, and they show us how to wake up to the divine energy sleeping in our DNA. That's how we speed up our spiritual evolution and ascend to the next level. See? That's where it gets its name."

A practiced speech. "You say Father Ray knows about all this?"

"He does, but he calls it by a different name."

"This is a group at the church, you said? He approves of this?"

He shrugged. "Not officially. But it is the power working in him all the same. He has received it as a gift, you see? God gave it to him with his illness."

"What illness?"

"He does not like to talk about it," Garcia said, his voice softening, "but we think he is a hemophiliac."

This was a revelation. My mouth fell open. "Are you sure? That explains his bleeding."

"No, not really," he continued, excited. "If he is — and I am pretty sure — it is precisely *because* of this that he is able to identify with the sick and absorb their infirmities. His suffering brought him closer to God, and so God allowed him to have this gift. But we believe others can achieve this in other ways."

"I don't know why you're telling me this," I said, feeling entrapped by a salesman. I pushed back my chair. "I'd better be going."

"It's about your brother."

I sat. "What about him?"

"He may have made contact."

"Contact? With what?"

"With *who*," Manny corrected. "The High Ones who give Ray his power."

"High Ones?"

"Archangel Guides who reveal and unlock levels of DNA that are hidden and untapped in us. Through an Ascension Consultant who receives these messages, you can reclaim your divine inheritance through four levels: Awakened One, Azreal, Avatar, and Christ Consciousness. Healing is often the outcome, releasing *dis*-ease and *dis*-order, you see? I think the first level is what happened to your brother."

"Don't tell me: you're one of these consultants?"

"Not yet. I'm training for my license. I'm still learning the language of light."

"The what?"

"The language of light. It was spoken by Jesus. It has one thousand levels of meaning in every word, enhancing its healing range. Spoken correctly, it attracts light from all levels of creation. I know that if I speak it over Dan, then he will —"

"No, sir. You'll do no such thing."

"— continue the process he has begun —"

"I said no. You mean well, Manny, I'm sure, but you can keep your religion to yourself."

"This is not religion," Garcia objected, hand to his heart. "This is alternative therapy for the whole person, body and spirit. We use this at the hospital all the time. Most insurance plans cover it under 'meditation and massage.' "

"They do?"

"It's very convenient. It goes right on the bill. A StarLight Analysis and a StarLight DNA Activation are very reasonable. You can put it on any major credit card." He pulled a business card from his shirt pocket. I read through the list of services and their prices.

I stared into his ice-blue eyes, gathering my composure. "Tell me, Manny," I said in a sincere whisper, "is the sex extra?"

He nearly spit. "What do you mean?"

"I think you know," I said. "But let me guess: some of these powers of light, as you call them, can be incarnated when two bodies united in an energy balance produce a star child without karma. In fact, you think that's what happened with Jesus' birth."

He leaned forward. "You've studied this, too? Is this why you were getting close to Father Ray?"

"I know that religious people might be fooled, but anyone familiar with classical Greece would recognize this as a 'mystery religion,' a Gnostic sect."

"Pardon me?"

"*Gnostic*, from the Greek word for 'knowledge.' It promises secret wisdom to escape the corruption of this material world into pure ethereal realms, right? *To return to the stars*, as Plato put it, usually with the aim of becoming divinities. And often accomplished through ritual sex."

His face darkened. "Father Ray has spoken to you about us already, hasn't he?"

"Not a word," I said. "You just picked the wrong guy to bamboozle. I'm a classics professor, and I know all about this Gnostic nonsense."

"I'm trying to help you and your brother."

"You can help by staying the hell away from my brother."

"He is at a critical juncture of his own ascension —"

"I said stay away."

"— and to interfere will be dangerous to him and to you."

I leaned forward and bore a sharp gaze into him. "Stay away, I said. I mean it."

"You'll be sorry," he said. He crushed his aluminum can, uttered a curse in his language of light, and left.

CHAPTER 14

"This is the first I've heard of them," Casey said on the phone. "They're probably harmless. It's like people who are into palm-reading or crystals. It's no big deal."

"No big deal?" I blurted. "He basically threatened me and Dan."

"He's just a religious kook, Reed."

"They're the most dangerous kind," I said. "In fact, he said just that. He said it was *dangerous* for me to interfere with Dan's so-called spiritual process. I asked the charge nurse to keep the guy away from Dan."

"Maybe she's one of them, too. Didn't you say this group works in the hospital?"

My hip ached from pacing; my head ached with worry. "Yes, I did. They have a group in the church, too. Say, I wonder if Ray knows about these Ascension people? Have they been a problem in the church? Has he opposed them? Is that why Dan would say that Ray is in danger?"

"Beats me," Casey replied. "It's either these kooks, or there's something to that business about Ray absorbing Dan's internal injuries."

"I can't believe that."

"What about his hemophilia theory? Do you believe that?"

"It's hard to believe anything that turkey told me."

"Makes perfect sense to me," Casey said.

"Not without proof," I said.

"There's one way to prove the 'absorbing illness' part, though."

"How?"

"If it's true, Ray will worsen as Dan improves."

"That wouldn't prove it logically," I said. False cause argument, I thought.

"Only one way to find out," she said. "Let's go see how Ray looks today. The Good Friday service is at three. Get some sleep, and I'll pick you up in time for it."

"I dunno —"

"That guy Garcia will be there, I guarantee. Maybe you can find out more about him and his group from Ray."

I agreed.

The service seemed normal at first, at least to an outsider like myself, apart from the packed house inside and the six TV news satellite trucks lined up in the street outside. Spotlights on tripods with silver reflective umbrellas lit platforms on the sidewalk for reporter stand-ups. Behind a ribbon of fluttering yellow police tape stood a pack of photographers from area newspapers and a few journalists poking microphones in people's faces. Police at the doors escorted Lance Boyle away, and anyone with a camera or video recorder in view was asked to check it. If they used metal detectors, they might have confiscated picture-taking cell phones and pocket-size digital cameras, too.

Casey and I edged our way to a standing-room-only spot, when jet-black heads turned and Spanish voices rustled. "It is the brother of Lazarus," I heard someone say, and the crowd parted like waves before Moses' rod to make a space in a pew for us.

Casey knelt, and I followed suit. No need to stick out more than I did. I folded my hands, not knowing what else to do with them. Casey bowed her head, but I surveyed the sanctuary, noting the altar was bare, without cross, candlesticks, or cloth. The door of the empty tabernacle hung open, agape in mourning. Even the life-size wooden cross that had been mounted on the wall behind the altar was missing. A light shadow remained where dust hadn't darkened the bricks.

Casey noticed my puzzlement. "He's going to carry the crucifix in later," she whispered in my ear. That's when everyone stood up.

Ray processed up the middle aisle alone, his face like flint, his stride slow, measured. Red vestments flowed over his shoulders like a curtain of blood. He sniffed back a nosebleed and dabbed at it. Once he reached the foot of the altar, he prostrated himself, arms outstretched as though crucified to the floor. Kneelers clattered down, and the congregation members crossed themselves.

After a few moments, Ray struggled up, ascended the dais to his chair, and with his bandaged hands folded, he called out, "Let us pray."

A series of readings followed his strained invocation, and I thought during the long reciting of the Passion as found in the Gospel of John, with everyone standing throughout, that Ray buckled and caught himself more than once. I dropped my gaze to the carpet for the duration of the long prayers that followed: prayers for the church, the clergy, the Easter baptismal candidates, the unity of Christians everywhere, the Jewish people, snapping my head up at the end when I heard Ray interceding for those who do not yet believe in God. He was looking at me.

But not for long. At the *Amen* the crowd sat, and he disappeared through a side door with the altar boys in tow. I wondered if he'd taken ill.

"He's going around to the narthex," Casey explained with a pat on my arm. "He'll process in again for the next part."

Sure enough, Ray re-entered the sanctuary, shouldering the dark beam of the church's cross. Two servers stood before him; an acolyte behind him held the cross's end low at arm's length so it wouldn't drag. Ray paused. The shadow of Gethsemane passed over his face. He took a ragged breath and chanted hauntingly, "This is the wood of the Cross on which hung the Savior of the world." Then he stepped forward, stooped with the sorrows of the world upon him, the sins and sicknesses of the congregation — all their groping, hoping, thronging, longing — borne by him toward the altar. His mouth grimaced, and he pinched his eyes as though he was being shouted at. He paused in the middle of the aisle and repeated the chant. As soon as he reached the front, he lowered the cross to the floor, leaning it against the steps for the veneration rite. He rose with difficulty, tears squeezing out of his eyes. When he raised the hand of blessing, everyone could see the Spandex wraps on his wrists were glistening and wet.

"Behold the wood of the Cross on which hung the Savior of the world," he intoned, the words echoing like the blows of a hammer in my ears.

Then he dropped his chin to his chest, swayed once, and fell in a heap as though he'd been cut down from a tree.

"*¡Madre de Dios!*" someone shouted; women cried out, and two men pressed their way to the dais — Manny Garcia and the other Hispanic EMT from the crash. Others rushed forward but the men shooed them back.

"Make way," Manny cried. "Give us room! *¡Por favor!*" He knelt, tore aside the scarlet vestments, checked Ray's pulse, and then shook his head. He leaned close to Ray's face and muttered words. Probably his language of light.

Hidden digital camcorders hummed to life, and cell phones beeped. Flashbulbs flared.

I had the sensation of being dropped in a fast elevator. While I tottered, the crowd all around me stood up, rubbernecking for a look, knuckles to their teeth, murmuring like bees. Some dropped to their knees, crossing themselves and praying. Others cried out in sobs.

Estrella Esperanza, the Fan, waved a handkerchief on the dais like a ship's distress flag. "Help! Please, help!" she wailed.

Police barked at the door to hustle people out, and two uniformed men muscled their way to the front to secure the area. One tapped the microphone at the lectern.

"Everyone please exit the sanctuary. Please exit out the back in an orderly fashion." He stabbed his raised fingers to the rear, like directing traffic. He looked annoyed that he didn't know Spanish. "*Exito,*" he said firmly, not sure if it was a Spanish word.

The exits jammed as congregants crashed into news-people pressing and shoving from the other direction, their fish-pole mikes swinging and camera lights ablaze. Lance Boyle slithered through the turmoil. I stopped him with my cane across the aisle.

"You again?" he said, gold tooth flashing. "Isn't this great? Can you read the headline? 'Stigmatic bleeds to death on Good Friday.' "

"We don't know that."

"One can hope." He jerked away, genuflected and snapped off three shots before an irate man tackled him. As the men wrestled, I noticed a sweet perfume of vanilla and almond.

The scent anointed Ray's dead body, sprawled over the cross, where a trickle of blood from his hand stained the wood.

CHAPTER 15

After the ambulance howled away and the yellow police tape had been strung around the church, Estrella the postulator gathered her flock on the lawn for a twenty-decade Rosary and a fine photo op. Away from the glaring TV camera lights and chattering reporter stand-ups, I asked Casey to drive me to the hospital.

"But they're taking him to the clinic, not the hospital," she said, glancing around, jotting notes. "It looks like lots of others are going there, too, but I don't think we'll get any information from Dr. Rashidi today."

"It's not that," I said. "I've got to tell Dan right away."

"Oh. OK," she agreed reluctantly. "Let me talk to a few people here first." She pulled out her pocket digital recorder, checked the battery level, and then hurried to join the gaggle of reporters vying for Estrella Esperanza's attention.

"He is a saint, in truth," the Fan declared. "What more proof do people like you need?"

Perched on the church's garden wall with a face like a leering gargoyle, Lance Boyle aimed his telephoto lens and squeezed off shot after shot.

Dan was awake when we arrived. Casey summed up the news while I nudged a chair closer.

"I knew it," Dan whispered. "I just knew it."

"You said he was in danger," I said tersely. "Is this what you meant? He'd have a stroke or something?"

"He was murdered," Dan said. "I know it."

"How do you know that?" Casey gasped. "Do you know by who?"

103

"I don't know," Dan said. "I just — I don't know — just felt it. When he touched me. Something was really wrong with him. Like he was full of poison."

Casey sighed. She turned to me, pain in her eyes, a look saying *he's not himself yet*. "Speaking from experience," she said, "we'll have to wait for a press conference or statement for the official cause of death. They're bound to have one, given the public interest."

"You know what those loonies outside are going to say?" I broke in, jerking my thumb. "They're going to say Dan killed him, that Ray absorbed his injuries. They'll say Dan should be the dead one, but Ray is dead instead. That's what they'll say."

"Maybe it's true," Dan said, his eyes welling. "Maybe I killed him."

"Danny, c'mon," I said. "This is just something that happened, and you didn't do anything."

"That's right, Dan," Casey said. "It's something else. It's got to be."

"I should be dead. Not him," Dan moaned.

"Stop it, Dan," I said. "*Post hoc ergo propter hoc* argument."

Casey looked at me quizzically. "Excuse me?"

"Just because Ray died soon after Dan was hurt doesn't necessarily mean that one caused the other. It's poor logic," I said.

"Are you kidding?" she scolded. "How can you be talking about logic at a time like this?"

I must have blanched.

"Besides," she added, "it makes perfect sense to those people out there, Reed. Isn't that what Good Friday is about? Someone dies in somebody else's place? Isn't that what you'd expect from someone like Ray?"

Someone like Ray. She meant "a stigmatic," one who shared the passion of Christ bodily and now shared his death in the same manner. On Good Friday, no less. Estrella Esperanza might indeed have a good case for his sainthood now. Unless one of her followers decided that Ray would have been a better saint alive than dead, and blamed Dan for his death.

The idea gave me a headache, and I rubbed my temple. "Look," I said, "we all could use a little rest now. Dan, I'm going to make sure you're closely watched, just in case some fanatic gets the wacky idea that you somehow contributed to all this and tries to get even. And for God's sake, don't give anyone else the idea Ray was murdered — by yourself or anyone else. If you think those people outside are upset now, there's no telling what they'd do with that rumor. OK?"

Dan pressed his lips together. He nodded feebly.

"Good," I said. I gave him a light knuckle-noogie on the head, like when we were kids. A silver medal winked from under his unbuttoned shirt.

"By the way," I asked, pointing to it, "what's this? A good-luck charm?"

Dan pulled it out and displayed the oval medallion on his palm. There was a figure of a robed woman on it, standing on a globe, light-rays streaming from her fingertips. "Ray gave it to me," he said. "It's called the Miraculous Medal."

"I guess it worked," I said.

"Just don't tell Dr. Rashidi," Casey said. "And say, when he comes on his rounds later, ask him what he thinks happened. He'll probably talk to you and not to us."

Always working her sources, I thought. Well, it's her job. "See ya later, Danny," I said. "Get some rest. We'd better go, Casey."

She knit her fingers in mine as we left the room, and her stride matched to mine. My pulse skittered.

On the way out, I asked the desk nurse to arrange tighter security. And I asked Casey to sit on the information she heard from Dan. "After all," I said, "how could it possibly be a murder, in full view of a whole congregation?"

"Maybe it isn't a murder," she said. "Maybe it's a miracle."

CHAPTER 16

At Tall Pines Park Campground, we idled on the shoulder while a caravan of RVs, fifth-wheelers, and pickups coughed out the gate. When the last one rumbled onto the highway, Casey pulled in. Beth Berger flagged us down. Her husband, a craggy man with a bulbous nose, dressed in hunter's camouflage and a blaze orange cap, accompanied her to the lowered window.

"We're real sorry to hear about your friend, dearie," Beth said, palm to her cheek. "Awful. Real awful."

"Guess you'll be leavin' too?" Hadley Berger said, leaning down and squinting inside. He looked like a mole with his close-set eyes. "Not much chance of gettin' healed yourself now, is there?"

"I'll be staying," I said. "I still have work to do here."

"Oh, this here's my husband, Hadley," Beth said. "This here is Reed. Don't think you've met proper."

"How do?" Hadley said. "An' howdy to you, Casey."

Casey dimpled her cheek.

"Well, it'll be kinda lonely now," Hadley said, eyes on the exodus. "Everyone come to see the padree. No sense in them stayin' now. All the other camps and motels will be emptyin' out, too, I betcha. Wouldn't be surprised if all them spics that come to town move away, too."

"Hadley, they live here now," Beth said, rolling her eyes. "They got jobs here — jobs we want these people to do."

"Jobs? Let's talk about jobs. First we send thousands of jobs to Mexico and whatnot, and then they send thousands of poor people here illegal to steal wages from votin' citizens," Hadley continued. "It ain't right."

"Look who's talking," Beth said, jabbing him in the shoulder. "Your grandpap come over the ocean from Germany on the boat in 1922 to find work. You got pictures."

"This here's a flood worse than the Sinnissippi overflow in '93, and we're drownin'," Hadley huffed. "You ain't seen these people hangin' 'round the park all day smokin' funny stuff afore getting rides to the big operations around here to slop hogs or to slaughter 'em. Their kids ain't immunized, they bring strange diseases with 'em, and they want all the healthcare and handouts the gov'ment can give 'em free with our tax dollars. Mister, you seen 'em at the clinic, right?"

"A few," I admitted.

"They got the run of the town, I tell you, and that padree sure didn't help. We got no more places to put 'em. Even our neighbors are rentin' out their garages and barns to these people for fifteen hunnert dollars per month. And where do they get the money? Not the canneries. Not the renderin' shop. No, sirree. Meth shops and mary-juana, that's where. That's a story for ya, Casey."

"I'll work on it," Casey said, uncommitted. She rolled up the window.

"You need somethin', you call," Beth said, her cheeks pinked.

Casey spun the wheels a little on the way to the cabin. In the rearview mirror I saw Beth wag a scolding finger at Hadley.

"So, does Hadley speak for the town, and not Beth?" I asked.

"Crime is up," Casey acknowledged. "But most of the immigrants are young men, and adolescents in general commit the most crimes. Our police — the few there are — are overwhelmed and don't even ask if a person is illegal. Thousands come in by railroad every year."

"Delivered straight to the shop doors, right?"

"At the owners' expense, some of them."

"Don't the cops know?"

"They're not allowed to arrest illegals or check work permits or ticket businesses for hiring undocumented workers. That's a federal job."

I gathered my coat and cane and levered out. "Care to come in?" I asked.

"I've got a story to write," she said. "You'd better get some rest. See you." She brushed back her hair, and the brassy strands shone in my eyes like filaments of lustrous glass.

Peggy's auburn hair glittered that way in the light, too. It was probably unfair to compare the two women, although Casey had that spunk and sunny smile that drew me at first to Peggy. Both outgoing. Independent. Ambitious. Unafraid to speak their mind. Peggy was unafraid, period. And in those last years, her serenity and courage and good humor revealed a depth, a beauty, and a faith I couldn't have seen as a younger man. The funny thing is that she was more worried about me being left alone. She said I was getting the raw end of the deal.

Casey's Grand Am reached the main road and stopped for traffic, the turn signal winking. I found myself looking forward to seeing her again. I pinched my eyes shut and shook my head. *This is like that summer camp fling with Patty Trilling when I was fifteen,* I scoffed at myself. *Where could this possibly go from here?*

When I looked up, she was gone.

"She's gone."

Peggy's hand felt like a dry sponge. The skin, pale as parchment and stained plum with bruises, wrinkled under my thumb. Her mouth gaped as though in disbelief, and the doctor, making as though to check the pulse at the neck, closed the jaw gently. A nurse with a clipboard stood in the shadows. The morphine she'd injected earlier had quieted the last struggle, and Peggy's breathing shallowed until she slipped away without pain. The toilet flushed in the bath between rooms, and the light snapped off. It's like that, a hospice worker once told me: turning out the lights in the rooms of the house, one by one, and then leaving.

The physician checked his watch, took the clipboard, clicked a pen and jotted the time. "I'm sorry," he said. "Would you like a moment alone?"

I nodded. They left.

Silence wrapped me like a wet shroud. "I miss you, Margaret Jean," I said.

No reply.

What else can you say? The other patient in the room, behind a scrim, snored softly. Still alive. For now. But no one gets out alive.

I kissed Peggy's hand and cheek. There was still a blush of warmth there. Why hadn't I kissed her more before? Held her more often? Said "I love you" more? I love you, Peg. Love you.

The shudder began deep in my stomach, made its way up to my mouth, and burned behind my eyes. I clung to her. Eventually, a rapping came at the door: the physician, back to ask about the disposition of the remains. Please, give me just another minute. Knock knock. Please.

"Mr. Stubblefield?" Knock knock.

"Reed Stubblefield? Are you in there?"

I shook myself upright. The blood drained from my head, and I felt woozy. A krypton beam broke through the window and searched the room.

"Sheriff's deputy, Mr. Stubblefield," a bass voice called. "You in there? Hello?"

Since the meds put me out soundly, I struggled to my feet. "Hold on," I croaked, dizzy. I fumbled for the light, Citizen Cane, and my wits. "Coming."

I pulled open the door and hung onto it for support. "Yes?"

Two men in rain-speckled overcoats stood on the stoop. The taller one showed a badge in a black wallet. "Otis Anderson, sheriff's deputy," he said, his breath steamy. "My partner, Detective Frank Gordon of the River Falls Police Department. May we come in?"

"What's this about?"

"Father Ray Boudreau over at Saint Mary's. We just have a few questions."

"OK," I said. "Sure."

They stepped inside, dripping. Anderson looked up and down, his steel-gray eyes measuring the room. He wiped his thinning mustache with a sleeve and brushed his comb-over blond hair. "Thanks. This won't take long," he said.

"Mind if I sit?" I asked. "I just woke up, and my meds make me foggy."

"Fine," said Anderson, noticing the cane. "My arthritis kicks up in wet weather, too. Taking something for it?"

"It's not arthritis," I said, my head bobbing like a birthday balloon. "It's — something else. I've got a pin in my hip. The doctor gave me something to sleep." *Routine investigation, I told myself*, grunting into the rocker. *Just like after the school shooting. But why talk to me?* "What time is it?" I asked.

"About eight p.m.," Anderson said. "Where were you around three today?"

"At St. Mary's, for the service."

"Go there regular?"

"Not really. I'm Presbyterian — sort of."

Gordon was scribbling a few notes.

"So why go there?"

"I was getting to know Father Ray. As a friend." *No, officer, to get healed, like everyone else who's been coming.* Isn't that what he wanted me to say?

"So you were close?"

"Not close. Just friendly. We have — we had — similar interests."

"Like what?"

"Aristotle. Greek mythology. Poetry. He loaned me some books."

"When was the last time you saw him, before the service?"

"Wednesday, I guess. After the accident. When my brother Dan was" — *was killed, officer. Ray touched him, and he sat up alive* — "was injured and taken to the hospital. They took Ray in, too, but I didn't see him there."

"And before that?"

"A week before that, I suppose. Yes, at the Friday Fish Fry the church has."

"I thought you said you weren't Catholic."

"I volunteered to help in the kitchen."

"Why?"

I shrugged. *I wanted to be with Casey Malone. Wouldn't you? Those peanut-butter fudge eyes. That coppery hair. The killer dimple. I've been feeling lonely*. "Why does anyone volunteer to help others? And Ray invited me."

"When?"

I paused to think. "When I borrowed some books at the rectory."

"Just walked right up and asked for books?"

"No, we met before. I met him at a used bookstore almost two weeks ago. I forget the name of it," I said. "No, wait: Books and Brews, I think. And we talked on the phone after that."

"You talked a lot?"

"Not a lot. Some."

"Did he ever tell you he had any enemies?"

"No. Wait, yes he did."

"Did he say who?"

"Not by name. He said some companies around here didn't appreciate him standing up for immigrant workers' rights."

"Did he say anyone in particular would want him dead?"

I thought about Dan saying *he was murdered*. "He told me the local slaughterhouse people were mad at him. Do you really think he was killed?"

"Do you?" The steely eyes drilled into me.

"No. I mean, I don't know. How should I know?" I gripped my cane to keep from shaking. "He was sick a lot. He had these awful bruises. My wife died from leukemia a while ago. Her skin spotted easily, too. I guess he had a blood disease or something. Like other people I've seen in the hospital. Maybe he had a stroke." Suddenly my breath came short.

"Did he ever talk to you about his medical condition?"

"Not really. I mean, no. He never complained. He was around sick people a lot, so he caught colds easily. Took some cough medicine, like anyone else would."

"Did he say what kind?"

"He might have. I forget. Something over the counter. Why? You think he overdosed on a prescription of some kind? Had an allergic reaction?"

Gordon penned something and spoke up. "Funny you'd ask. What'd you say your prescription was for again?"

I felt queasy. This didn't sound good. "Nardil," I said. "It's an antidepressant." They'd find out anyway.

"Never heard of that. Izzat like Prozac?"

"Yes, like that. Not very common."

"How'd you feel about the Father's healing ministry, Mr. Stubblefield? Ever go to a service for that?"

I was hesitant to admit it. No sense in lying, though. Too many witnesses. "I went once. Just curious."

"Looks like you weren't healed," Anderson said, pointing to the cane. "Must feel bad about it, coming all the way out from Chicago and all."

"I didn't come here to see him. I —"

"Someone who wasn't healed might be angry about it," Gordon said. "Even revengeful, huh? Wouldn't you say so?"

I was beginning to think I'd said too much already. "I couldn't say."

"How'd you feel? Disappointed, huh?"

"Just curious. Puzzled, really."

"Puzzled?"

"Well, I don't believe much in that stuff," I said. "It's not logical."

"Sounds like what Mr. Lance Boyle would say. Know him?"

I pinched my lips. "We've met."

Gordon flipped his notepad shut and pocketed it.

"That's enough for now, Mr. Stubblefield," Anderson said. "If you think of anything else, give me a call." He produced a card. "Thanks for your time. Don't bother getting up on our account."

As soon as they left, I hauled myself up, staggered to the bathroom, and threw up.

CHAPTER 17

Local Cleric Collapses,
Dies During Church Service
By Casey Malone, Sinnissippi County
Weekly Observer staff reporter

The Reverend Raymond Boudreau of St. Mary's Parish collapsed suddenly in front of hundreds of horrified worshipers at the height of celebrating Good Friday services last week and was pronounced dead shortly afterward.

Two emergency medical technicians attending the 3 o'clock service hurried to the priest's aid to no avail. River Falls police officers pronounced the stricken cleric dead at about 3:30 p.m.

The body was transported by the Sinnissippi Rescue Unit to the Coroner's Morgue for a preliminary examination while dazed parishioners gathered on the church lawn to pray. Dozens wept openly.

Sinnissippi County Coroner Doreen Gates, in a brief written statement, said the cause of death is under investigation. She declined to comment directly, saying only that a coroner's inquest was likely, given the high public interest in the case and the "unusual circumstances" of the priest's sudden death.

Eyewitnesses said the cleric looked stressed at the altar, and appeared to be bleeding at the wrists and hands, which were heavily bandaged. Some said he was sweating droplets of blood before he fell unconscious.

"Father Ray just looked terrible up there," said Mabel Diehl of River Falls, a lifelong parishioner. "We knew he was ill. He always looked ill, but not like this."

"I'm very upset," said Maria Rivera of River Park. "Why did God take him from us? We needed him."

Angel Hernandez of East Bluff agreed. "He was for the people. He fed the people. He healed the people."

This was the part of Father Boudreau's brief ministry that attracted the most attention since his arrival last September. In fact, dozens of people from every parish he has served claim that they have been made well from various ailments following a service conducted by Father Boudreau.

Many further claim that his bruises and bleeding prove he had been given "the stigmata," the crucifixion wounds of Christ in the hands, side, feet, and brow, a sign of particular holiness or spiritual ecstasy, traditionally linked to healing powers, and always most evident during Holy Week.

There is even speculation that Father Ray's timely intervention in a local traffic accident last week resulted in one victim's resuscitation despite being pronounced dead at the scene.

Such reports attracted television news crews from the Quad Cities area for the Good Friday services. *The Weekly Observer* office has received calls from wire services and media from as far away as Massachusetts, Texas, and the Phillippines for information.

Church officials will not comment on such speculations. The diocese will only confirm Father Boudreau's service record, which indicates transfers every two or three years throughout northern Illinois.

Local law-enforcement officials, too, remain guarded in their comments. Sinnissippi County Sheriff's Deputy Otis Anderson said a routine investigation is pending.

"I'm waiting for the written report from the pathologist," Anderson said.

Detectives from the River Falls Police District, meanwhile, were talking to colleagues, friends, and acquaintances of Father Boudreau on Friday and Saturday. Although crime-scene specialists were on church property most of Friday afternoon and again Saturday morning, they refused to say that the death was being treated as suspicious. Anderson acknowledged that pending permission from diocesan authorities, an autopsy would be ordered to determine the cause of death.

"It is too early," Anderson said, "to rule the death accidental, natural, or suspicious."

In the confusion immediately following the cleric's collapse, the vestry was burglarized. Bottles of communion wine were smashed or stolen by an intruder who pried open the rectory door and gained entry through the residence. Police are looking for a suspect they will not name at this time.

No one was in the residence at the time; parish rector Rev. Brian O'Neal was assisting Rev. Boudreau with the service at the time of the break-in.

O'Neal said a private funeral Mass closed to the public would be held once the coroner had released the remains. This would be conducted at an undisclosed location, he said, to avoid undue attention.

O'Neal suggested prayer cards and memorial gifts for the support of the County Food Pantry or the Sinnissippi Literacy Council, charities supported by Father Boudreau, be sent to St. Mary's Church. The 11 a.m. Mass on the First Sunday of Easter will be celebrated in his memory, he added.

O'Neal also said that the diocese would be appointing a special investigator of its own.

"The bishop would do this in any case," O'Neal explained, "but this merits special attention because of the many things people have speculated about Father Ray. The Church is not interested in pious rumors, but in the truth."

Local parish member Estrella Esperanza said the truth is plain. She is the postulator and chief advocate for "The Cause of Father Raymond, Inc.," an organization dedicated to having Reverend Boudreau declared a "Blessed" and then "raised to the altar," that is, "canonized" or pronounced a saint by the Roman Catholic Church.

Normally, such a procedure begins long after a candidate's death, but Esperanza has followed Father Boudreau from one parish to another for years, documenting his alleged miracles.

The canonizing process usually takes decades of cautious judicial review by local and Vatican officials. During his

tenure as pontiff, however, John Paul II sped the canonization of 450 saints and pressed for Mother Teresa of Cal-
cutta's cause immediately upon her death.

What chance would Father Boudreau of River Falls have?
Esperanza has no doubts: "He healed many because he
bore the wounds of Christ himself," she declared. "And now
he has borne his death."

"So, Reed, you believe it?" Dan asked, folding the paper.

"Believe what? That he was killed?"

"That he's a saint?"

"It doesn't matter what I believe," I said with a shrug. "What matters are the facts."

"The fact is," Dan said, pointing to his heart, "that I'm alive, and
he's not."

"That doesn't make him a saint."

"It does in my book."

"C'mon, Danny. You skipped Sunday School to smoke butts in
the alley and never came back."

"I'm different now."

"Look, it's common for people coming out of accidents or heart
surgery to ask big questions before their reason can kick in —"

"Something happened to me, Reed, for Christ's sake."

I decided to shut up. His breathing was labored from the broken
rib, and the color was rising in his face. I felt it rising in mine, too. After a sip of water, I began to cool off until he said:

"The cops came last night to ask me questions."

"What'd they ask you?"

"How I knew him. Where I'd seen him. Made me feel like a suspect. Like I'm the one who killed him. Maybe they're right."

"Don't be dumb," I rebuked him. "They're not going to believe for
a minute that Ray somehow absorbed your internal injuries and bled
to death instead of you. They're scientists, like Rashidi."

That's when a rock dropped in my stomach. I asked, "What has
Rashidi said about all this to you? Anything?"

"Not a thing. He's all business. Tells me what tests they're doing, and how long it's gonna take for results."

"How long?"

"Looks like I'll be in here a week at least. He's still worried about the brain. Liver and kidneys." His breath struggled. "Lungs. Well, crap. Everything."

"I wonder if that's all he's worried about."

"What do you mean?"

"Why do you think he drives up here every day to check on you?" I asked, suspicion creeping in my voice.

"To see if I'm still alive," Dan said. "According to him, I shouldn't be."

"That's exactly right. He turned white as a ghost when you came back after he pronounced you dead. Not only was he embarrassed in front of those EMTs he was training," I said, more convinced, "but he was angry. He said, 'It can't be.' *Can't*. The doctor had been made to look like a fool by a healer he didn't believe in."

"Just jealous."

"Enough to kill him?" The stone in my stomach turned. "Enough to kill you?"

Dan's brow wrinkled, looking mystified.

"Maybe he thinks you're proof that he was wrong about Ray," I said.

He sucked in a whistling breath, painfully. "Am I proof that you were wrong about Ray, too?"

So we were back to that. "I'll know I'm wrong when Ray strolls back into St. Mary's on Easter morning."

"That's tomorrow."

"So you want me to go there and wait for him, is that it?"

"If you want to."

"I don't."

I stood, found my leg, and turned to the door. "Keep the paper," I said.

Dan underlined Casey's byline with his finger. "How is she?"

"Who?

"Casey?"

"Fine," I said shortly.

"She seems nice."

I limped away. "I'll see you tomorrow, same bat-time, same bat-channel. Don't absorb anyone else's illnesses, OK? Hospitals are full of them."

"Reed, it's OK with me," Dan said. "And I think it would be OK with Peggy."

Illinois prairie violets, coreopsis, and coneflowers fringed the sunlit meadow where we snapped out the plaid picnic blanket. The wild bergamot was in bloom, and the royal catchfly would soon be out.

"Hear that?" I asked Peggy. "Meadowlark. She must have her nest somewhere in the shade over there."

"Protecting her babies."

Our talk last night about having one of our own was short and uncomfortable. It just wasn't a good time, I argued, with us moving to a new neighborhood, a new school, tenure-track position, five preps, student advisement, committee work.

"Should we move up the trail?" I asked.

She shook her head, smiling. The June light danced in her auburn hair. "No, honey. This is fine."

I unpacked the basket. It wasn't a long walk from the Forest Preserve parking lot, but Peggy looked fatigued already, and she rubbed her arms as though chilled.

"Still fighting that cold," I observed.

"Seems to be hanging on," she said. "I should have brought a sweater."

"Maybe we shouldn't have come."

"Didn't I say I could use the fresh air? I've been inside two weeks." She sniffed, sounding stuffed.

"Sinus infection still bothering you?"

"Not bad. The amoxycillin helped." She shivered; getting out into the warm sunshine wasn't helping as much as we thought it might.

She scissored down to the blanket, bent her arms stiffly and flexed her wrists.

"Still sore in the joints, too?" I asked.

"The ibuprofen isn't doing a thing. Getting old already, I guess."

"Ibuprofen won't help that," I said. "Try this."

I drew a bottle of Prairie State Barn Red, our favorite table wine, from the basket. Made in Illinois. "They say the antioxidants in red wine slow aging," I said, digging in the corkscrew and twisting it with a squeak. "It's why Italians live so long."

"Nah," she said with a sly smile. "It's the lovemaking that comes after the wine."

I laughed. A warm breeze rustled the milkweed and puffed my hair in my face. I blew it aside. A fluttering swallowtail caught my eye and when I glanced up, Peggy was massaging her elbow with her thumb and inspecting her forearm.

"What is it?" I asked.

"I wonder if I'm allergic to something out here," she said, nose wrinkled in puzzlement. "I've got a rash — or something."

People with leukemia have less than the normal count of healthy red blood cells and platelets. Because there aren't enough red blood cells to carry oxygen throughout the body, patients look pale and they tire easily. And because there aren't enough platelets, patients bruise and bleed easily. Some develop red spotting under the skin and display flu-like symptoms: fever, chills, infections, and bone or joint pain. It can be difficult to detect in some chronic cases, and it sometimes develops rather suddenly. In such acute cases, abnormal cells collect in the brain or spinal cord and cause seizures.

"All of this fits Ray's symptoms," I told Casey while feeding more logs to the cabin fireplace. "I should have recognized it sooner."

"Mystery solved," she said, "although he could have been a hemophiliac, too, like that guy Garcia said."

"It's a good theory," I acknowledged. "That could better account for unstoppable bleeding and the constant bruises. Maybe Rashidi is free to say so now publicly, given the fact that Ray is dead." I brushed my hands and sat beside her. "And who knows? Maybe he was making it worse, in order to do him in. After all, Ray was healing more people than the doctor was. Rashidi was losing money. The clinic was scheduled to be closed by his HMO for lack of finances. Maybe the Medicare claims of immigrants that Ray was attracting here were driving down profits, or Ray's healings were making the clinic unnecessary."

"That's a stretch. You're sounding like Lance Boyle."

I made a lemony face. "But here's the real problem for me: why wouldn't Ray or someone else in the church hierarchy openly admit to such an illness? Why deceive the public and make them think he was a stigmatic instead of simply being sick?"

"That's just it," Casey said, fingertip to her button nose. "People would know the truth, and people would stop coming. They wanted people to believe in him so they would fill the pews and the collection plates. People have been leaving the Church; this brings them back."

"Either that," I ventured, "or they were really getting healed, as long as they believed. So why spoil that? It's just that the healer couldn't heal himself."

"I'd say you had too much wine, but you haven't touched it," she said, running her mischievous tongue along the rim. "This is good. What is it?"

"It's called Prairie State Barn Red," I said.

I watched her sip it, and a warm glow spread in my body.

When the sun arose on Easter morning, it turned the feathery bands of cirrus clouds blood red. I rubbed the sleep from my eyes and wondered whether Casey was, at that moment, watching in astonishment as Ray appeared in St. Mary's sanctuary in time for the first Mass of the day.

Why should we marvel at the Resurrection, I asked myself, since we all experience it every morning when we return to life from the "little death" of slumber? Do we not willingly surrender our consciousness every night, believing, in faith, that we will arise to new life in the morning?

That is why it is said the happy are no better than the wretched for half their lives, Aristotle said wryly, *because they sleep.*

I wriggled my toes and fingers to get my blood moving. Edging into alertness, I smelled a subtle sweet-sick stink of death in the air. Just my imagination, I chided myself. Next thing, I'd hear foot shuffles and Ray knocking at the door and saying, in a voice dry as dust, "Hi, Reed. About my books you haven't brought back yet —"

When I stretched my neck left and right and faced the wall, the stench increased. Yes, that was it. The mice, shrews, chipmunks, or bats — whatever they were — had finally succumbed to the slow-working warfarin and were now decomposing behind the paneling.

Add air freshener to the shopping list. I'd get some on my next visit to the Value Mart to refill my prescription. In the bathroom, I shook the bottle. It rattled flatly. Considering the dwindling supply, it had been a tough week.

But tougher for Ray. At this moment, his blue-gray body probably lay on a stainless steel table, his scalp folded over his face for a cranial exam and his torso sliced in a Y incision from nipples to nuts, his organs removed and weighed in scales while his blood drained into test tubes for a toxicology lab. Nail holes and a spear wound are no big deal for a comeback; a dissected carcass is a real challenge.

Yet isn't that what awaits many of us?

And what happens after that?

Death is not the worst thing that can happen to men, Aristotle answered.

CHAPTER 18

When the Princess phone jangled the Thursday after Easter, I sat bolt upright and the blood drained from my head. Ray calling from beyond? I fished the receiver from beneath the bed.

Father Brian's voice said, "Your brother just went into shock. The hospital couldn't reach you by phone. I don't know what the problem was exactly, but they called me and —"

"Thanks," I said, spangles in my eyes. "I'll go right away." I nearly dropped the phone.

"Need some company?" Father Brian asked. "I'm going that way now. I'll pick you up."

I agreed, hung up, and breathed in short, rapid gasps.

"It's acute kidney failure," Dr. Rashidi said, clutching a clipboard to his chest like a shield. "I was afraid it might happen, given the blood tests we ran. This often happens after a trauma injury."

"What's that mean?" I asked. "He needs a transplant or something?"

Rashidi shook his head. "I don't think so. Transplants and dialysis are only needed in chronic, long-term cases when the kidneys have eroded to ten percent of their regular workload. That's not the case here. The good news about acute kidney failure is that this organ has an excellent capacity to heal itself after damage."

"I guess we won't need another miracle, then," I said. I thought of Dan's medal.

Rashidi soured. He raised an eyebrow in Father Brian's direction. "With respect to present company, miracles are a violation of natural laws." He said it as though he was in natural law enforcement.

The pastor didn't bite. "How soon will he recover?" he asked calmly.

125

"Most people with acute kidney failure recover within a month or two. We'd best keep him here. Given his other issues, he must remain under close observation. The kidney treatment itself is fairly simple: diuretics and urine-stimulating medications. The idea is to restore fluid balance in the body."

Now he was sounding like Aristotle. "When can I see him?" I asked.

"Tomorrow morning, perhaps. We'll keep him in Intensive Care, but we should have him stable by then. I'm listing him as 'serious' for now."

After I said thank-you with a resigned sigh, Father Brian led me back to the elevators.

"I'm glad I could reach you," Father Brian said, making small talk. "I imagine your cell phone is in a 'dead zone.' Either that or you should check the battery to see if it's dead."

Dead, dead. "Yes, I'll check it."

The mystery of the dead phone didn't trouble me much at the moment. This did: *Ray is dead; Dan isn't.*

I knew that the kidneys perform a vital function by continually filtering blood, ridding the body of poisonous substances. Had Ray been poisoned? Was Dan? Rashidi himself may have aggravated Dan's condition, hoping to dispel any "superstition" about his unexpected roadside recovery and thereby rescue his own reputation.

When the elevator doors rumbled open in the lobby and we stepped out, Manny Garcia brushed past us and stepped in.

"So chilly all of a sudden," Father Brian said, buttoning his raincoat.

I glanced behind me and met Garcia's frosty stare. I swung around. I thrust Citizen Cane between the closing doors. They stuttered and slid open.

"Stay away from my brother," I warned him. "Don't go near him. Understand?"

The doors whooshed back on their track but I elbowed them open.

"Hey, do you mind?" an orderly in scrubs said.

"Take this outside, you two," a man said.

Manny shouldered his way past the other passengers, all politeness. "Excuse me. Sorry. Thank you."

The doors shuddered behind him and the occupants' grumbling cut off. "Jesus Ch—"

"I work here, sir," Garcia said. "There's nothing wrong with me using the elevator."

"Look, if any of that Star Stuff appears on the bill, I'll sue, you understand? I won't have it."

"I'm sure Mr. Garcia will honor your request," Father Brian said, standing by me. "Won't you, Mr. Garcia?"

Manny returned a poisonous stare. "We are both in the business of helping people reach their potential," he said. "As the Master said, 'I came that they might have life abundant.'"

"We don't agree on what he meant by that," the clergyman said.

"It's all a matter of interpretation," Manny parried. "What's yours, Mr. Stubblefield?"

"Well, I —"

He didn't wait for a reply. He spun for the stairwell. The door hissed behind him.

"You know about this fellow, right?" I asked.

"Manny is part of the parish."

"I mean his group. The Ascension."

"Oh, yes. They've been around for, oh, let me see —"

"Let me guess. Seven months. Since Ray arrived."

"Long before that. Since the faith entered Greece, for about two thousand years, in one form or another."

"Sure," I said. "The Gnostics. A little Persian dualism here, some Greek sensuality there, sprinkle with Egyptian mysticism and stir in pseudo-science with a Christian spoon. Voilà — you, too, can be divine."

"Counterfeits are always convincing. People in dire need will often settle for a half-truth. We have made it clear from the pulpit many times that we do not endorse this group, but it seems that many of our parishioners still cannot tell the difference as you can," Father Brian said with a disappointed sigh.

He glanced up to the elevator's floor-indicator light and sucked in his breath.

"What's the matter?" I asked.

"It's stopping at Dan's floor. Come with me. Hurry."

"I already told the head nurse not to allow —"

He had already stepped away to the reception desk. He asked to speak to the Charge Nurse on Dan's floor. "That's right, Beverly," he said into the phone. "The family requests that under no circumstances should that man visit with Mr. Stubblefield. Yes, he's right here with me. Want to speak with him? Fine. Yes, thank you. I appreciate it. God bless you, Beverly."

He thanked the receptionist and turned to me. "She's pretty good about such things," he said. "She runs the floor like a drill sergeant. And I'm certain Dr. Rashidi won't allow any hocus-pocus with his patient."

He pulled up his collar to leave, and I followed reluctantly. He resumed small talk about the weather, but I fretted over Dan. Fanatics do not give up easily. If Manny and his crew believed that Dan somehow carried a secret to their own salvation, their own transcendence, what might they do? Shouldn't I be on guard at Danny's bedside?

Outside, the icy rain spat in my face and further dampened my spirits, although it had dispersed the usual clutter of candle holders.

Father Brian snapped open a black umbrella. "I'd like you to come back to my place for lunch," he said. "There's someone there I want you to meet."

"Who's that?" I said, huddled with chills.

"Monsignor Antonio DeMarco. The bishop's special investigator."

"Investigator?"

"Concerning the circumstances of Father Ray's case," he replied. "There are some things, you know, that we don't take by faith. He has some questions for you."

DeMarco rose to greet us, a saturnine man with brilliantine hair and dark brows knit across a hawkish Roman nose. Many secrets lay sunken beneath the still, gray pools of his eyes. Muscles rippled under the tight black shirt, and he seized my hand with a wrestler's grip. Why I had expected the fumbling, dumpling-faced charm of Chesterton's Father Brown, I don't know.

"I'm very glad you could come for lunch, Professor Stubblefield," DeMarco said after the introductions. "Father O'Neal speaks well of you."

"How kind," I said, on guard. He spoke without an Italian accent. Maybe the "Antonio" had thrown me, or my own wild supposition that the Vatican itself would deploy an operative.

"How is your brother doing?" DeMarco asked.

I told him while Father Brian took my coat.

"The prognosis sounds positive," DeMarco said. "Still, you must be concerned."

"He's been through a lot recently."

"So I've heard," DeMarco said. He motioned to the kitchen dining area. "Come, have a seat. I'm told you're working on a book about Aristotle?"

I settled in a chair. "I haven't really started," I answered. Father Brian positioned himself behind me discreetly, in case I needed assistance. It comes by habit when you live with a sickly companion like Ray, I guess. "Ray — I mean Father Ray — was helping me some with the research."

"Yes, his acquaintance with Aquinas and the classics was well regarded," DeMarco said. "Coffee?"

"Just lemon-grass tea, if you don't mind? I'm on medication, and some things disagree with it."

Father Brian raised the heat on the kettle.

"I should have asked about the memorial Mass yesterday," I said. "How did it go?"

"Well attended. It was, on the whole, a celebration of his life," Father Brian said.

"I couldn't come," I apologized. "I just wasn't feeling well."

"That was why you sought out Father Ray?" DeMarco inquired. "Your — incapacitation?"

He gets down to business fast, I thought. "No, not at all," I said, patting my cane. "I'm not really a believer, I'm afraid."

"That's one reason I wanted to speak with you so eagerly," DeMarco said. "Not enough doubters around."

I cast him a quizzical look.

"We take a decidedly skeptical approach concerning unusual phenomena," he explained, steepling his thick fingers. "In fact, at one time in our tradition, a man in my position was ordered by his superiors to aggressively disprove any extraordinary claims. That's why he was called the devil's advocate."

"What is the title now?"

"Simply an investigator, who is trying to solve a mystery, you might say."

"But tell me," I said, the tea water hissing, "which mystery are you trying to solve?"

DeMarco smiled dryly. "The mystery of his death I will leave to the police," he said. "I am interested in the mystery of his life."

"So you can make him a saint?"

The monsignor smiled benignly and poured cream into his coffee, forming clouds in the cup. "Heavens, no, Mr. Stubblefield. That is quite the wrong phraseology. Neither the local diocese nor the Vatican's Congregation for the Causes of Saints 'makes' saints. They only discover and confirm those whom God has raised in our midst, and it is the Spirit who moves the faithful to recognize an authentic reputation for sanctity."

"There are some people around here who are moved to recognize Ray in a hurry," I said, taking tea.

"Yes, I am aware of them," DeMarco said. "They are certain — and noisy. All the more reason to speak with another quiet skeptic like myself." He saluted with his cup and took a cautious sip. "You see," he continued, "Canon Law says that a 'cause' cannot be officially launched until the candidate has been deceased at least five years."

"But Father Ray has hardly been gone five days," I said.

"Quite so. And while it is never to be a matter of urgency nor popular opinion nor the power of the media, but a matter solely of what we call 'heroic virtue,' it is nevertheless important to begin the investigation early, while there are still fresh witnesses." DeMarco leaned forward, lowering his voice to confessional level. "Let me tell you: the current *Index ac Status Causarum* lists 1,369 active causes in progress. Most causes will be killed."

An interesting choice of words, I thought. "How is that decided?"

"It is a long legal process."

"How long?"

"Decades, usually. It takes that long to compile his *vitae*."

I must have looked very puzzled.

"Oh, not like your *curriculum vitae*," he hastened to explain. "Not a resume. It's a documented biography of about a thousand pages, with a compendium of witnesses' affidavits, letters, diaries, or other writings that support the holiness of the candidate. Then there's the legal brief summarizing the testimony of psychologists, physicians, and such — often people who are not Catholic, and not even believers. Agnostics are preferred for objectivity. Ah — the soup is ready."

Porcelain bowls clinked, and while the two clerics recited a brief grace in unison, my hands lay on my lap like two pork chops. My ears were ringing from the monsignor's words.

After the *Amen* I asked, "So, Father, are you recruiting me as one of these agnostic 'consulters'?"

"Not exactly. But I would like to confer — share information. The truth is: I need a fellow skeptic to challenge me. Especially someone so well-versed in Aristotle."

"Why is that?"

"The Congregation for Causes is precise in its tests of the grace of God at work in a person," the investigator said, dabbing his lower lip with a napkin in that practiced way priests do hundreds of times at the altar. "There are seven tests: three supernatural virtues of faith, hope, and charity, and four cardinal, or moral, virtues. You should know them: prudence, justice, fortitude, and temperance."

"Aristotle's four criteria for a life of excellence," I said. "But these can be found in any decent person."

"See? You are challenging me already. I like that," he said.

I felt as if I had passed a test.

"A 'saint' exemplifies these moral qualities to a 'heroic' or exceptional degree," the monsignor continued. "As you might already know, the term 'heroic virtue' comes to us from Bishop Grosseteste's translation of Aristotle's *Nichomachean Ethics* in 1328."

I nodded as if I knew. I didn't. Community-college instructors who are generally MAs haven't done as much research as PhDs. But we don't like to admit it.

"Aristotle's phrase was also adopted by Thomas Aquinas to define exemplary believers. Heroic virtue thereby became synonymous with holiness, and since that period, all candidates for beatification or canonization have had their lives investigated according to this rubric."

"Why not judge them by uniquely Christian virtues," I argued, "like humility, or mercy, or for God's sake, the Beatitudes?"

"I thought you said you weren't Catholic," Father Brian said, bemused.

"I'm not."

Father Brian snickered. "This reminds me of a M*A*S*H episode where Father Mulcahy asks a wounded soldier, 'Are you Catholic?' and the soldier says no, and Mulcahy says, 'In due time, my son, in due time.'"

I smiled politely but squirmed a little. Father Brian went back to his soup, pleased by his own anecdote.

"The answer to your question, Mr. Stubblefield," DeMarco said, "is that the early Church fathers adopted the Greek model of the morally excellent person after the age of martyrs." He spoke as though he were pacing a classroom. "Those killed in the Roman persecutions achieved moral perfection, it was said, by surrendering their lives as Jesus did, in complete faith, hope, and love. In non-martyrs, however, perfect love of God is not so obvious. Thus, the claim to sanctity is not in how they died but in how they lived."

"Even in this case?" I asked.

"Especially in this case," DeMarco said emphatically. "Religious ecstasy and psychological trauma are quite similar. Mystics and manic depressives often look alike."

"You think Ray was disturbed?" I asked.

"That would be for a consulter in psychoanalysis to determine," he replied.

"How can anyone tell the difference?" I pressed.

"Training, and experience, and some investigation — and some instinct — much as you can spot a plagiarized term paper, perhaps," he said. "I once managed a case with a French nun who said she was besieged by the Devil. The other sisters in her order knew nothing about it, for the abbess kept it quiet. She died young, and afterward, when they found her diary and letters, they thought she was a saint because she described how she had wrestled with the Devil. It turned out to be a young man in the village who had, shall we say, captured her affections. They killed the cause."

"That's an easy one," I said. "But you have some empirical evidence here — people healed, bleeding hands."

"*Claims* of healing, bandaged hands," he corrected. "That is all anyone objectively observed."

"So what's your explanation?"

"It is too early to make a proper inference," he said.

"What's the usual explanation?"

"The *usual* explanation is something quite natural."

"Did Ray have leukemia?" I blurted.

DeMarco looked to O'Neal. O'Neal shook his head. Did it mean 'no, he didn't have leukemia' or 'no, don't tell him anything'?

"He did not have leukemia," DeMarco said.

"Hemophilia?" I shot.

133

DeMarco took a breath. "Name as many conditions as you like. Even if he did have a chronic condition of any sort, it would not fully explain the phenomenon. We believe that some people experience a closeness with God that surpasses the intellect and imagination, and that such a grace given to a contemplative person passes back through the intellect and the imagination to the body. Thus, in a genuine mystic, there are ripple effects of the immediate intellectual apprehension of God in the imagination and the body, an imitation of God in the flesh crucified, as in Francis of Assisi: the stigmata. Are you following this?"

"So it's all in the imagination?"

"In a manner of speaking, yes, whether the mystic's experience is authentic or not. The mind — intellect and imagination — are fully engaged, and the body simply follows. The truth is: most mystics in the past who have had the stigmata tend to copy the crucifixes they see. If the nail-holes are in the wrong places, they appear that way on their bodies."

"Still," I rejoined, "they do appear."

"Sometimes the nail wounds appear, sometimes they are closed, and sometimes they appear only on certain days such as Good Friday. In any case, it is possible they are self-induced," he said.

"You think Father Ray wounded himself?"

"I don't mean to imply that. I mean to say that the imagination has a powerful effect on the body. If a Spanish visionary is accustomed to seeing Mary dressed in blue and red, as in some Spanish art, instead of the usual blue and white, then that is the way she will be dressed in their visions."

"In order to be recognized," I suggested.

"So, who is the devil's advocate now?" DeMarco said.

I had to chuckle. "You have me there. So, what you're saying is that visions and even the stigmata are not proof of sainthood?"

"Even if it causes considerable excitement," DeMarco said with a questioning smile, "it is not proof. In strongly probable cases, the Church does not forbid belief in such things, if it appears authentic. Rather, the Church is interested only in the heroic virtues."

"Not interested in miracles?"

"If you mean medical cures, the answer is: not really. Beginning in 1983, the criteria were decreased from four verifiable miracles to one, although two are preferred. Besides, doctors are limited to saying whether or not a cure is officially 'scientifically inexplicable.' "

"Dr. Rashidi might admit that," I said. "But he'll never call anything a miracle."

"No doctor can decide if it is a miracle. That decision is left for the theological consulters, whose conclusions must be ratified by an army of cardinals and ultimately by the Holy Father himself."

Father Brian cleared dishes and offered more tea. I put my hand over my cup.

"The truth is," DeMarco said, "asking for miracles is an impediment to the process. I've heard of nuns waiting outside emergency rooms praying to their founding abbess for a miracle every time an ambulance pulls in."

Father Brian tapped his watch. "Your appointment, Monsignor?"

"Quite right," DeMarco said. "Mr. Stubblefield, I'm glad to have met. We'll talk again, I'm sure."

We shook hands. He had a wrestler's grip. Father Brian had my coat waiting, and I shrugged into it. "I thought you might ask me more questions about Ray," I said.

"Another day," DeMarco said. "I just have one for now. When he fell at the altar, did you notice any odor?"

"Odor?" I repeated, puzzled. "Let me think — yes," I recalled. "Vanilla, or almonds. I thought it was the candles. Why?"

"That's a good question," he said. "We must keep asking it."

"It's called the aroma of sanctity," Casey said.

"That's not what you're wearing now," I said.

"That's Tabu." She swung her honeyed hair beneath a black beret, cocked in a rebellious tilt.

I took a deep breath and exhaled luxuriously. The wooded path smelled of moist humus and shaggy-bark cedar. April snow receded beneath the feathery spruces while the early spring trout lilies, blue phlox, and bloodroot took advantage of the sunlight cascading though the bare-branched butternuts and burr oaks. "So that's what we smelled?"

"Maybe. It's an aroma associated with saints," she said. "They say that exhumed bodies of saints sometimes show no decay, like Padre Pio's, and a sweet perfume persists even after death."

"Maybe that's why they're delaying the autopsy," I said. "To see if he decomposes naturally or not." The dead leaves from fall squished beneath my boots.

"If I remember right, the smell of almond is a sign of cyanide poisoning," Casey said. "Even a small amount would cause hemorrhaging. It would show up on the toxicology report."

"Would we have access to that?"

"Sure, if there's an inquest. All the evidence submitted to the coroner's jury is made public. You can get copies for a small fee. But that might not be for another month."

"What if there's no inquest? What if the coroner just declares the death accidental, or by natural causes? And if it's ruled a homicide, wouldn't the medical report be sealed as evidence or something like that?"

She laughed a silvery laugh. "You watch too much television, Reed. Sure, I could still get it. Just like I'm getting the police investigation report."

"You can get that?"

Her dimple creased naughtily. "Already got it. I'll bring it tomorrow."

The leaves rustled to my left. A robin red-breast hopped away from us and launched up to a hickory branch. It chirped, annoyed.

"You owe me a quarter," I said.

"A quarter? For what?"

I had said it as a mindless reflex. I repented. "What I mean is — well — Peggy and I used to have this bet every spring. The first one to see a robin gets a quarter."

"Oh, that's so sweet," she sing-songed. "You must miss her."

"It's little things like that. Forget it."

"No, it's OK. It's nice."

"You miss your ex at all?"

"No. Not a minute. Let's not discuss that. You mind?"

The robin scolded me again.

"A quarter, did you say?" She dug into her pocket. "I don't have a quarter. Will this do?"

She turned my chin with a finger and gave me a warm kiss.

I nearly dropped Citizen Cane.

CHAPTER 19

INVESTIGATION SYNOPSIS: NARRATIVE STATEMENT

1. Basis for the investigation

At approximately 3:25 p.m., Friday, April 9, Detective Frank Gordon, Badge 106, received a phone call from Lt. Francis Haloren, Commander of the Communications Section of the Sinnissippi County Sheriff, dispatching him to meet Sheriff's Deputies at 300 Union Street, River Falls, relative to a death from unknown causes and a burglary. Officer Black also stated that he had notified the Crime Lab and the Coroner's Office.

2. Detective's arrival on the scene

At approximately 3:35 p.m., same date, Detective Gordon arrived on the scene and spoke with Officer Black of the Sheriff's Department. He related to Detective Gordon the following account, given to them by various churchgoing witnesses as well as ESTRELLA ESPERANZA, W/F, age 47, residing 12847 Hill Road, River Falls:

3. Summary of witnesses' accounts

Shortly after 3 p.m., same date, the officiating priest for the Good Friday Mass, REV. RAYMOND BOUDREAU, W/M, age 35, fell unconscious and was immediately attended by two EMTs present who tried without success to revive the victim. An ambulance was called while officers cleared the area. During this time, a white male (later identified as KENNETH DURROW, age 45, of an unknown address) had apparently entered the church vestry area (300 Union street), forcing open the cabinet storing communion wines, and opening at least one bottle by force, breaking it. The sound led a witness, ESTRELLA ESPERANZA, W/F, age 47, residing 12847 Hill Road, to enter the vestry and see him and call out for help. The subject threw a tire iron at her and then fled on foot in a northerly direction on Union Street from the church rectory toward the Red Oak Trailer Park.

4. Detective's observation of the body

After obtaining this information, Detective Gordon went to the chancel area by the altar, where he observed the body of a white male (identified by witnesses as REV. BOUDREAU) lying face up, apparently dead. This male had noticeable bruises on the wrists which had split and bled, and bruises on the brow indicating the possibility of internal bleeding. An extended right arm showed signs of bruised needle marks from recent injections near the inside elbow. The position of the body was as follows: the head was in a westerly direction, the legs extended in an easterly direction, the right arm extended in a southerly direction, and the left arm was under the body.

5. Description of victim's clothing

The body of the deceased was clad in the following: Roman Catholic clericals with embroidered red vestments. Brown athletic wraps on both forearms extending to wrists and hands, crossing thumbs and both palms, and white athletic wrap on knees, ankles, and feet, black socks, and brown leather clogs.

"Clogs?"

"Easy to slip in and out of," I said. "Maybe his ankles had swollen so much that the zippered boots he usually wore were no longer tenable."

6. Search of the scene

At this point Detective Gordon examined the scene with other officers, who had secured the area. As to the deceased, there was no evidence of an accidental fall, weapons, narcotics, or poisonous substances. The victim had collapsed in full view of the congregation in what appeared to be a faint. As to the burglary, entrance was gained to the vestry via the attached residence's main door, which faces the rear parking lot. The Subject forced the door open with a tire tool measuring 14½ inches, and then proceeded to the vestry through a hallway.

7. Search continued inside
From the residence's entry door Detective Gordon followed the hallway to the vestry, where a series of red stains marked the carpet 3 ft. from the north wall. These were determined to be wine spills from an open bottle carried by the Subject in his escape. Detective Gordon found a broken wine bottle on the vestry floor 6 in. from the west wall cabinets where communion wine and other materials were stored. The Subject apparently forced open the cabinet with the same tire tool used for the entry door. Upon being discovered by the witness ESPERANZA, the subject threw the tire tool at her, dropped one bottle, smashing it, and fled with another bottle through the hallway and out the main residence door. Detective Gordon checked other rooms in the residence for signs of disturbance but everything was in an orderly condition.

8. Search continued outside
In checking the area outside the residence, Detective Gordon found a gray glove for a man's left hand 2 ft. from the entry door.

9. Activity of lab technician
At 4:15 p.m. Tech. Farrell arrived on the scene and took the following photographs:
    a. One tire tool measuring 14½ in. found 1 ft. east inside frame of vestry-to-chancel entry
    b. Sample of blood stain located 3 ft. south of altar

    c. Sample of wine stain in hallway, 3 ft. from wall on carpet
    d. 1 man's gray glove
    e. Broken bottle and pieces 1 ft. from vestry cabinets
    f. Splintered cabinet frame
    g. Broken entry door
    h. Body from all angles, with particular attention to the bruises at the wrist joints and head, and the needle marks on the right arm

"Remember I told you about the needle marks?" Casey said. "Could be a diabetic, too. We just don't know."

During the taking of these photographs, Detective Gordon retrieved items a-f above as evidence.

10. Disposition of evidence

Items a-f above were placed in individual plastic bags and a container for the blood sample. Evidence cards were filled in and initialed. Bags were sealed by Detective Gordon. All items were later entered in the River Falls Police Department's Evidence Book, page 22, under Evidence No. 1126 and were then turned over to Tech. Farrell.

11. Personal items removed from body

A check of the body for personal property was made, and the following items were removed and secured for the Coroner's Investigator: 1 silver metal wristwatch with leather band taken from the left trouser pocket, one 1½ in. hard cut masonry nail from the right trouser pocket.

12. Sketch

After the body had been checked by Detective Gordon, Tech. Farrell, and the EMTs, Detective Gordon and officer Black took the necessary measurements of the scene so that a sketch could be made for use at a later date. Sketch is attached to this report.

13. Disposition of body and coroner's examination

At about 3:35 p.m., the River Falls Rescue Unit arrived on the scene and EMTs pronounced the victim dead at approximately 3:45 p.m. Detective Gordon tagged the body on the left ankle. The Rescue Unit technicians then wrapped the body, placed paper bags over the hands, and transported the body to the Coroner's morgue for a preliminary pending the authorization for a medical-legal autopsy to be performed in the presence of Detective Gordon and Sheriff's deputies at a date to be announced.

"Paper bags over the hands?" I inquired.

"Preserves the hands as evidence. They look for residue under the fingernails, stuff like that."

14. Detective's interview with witness

After the body was transported from the scene, Detective Gordon spoke with witness ESTRELLA ESPERANZA. Witness ESPERANZA related the following: She was in attendance for the 3 p.m. service when REV. BOUDREAU fell. She hurried forward to assist him, as many others tried to do. She heard a noise of breaking glass in the vestry and opened the door. She saw a white male whom she identified as KENNETH DURROW, age 45, who lives in the area as a drifter. He held a metal crow-bar-type tool in one hand and a bottle of wine in the other. The Subject DURROW threw the metal tool at her. The tool missed ESPERANZA. The Subject ran away toward the residence behind him. She called for help, but in the confusion, she was ignored. She ran after the Subject, and saw him escaping on foot in a northerly direction toward the Red Oak Trailer Park. Attached is a copy of ESPERANZA's full statement.

15. Notifying appropriate divisions

After taking her statement, Detective Gordon notified HQ and placed an APB via police radio, giving a full description of Subject DURROW (see above). The Subject remains at large.

16. Check of Record Room File

At 4:30 p.m. Detective Gordon left the scene and proceeded to the City Police Record Room to obtain a mug shot and records on Subject DURROW. The Record File revealed that the subject DURROW, W/M, DOB 1-7-59, last known address 1117 Red Oak Trailer Park, River Falls, had two previous arrests in the last year, RS 45, Art. 3, Vagrancy, and RS 14, Art. 187, Simple Burglary.

17. Status of case

Investigation continuing. Supplementary Report to follow.

18. Signatures

I shut the manila folder and handed it back to Casey. "Standard and familiar diction, rarely rising above the commonplace and colloquial. Unoriginal, and substitutes repetition for development," I said. "I'd give it a C."

"It's not a term paper, silly," Casey said, opening it again. "It's an official report. That's how they're written."

"It doesn't report much more than we already know. The masonry nail in the pocket is interesting, though."

"Cutting himself with it, you think?"

"No. A masonry nail is small and blunt, and hard to cut with. Besides, they would have reported blood on it," I said. "It looks like a miniature spike, so it's probably just an innocent reminder in his pocket of the day's meaning, that's all. At least there's more useful information on the burglary. Now we know they're looking for Kenny. Looks like he saw an opportunity to go after the wine."

Casey pointed her pencil to that paragraph. "Could be. Or he was removing evidence."

"Evidence?"

"Remember what I said about the almond smell? About cyanide? Maybe he put some in the bottles."

"C'mon, Casey," I said, dubious. "What would a bum like Kenny know about poisons? And why would he want to poison Ray? And how did he get cyanide in the bottles? And why remove them? And then —"

"Hold it, Sherlock," she said. "One thing at a time."

"OK," I said. "Let's start with motive. Why would a vagrant and a thief like Kenny want to hurt Ray?"

"You saw how he reacted when Ray touched him at the fish fry."

"He freaked."

"He said, 'You freak,'" she clarified. "He's clearly psychotic. Everyone knows he's mentally ill. Many of the homeless are. He's been known for odd behavior — talking to himself, hearing voices."

"A schizophrenic?"

"Probably. Along with that, he might have had some weird paranoia about Ray, about church conspiracies, and saw it as his mission to destroy him. Maybe his voices told him to do it."

"Probably. Maybe. It's all guessing. The rhetorical fallacy of *Inexpert Opinion*. And to say, 'Everyone knows he is mentally ill' is an error in logic called *alleged certainty*. What do we really know about him? Military vet? Local man? Family in town?"

She shrugged. "Nothing."

"OK, then. We'll have to assume a few things for now. Let's think about the means, then. Where would a mentally ill drunk get cyanide?"

"I don't know. There might be a common household product, like a bug killer or something, that contains it or a form of it. Ever seen those warning labels? They're scary. Or, since he's a thief, he could have taken something from the last hospital he was in."

"He'd need some prior knowledge of the ingredients in household products or medicines."

"There's plenty of meth labs around — drug-dealers who know stuff like that."

"Or the town pharmacist told him when he asked," I joked.

She didn't laugh. "And farmers use pesticides and fertilizers. They're spreading ammonium hydroxide in the fields now. There's lots of poisons around in unlocked barns and such."

"Even if he managed to get something," I persisted, "how did it get into the wine bottles? He had to sneak in the vestry in advance, open the locked cabinet, remove the foil and corks, sprinkle in the powder, and replace the corks. All undetected?"

"Maybe they're twist-off caps."

"I doubt the church uses mass-produced wines," I said, regretting the pun.

"So maybe the wines are so specialized, they don't have foil over the corks. Then he could remove and replace them."

"You could see the corkscrew hole."

"Not if you turned them upside down."

"You'd see the stain." I scratched my head. "I don't think our friend Kenny would have the presence of mind for such a plan. The best explanation is that the town drunk saw a chance to get to some cash or good wine while everyone else was distracted. He broke in, was surprised by a bystander, dropped some of his loot, and ran off."

"We're still left with the almond smell."

"The candles. Or," I added with a light sniff, "a woman's perfume, activated by anxiety and a little warmth."

"Those older church ladies don't wear Tabu, Reed," she said with a flirty smile.

"If you say so," I said. "But tell me: what other poison might give off an almond or vanilla odor?"

"Only one way to find out," she answered. "Check the Merck Manual at the library. There's one in the reference section. We can go tonight after I leave the office. About six?"

"It's a date," I said, thinking that the last time I went on a date to study at a library was at least thirty years ago, when I was an undergraduate and Casey was still an infant.

I waited in the parking lot, listening to the Cubs on WGN radio. When they were down seven-to-one early in the game and going to the bullpen, and Casey hadn't shown up yet, and I was getting chilled in the car, I decided to go inside.

Two teenagers were doing homework at the Internet station, giggling softly. An elderly gent in an oversize chair rustled his way through a week-old *New York Times*. Otherwise, the place looked dead. I browsed haphazardly in the two-shelf reference section across from the checkout desk. Dictionary of Philosophy. Encyclopedia of Science Fiction and Fantasy. Master Plots. Illinois Bike Tours.

"Help you find something?" The librarian, a sixty-ish woman in a flower print dress and bifocals on a necklace, spoke from behind the counter. She aimed a bar-code scanning tool at me like a pistol.

I swallowed hard. "I'm waiting to meet someone."

"Who would that be?"

Small towns. None of your business, lady. "I'm supposed to meet Ms. Casey Malone."

"Casey Who?"

"Casey Malone — a reporter for the *Observer*. Know her?"

"Oh, sure! *That* Casey. Known her since she was yea tall." She hovered her hand a few feet off the floor, and then eyed me up and down. "You related?"

"We're just friends."

"Oh, sure," she said, a doubt wrinkling the corner of her pruny mouth. "Fact is, she just left. Said to be on the lookout for a good-looking guy in deck shoes. I expected a younger man." She reached beneath the checkout counter. "She said to give you this."

She handed over a number-ten business envelope. Unsealed. There was a hint of Casey's Tabu on it. The librarian fluttered her heavy eyelashes.

I thanked her and found a study carrel, where I opened the letter away from the librarian's prying gaze. It said:

Dear Reed: Something came up and I had to run. It's always something. I'll call. Casey.

Reporters are always on duty. No sense in wasting time, I thought. I hunted the information I'd come for. I thumbed through The Merck Manual's index to find "cyanide." It didn't tell me much: cyanide's scientific name and forms, its sources in a variety of fruit seeds, antidotes, and more interestingly, its presence in certain pesticides and fertilizers, in abundant supply locally. Any farmhand would have access to some.

The odor of bitter almond may be noticeable at an autopsy. Not before? At least the symptoms of poisoning matched fairly well: rapid respiration, flushing, headache, dizziness, unconsciousness — and all occurring quickly after ingesting a small amount.

The article mentioned Laetrile, claimed as a cancer cure. It was made from apricot kernels and widely available in Mexico, where many desperate patients traveled for treatments. If roasted at 300 degrees for ten minutes, about forty apricot kernels can fatally poison a man.

It wasn't likely that forty kernels were crushed into his food and unnoticed.

But Father Brian, I recalled, made his own apricot preserves. And there was also a good chance that, with the influx of Mexicans in the region, Laetrile could be one of the illegally imported drugs they brought with them.

Before turning in that night, I pulled out Ray's paper on Aristotle and a stack of index cards, pen in hand.

It was like hearing his voice again.

"We know that Aristotle rejects the idea that the suffering of the hero comes by vice or depravity," Ray said, "otherwise the suffering would not evoke pity. Therefore, the *hamartia* (shortfall) that causes the suffering should not be understood as 'sin' or 'vice' but rather should be taken to mean a good quality that becomes a liability."

An excellent point, I thought, and a fine employment of *distincto* to clarify a definition. One would anticipate a tactic of *exemplum* to follow. It did.

"For example, Antigone's loyalty to her family and religion force her to act in ways that risk her life. Her action — to bury her brother when such an act is against the king's law — is seen as a 'vice' by the state. But we know that it is a noble thing that she does. The same is true of Jesus, who is regarded as a threat by the religious establishment."

The *analogia* was fair enough. But it got me wondering: Was the same true for Ray? Did he threaten someone's position — like Father Brian? Offend someone's theology? Was he becoming a liability to the religious establishment? *Is that why you were thinking about this subject and wanted me to see it, Ray?*

"In Greek tragedy, the hero is destined to suffer vicariously," Ray said. "The original function of Greek drama was, after all, religious. It accompanied the ritual sacrifice of a scapegoat called a *pharmakos,* and in identifying with the actor-priest's dramatized death, the people experienced a sense of release and healing."

Yes, that was certainly Aristotle's medical analysis of drama. And just as a scapegoat cured a spiritual problem through a *pharmakos*, the modern *pharmacy* cured physical problems. An interesting confluence of etymology. And that reminded me: I needed to check my supply of Nardil.

I returned to the paper. It might have been Aristotle's analysis of the Roman Catholic Mass. After all, didn't the Roman Church insist that the Mass was a re-presenting of a ritual sacrifice, a drama of sorts carried out by a priest acting, as it were, in Christ's stead? Did Ray's death lead to someone's sense of release? Whose?

When finished, I gathered the papers and cards. I'd taken all the notes I wanted; it was time to return it. I arranged it with Father Brian by cell phone. I had vowed, after our last call, to keep the battery charged.

In the morning, when I arrived with the paper and Ray's books, I told Father Brian that Ray's work was potentially publishable, and that I'd be glad to recommend a suitable journal for submission. "That is, after I've tracked down some of his citations. Oh, and it should be re-typed in the proper format."

"Father DeMarco might like the original," he said. "He's collecting all of Father Ray's papers for the *Positio*."

"The what?"

"The portfolio of evidence. For the Cause?"

"Ah, I understand. Is he here?"

"No, he's at —" The cleric paused. "He's attending the autopsy." He glanced at the mantle clock. "I'd offer you tea and muffins, but I'm due to meet Monsignor at the county courthouse soon."

"That's too bad," I rejoined. "I'd really like to try that apricot spread you make. You use real apricots, isn't that right? Not dried or boxed apricots?"

"Real ones, naturally," he said. "When they're in season."

"How many do you need?"

"Oh, I don't know — a large basket. Really, it's just for myself and a few gifts. It's a lot of trouble for such a small amount, really. But it's a way I remember my mother's cooking."

"What do you do with the pits?"

"Discard them. Why?"

"I just don't know a thing about jams and preserves and that sort of thing," I said with a shrug. "City boy."

"You know they're poisonous, don't you?" Father Brian asked.

"Are they?"

"That's why I burn them in the fireplace. No need for an adventurous raccoon to be dispatched by my cooking leftovers." He shook the papers. "I'll ask our secretary Lois to copy the essay for you in the church office."

"Thank you," I said. So much for the apricot theory.

Maybe. How many in a basket? Forty?

Father Brian pivoted away and said over his shoulder, "Why don't you go ahead and replace the books on Father Ray's office shelves? You know where they go."

Not that Ray would need to find them again, I thought. I thanked him yet again and found my way to Ray's office.

Re-shelving the books took but a minute. I admired the bronze bookends again: a replica of the Parthenon on one side and a domed basilica I didn't recognize on the other. Who was it that asked: *What has Jerusalem to do with Athens?* Ray would know. He had spent his life answering the question. I recalled his poem with the Greek gods at table with the risen Christ, and thought DeMarco should see it. What *did* Jerusalem have to do with Athens? It was a good question and much depended on who was asking it. All too often, I observed, those in Jerusalem — religious people — spurned the life of reason, while those in Athens — academic types — scorned the whole idea of faith as antithetical to reason. Extremists, both. Where was Aristotle's Golden Mean?

It is obvious that there is some First Principle, and that the causes of things are not infinitely many, Aristotle said.

It sounded logical: in the beginning was the Prime Mover, One Who Acted and could not be acted upon since he was before all things, not existing as an impersonal force, but an agent with a will. Could it be?

God is a living Being, eternal, most good, and therefore life and continuous existence come from God, Aristotle insisted.

Maybe, I replied. He was hard to argue with. He was wrong about women; maybe he was wrong about God, too.

I replaced the last book on the shelf. The span of books between the Parthenon and the basilica represented Ray's effort to bridge the two. It's certainly what Thomas Aquinas set out to accomplish. I wondered where I stood now on that bridge.

I brushed the swivel chair where he had sat and studied the glass-top desk. My face reflected in it like a weary ghost. That's when I realized the desk was cleared of the correspondence, catalogs, and coffee mugs that cluttered it before; Father Brian or family members had begun the sad business of clearing Ray's effects. One reviews a whole life that way, sorting through the little things that we scatter in our trail: ticket stubs, keys, combs, receipts, souvenirs, pens, post-cards, the class ring we never wore after high school, orphaned socks, cosmetics, medicines. Most of it ends up on the curb in a plastic sack. It's lonely work.

The work wasn't done; a stack of junk mail and magazines had spilled over a gilt-edged commemorative mug and a box of facial tissues. I straightened the mail so it wouldn't drop to the floor. The mug held stubby pencils, elastic bands, and a shot-glass cough-syrup cup with a trace of orange crust, a reminder of his persistent cold. If I told Casey about it, she'd say Kenny poisoned the cough syrup, not the wine.

"Here's a copy of the paper," Father Brian said, entering. "I'm sure Father Ray would have appreciated your comments."

"I looked forward to talking about the paper with him," I said, folding the sheets. "I'll miss him."

"We all will," the priest said.

I said thanks and picked up my cane.

"Wait, don't go yet." He reached for the bronze bookends and pulled them to his chest. Books flopped on the shelf. "I know Father Ray would have wanted you to have these," he said.

"But, Father," I objected, "I hardly knew him. Are you certain? Wouldn't his family want them?"

"I doubt it," he said. "I've delivered all his other personal items to them myself."

I took one, hefted its weight. "You're quite certain they won't want them?"

"No more than they wanted his books," he replied. "And those have been left to his school in Dubuque."

"So that's where his family is, too?"

"He has some relatives here that I know of. His first cousin lives right here in town, in the River Road Apartments. Estrella Esperanza? Surely you know of her?"

CHAPTER 20

I was perspiring by the time I reached the River Road Apartments, still arguing with myself about making this unannounced visit. Father Brian gave me the address when I said I wanted to deliver my condolences personally. But it was delivering the bookends that gave me a solid excuse to research Ray's background firsthand.

I drove past the building twice before finding it. The River Road Apartments were a row of brick tenements sandwiched between an auto body and detail shop and a cheesy-looking pizzeria in a failed gas station. By the taped windows and faded signs on the first floors, it looked as if the downstairs housed businesses once, a dry cleaner and a gunsmith. One building combined a *Lavendaria* and a *Musicas y Videos* shop. I checked my driving directions; the ½ in the address indicated that the apartment entry was in the back. A light rain sputtered from the silver sky, and I was glad Father Brian had given me a plastic shopping bag for the bookends. I carried them around to a covered stairway and made my way up one creaky stair at a time. In the air there was a heavy smell of frying tortillas, a hint of cayenne pepper, and the thump of Salsa music. A Mexican flag hung as a curtain over one window; there was light behind a shade. I tapped the door with Citizen Cane.

Estrella answered the door. If she was surprised to see me, her prim face did not betray the surprise. A glint of hostility shone in her onyx eyes.

"What is it?" she asked brusquely.

"*No hable con ningun policia,*" a voice called behind her.

"It's not the police," she said over her shawl. She measured me with her dark eyes. "I told the police everything. Or are you a reporter?"

"No, I'm —" What should I say? A professor on a field trip? "I'm Reed Stubblefield. Father Ray and I got to know each other and — well, I came to give you something of his." I shook the bag.

She backed away from me and there was something in the backward steps that showed her unease, her lack of preparedness for a visit from a stranger. Her eyes narrowed. "You are the brother of the Lazarus."

I nodded reluctantly and gave my name.

"Come in," she said.

I stepped into a plain room, furnished with a plaid Goodwill couch, wooden chairs, and a pitted brass lamp with a fringed lampshade. A circular oil stove heated the parlor, framed by a gaudy lithograph of the Sacred Heart and a framed poster of Our Lady of Guadalupe.

A cabinet TV played a Spanish telenovela on cable, and a trio of young women who had gathered around it turned to me with a glare. One of them was the server Bianca who had hustled Casey and me out of the saloon. She cradled an infant in her arm; a pair of toddlers fussed near the couch. A baby cried from another room.

I handed over the bag. "Father Brian gave me this, but I thought you should have it." I looked regretfully at the puddle of water I'd brought into the well-swept room.

She peered inside and shook her head. "You mean to be kind, but I already told Father Brian I did not want them," she said. "We have no books. Half of our people cannot even read Spanish, and the ones that read the English have the third-grade level."

"I didn't mean to insult you."

Her eyes softened. "No. Of course not." She studied the bookends, reconsidering. "These can remind us of his learning and his goodness, *si*? The school and the church. His mind and his heart."

"Yes, a knowledgeable man," I agreed. "And a man of compassion. A rare combination."

"He knows we have the low reading rate, the high dropout rate from the high school," she said. "Ray teaches us the English, but the schools, they are not very open to him."

"I'm a teacher," I said, quick to show my well-versed multicultural sensibility, "and at my school in the city we had many Latinos — a Literacy Program, bilingual classes —"

"That's the city. There is no money for that here. There is a reading program at the library with a few volunteer tutors, that is all. The people here, they do not like that half of the students are Latino. Here, you assimilate or leave."

The word *assimilate* hissed from her mouth. It sounded like something Hadley Berger might say.

"Yes, you lost a fine advocate in Father Ray."

"That is why I must now speak for him," she said with fervor in her unblinking shoe-button eyes. "He gave us all the hope. Hope is all some of us have."

A little girl shyly buried her face in Estrella's skirts. The woman kissed her dark head and said, "He taught us to hope in God. It was for the love of God that he served the poor and the sick, you know."

"I'm sure," I said sincerely. "A great loss to your community, and your family. Were you very close?"

"We shared a grandmother, but my sister, she come to America long ago. We never know each other. I hear my American cousin, by letters, that he does well — go to the school, be made a priest of the Holy Mother Church. We are very proud of him."

"Did you hear he was often sick?"

She gripped the bag, a crease of doubt in her forehead. "Now you sound like the policeman."

"He asked the same thing?"

"I will tell you the same thing. We heard he suffered much, from the childhood. We did not know with what. But now we know why, *no es verdad?*"

The young women behind her nodded. One said, *"Creo que si."*

"I believe so, too," she repeated for my benefit. "Sometimes, Mr. Reed, it is a lifetime of suffering that makes a man a martyr, not the man's death. But Ray, he has both. He joined his suffering to the suffering of Christ, and now he has joined him in his death. He is gone

155

but the hope, it is not," she continued. "Not as long as we have Father Ray, who is with Christ, as our protector." She hugged the child. "Do you know what you can give to us, Mr. Reed? Ask Ray to help us."

Was she asking me to pray? "I don't think I can do that."

"You must. He will listen to you. Your brother, because of Ray, he is alive, *sí*? He will listen to you."

"But you're his cousin, his own family," I protested.

Bianca, the server from the saloon, came over. She looked sixteen; she might have been one of the dropouts Estrella mentioned. "You still do not believe." She set her lips tightly.

"And you do?" I asked.

"*¡De todo corazon!*" Bianca said, stroking the infant's fuzzy hair. "My little José-Marie — he is cured of the cough. He almost die. But Father Ray, I ask him for help, and he saves him. Is your brother not the proof enough for you, also?"

"I just don't think we have the full truth yet," I said.

"*Dios sabe la verdad de todo*," she said, turning on her heel and walking away.

"God knows the truth in full," Estrella translated. "And you will know it soon as well."

"It sounds like a threat to me," Casey said.

"She wasn't very happy with me," I admitted. "Maybe I shouldn't have gone."

"You did the right thing," she said, raising her cup for more coffee. A waitress complied. "You just surprised her by dropping in, that's all."

"So what surprise do you have for me?" I asked. "You sounded a bit giddy on the phone."

"They got Kenny last night," she said, leaning forward on her elbows, eyes bright. "Charged him with burglary and they're holding him for questioning in the death of Father Ray."

"That's where you ran off to, then. So, they suspect foul play for sure?"

"They're not saying. But what do you think? Why else would they hold him for questioning?"

"I don't know."

"Isn't it obvious? They want to know how he got the cyanide. That's not hard. I did a little checking: it's a common ingredient in pesticides and fertilizers. There's lots of that around here."

I didn't mention the Laetrile idea. Too far-fetched, even if Estrella had suggested a long struggle with a disease. And DeMarco said plainly that Ray didn't have cancer. "And they'll want to know how he got it into the wine," I said.

"That's harder," Casey conceded. "Let's say he tampered with it sometime Wednesday while everyone was occupied with your brother's accident. He knew exactly where to go. Then Father Ray drank some for the Holy Thursday Mass. So by early Friday, it might have been enough to cause a seizure."

"Wouldn't parishioners be affected?"

"Not enough in a tiny sip."

"Why does Kenny risk coming back?"

"He forgot to wipe off his fingerprints or something."

"Or maybe he just got greedy for the wine he knew was in there," I suggested.

"Or," she said with a snap of her fingers, "Father Brian set him up. Sure. That's how the cyanide got in the bottles — he put it in."

"You're kidding."

"He was jealous. The parish is dying off, and along comes this young guy with the power to heal, or so it seems, and things start hopping. He can't stand it."

"So he poisons the wine and he somehow lets Kenny know how he can come and help himself to some bottles during the service so he looks like the guilty one, and Father Brian has an alibi."

"There you go," she said victoriously.

"You've got it all figured out, don't you?" I said with a laugh.

She winked. "Not quite. But we'll find out more at the inquest. The coroner's office announced the date today and issued summons for a jury. She might issue subpoenas for witnesses, too, but it's unusual. It's in three weeks."

"Pretty fast, isn't it?"

"It looks like the pathologist's report came back quicker than expected. That church investigator probably had some pull."

"You mean Monsignor DeMarco?"

"That's the man," she said. "He looks like a vulture. Did he talk to you?"

"A little."

"What'd you tell him?"

"Not much," I said. "He did the talking. Told me how they make saints nowadays."

"I could have told you that," Casey said with a playful smile. "As fast as they can."

With time to kill before the inquest, I cozied into the cabin to begin my book. I fussed with arranging my books between Ray's heavy bookends and stared at them a long time before beginning.

Isn't this what writers dream about: an undisturbed hermitage in the woods, St. Anthony in his cell away from the world, solitude and space and silence? It isn't the dead silence of the crypt so physical that one begins to gasp for breath. Nor is it the metaphorical silence of an empty house, with its snuffles and creaks and the dull distant wheeze of traffic through Chicagoland's choked arteries. Rather, this is the silence before a sentence, the whoosh of air into the lungs before a spoken word, a silence in which you can hear the rush of blood in your ears if you choose to listen. And it is only by entering the silence that we can hear our voice.

I clicked "stop" on the laptop and the VoiceWare paused. A jittery line, like a patient's erratic cardiogram, stretched across the screen. It flatlined at the end where I had stopped recording. It was silent again.

I clicked "playback," and my reedy voice drifted through the tinny speaker: *Isn't this what writers dream about: an undisturbed hermitage in the woods.* With a cut-and-paste function, I could re-arrange the voice pattern in the manner of a word processor, and then print it all out. The drawback: one had to self-edit the *ums* and *now whats* and *oh hells.* A sneeze came out as *yaysnitch.* It might suit the improv jazz style of a Kerouac or the stream-of-consciousness of a Faulkner, but not the dense precision of — well, Aristotle.

I heard that some writers dictate their work: Erle Stanley Gardner, for example, while practicing law full time, dictated three Perry Mason stories concurrently using old-fashioned Dictaphones, but he had his personal Della Street to type it all out legibly.

I put the laptop in "sleep" mode. Maybe I'd use the VoiceWare for journaling. Then I could honestly tell the broadcasting instructor back at the college that his gift had been useful. He said he'd downloaded the shareware version for free and *it's OK if you can't use it,* but I knew he'd ask about it. I'd tell him it was great. Our lives are composed of such little fictions.

And speaking of fiction, I figured I should replenish Dan's supply of paperbacks. Funny how he'd gotten into detective novels.

CHAPTER 21

A buzzing throng of people shoved their way into the hardwood benches; a tangle of news-people jockeyed for position in the balcony, and Lance Boyle oiled his way to the front. A knot of latecomers jostled at the doors; a bailiff barked, and Spanish words were exchanged. The quaint nineteenth-century country courthouse could not accommodate the unruly mob; the doors jerked open, and a tumble of dark faces peered in, craning, jabbering, and gesturing excitedly to people pressing from behind.

"Now we'll find out why this happened," Casey said over the clamor.

All human actions, Aristotle informed me, *have one or more of these seven causes: chance, nature, compulsions, habit, reason, passion, desire.*

"They can't decide any motives here," I said. "Only *how* it happened — the cause of a sudden or suspicious death. Isn't that what you told me?"

"Right. Anything unnatural."

That was certainly the case here. But the glowering Dr. Rashidi, taking a seat in a reserved section for witnesses, would never say so.

"The jury has five choices," Casey said close to my ear. "They can rule it an accident, a suicide, a homicide, by natural causes, or undetermined."

"But not a miracle?"

She wrinkled her nose at me.

The jury of six strode in, four women and two men. The crowd rustled like a cornfield in a storm.

The sheriff said, "All rise, please."

Coroner Doreen Gates marched in from the judge's chambers, a smallish woman in an ash-gray pantsuit and half-spectacles on a strap lying on her lapel for reading. Her deputy followed, a lanky man in an ill-fitting store-rack suit. The audience stood. Once she ascended to the judge's seat and perched there, the crowd sat in unison, shushing one another. A court reporter poised her fingers over her keys, and Sheriff's Deputy Anderson stood before the bench, hands knit in the Adamic clasp below the belt buckle. Once I saw the gun at his side, my palms dampened.

"Good evening, ladies and gentlemen. This is not a trial," the coroner began, lifting her glasses to her face.

It sure looked like a trial to me. "Why isn't there a translator?" I whispered.

"Shh," Casey hushed me.

"The purpose of this inquest," the coroner read woodenly from a prepared statement, "is to provide a public inquiry into the causes and circumstances surrounding the death of Reverend Raymond Boudreau in River Falls, Illinois, on April 9. It is not the purpose of this gathering to determine the criminal or civil liability of any person or agency. However, a formal determination of the cause and manner of death may allow further legal proceedings."

That explained the huddle of suits and collared clerics at the two tables reserved for lawyers up front. Estrella Esperanza, as a family member, sat in the first pew, dabbing her eyes with a hanky already. The three women I saw in her apartment hemmed her closely, along with burly brown men who looked like their husbands or boyfriends. They needed their hair combed.

Coroner Gates turned to the jury box. "Members of the jury, you have been empanelled to hear the evidence and answer questions according to instructions which will be given to you at the close of the proceedings. The deputy coroner's role is solely to assist in presenting the evidence. The Coroner's Office and the Sinnissippi County Executive have determined who will be called as witnesses and the issues you will be asked to consider. Sheriff's Deputy Anderson will now swear you in."

While the panel members raised their right palms and repeated-after-me, I noticed Monsignor DeMarco ticking off items on a legal pad, looking like a football coach on the sidelines, checking his plays. Father Brian O'Neal sat next to him, smoothing his gray hair with his fingers like the anxious team owner.

With the jury seated, the coroner proceeded with a brief statement of facts as though the jury wrote it.

We, the undersigned jurors, sworn to inquire into the death of Raymond Boudreau on oath do find that he came to his death by a cerebral aneurysm as indicated in the coroner's report . . .

People rustled and whispered. *Not blood loss?* It just looked that way to some people in their selective memories. The hand coverings looked damp, but it could have been sweat. Besides, Ray had to lose 30 percent of blood volume fast to die from bleeding alone.

She described the scene, a narrative paraphrase of the police report. She listed the documentation the jury would consider in its decision: an autopsy report, a toxicology and pathology report, photographs of the deceased, a police investigative report, and a sketch. Transcripts of sworn testimony would be available to the jury panel immediately following.

"We are now ready to call witnesses in an order agreed upon with the Sinnissippi Diocese, the sole party of standing with whom we have shared discoverable material. Mr. Lang, please call the first witness."

The deputy coroner called, "Detective Frank Gordon, please take the stand."

Gordon, the originating officer, took the oath and sat, arms folded. He was accustomed to doing the questioning.

"Tell us what you saw when you first arrived at St. Mary's parish church on April the ninth," the deputy coroner said.

"When I arrived at 3:35, the deceased lay fallen face up beside the altar on the south side. Witnesses said it happened just after three. Two EMTs were still trying to revive him with a heart massage. They happened to be attending the service and so they weren't called, and therefore they had no equipment."

Manny Garcia squirmed in his seat, eyes penetrating. He mumbled, perhaps praying in his language of light.

"An ambulance was called," Gordon continued. "It came the same time I did."

"And they failed to revive him despite advanced lifesaving protocols?"

"It was too late by that time. I had the authority to pronounce him dead at the scene, but I waited for the coroner to show up." He gestured toward the judge's bench. "Coroner Gates made the official pronouncement around 4 p.m., and I sealed the area for a coroner's investigation."

"In the meantime there had been a break-in through the church residence area and in the vestry?"

"Yes. We have a suspect in custody."

"What was the suspect's apparent interest in the breaking and entering?"

"The wine. He ran off with a bottle and broke one on the way out after being seen by a witness."

"You took samples of the wine from the vestry storage cabinet, the spill, and the altar area, correct?"

"Yes."

"They were all the same type?"

"Yes."

"What kind?"

"Christian Brothers — what else?" He smirked.

The crowd murmured.

"Quiet, please," the judge said. "Go on."

"A dry red, 12 percent alcohol," he said.

"Thank you."

"Not really my favorite."

As though he knew the difference between claret and a cabernet sauvignon.

The deputy coroner wasn't amused.

Coroner Gates leaned forward. "Are there any follow-up questions from the party with standing?"

"None, madam," Monsignor DeMarco said.

"Step down, please," Deputy Coroner Lang said. "I call Dr. Ahmed Rashidi to the stand."

An anxious buzz filled the room, translations in progress. I leaned toward Casey. "What about the almond smell?" I said in her ear. "Why didn't they ask him about that?"

"He can't say. He's not a crime-lab guy. It's probably in the toxicology report, though. Rashidi will be asked, I'm sure."

Rashidi tugged his camelhair sport jacket smooth and waved away the Bible brought to him with a look of distaste. He raised his palm for a secular affirmation and sat stiffly.

"Doctor Rashidi, please describe your relationship to the deceased."

"Reverend Boudreau was my patient from the time of his arrival last September. In addition, I assisted with the medical autopsy and consulted with the pathologist for the toxicology report."

The doctor wanted to be sure no one sat up this time, I thought cynically. And maybe he made sure no mention of cyanide made it into the report.

"From witnesses, photographs, and the police investigative report, we know that Father Boudreau experienced visible bruising and bleeding in the areas of the hands, wrists, and brow," Lang said.

The crowd mumbled, restless; Estrella and the other women bowed heads and crossed themselves.

"Quiet, please," Coroner Gates called again.

"Yes, that is correct," Rashidi said coldly.

"Were these symptoms of a medical condition for which he sought treatment?"

"Yes."

"Since Father Boudreau is now deceased, and patient confidentiality is no longer necessary, are you able at this time to describe for us the nature of his condition?"

Medically inexplicable. Was that the term?

"Yes," Rashidi said, knitting his fingers at his chest. "Reverend Boudreau was a hemophiliac."

The audience erupted in swoons and shouts. *¿Como puede decir eso? ¡No es posible!*

"I *knew* it," Casey said, snapping her fingers.

The coroner, having no gavel, pounded the table with a book. "Order, please! Officers will remove you if you interrupt this proceeding."

"*¡Silencio! ¡Sientese!*" The audience settled into an uneasy silence. "*¡Se calman!*"

Rashidi, stone-faced, waited for his cue.

"Could you briefly describe this disease for us?"

"Hemophilia is a genetic bleeding disorder caused by a lack of clotting factor number eight in the blood. A person who has this problem often needs some form of intermittent treatment to prevent severe blood loss even from a small injury, and to stop internal bleeding. Reverend Boudreau had type A hemophilia, the most severe type."

"What are the particular symptoms of this severe type?"

"Easy bruising. Abnormal bleeding after an injury, even a minor one. The most common problem is bleeding in the joints, without any injury to cause it. Knees, elbows, ankles, and wrists are usually the target joints, as we say. The joints bruise and swell, and it is quite painful."

No wonder he wore the athletic wraps and limped, I thought.

"What is the treatment?"

"Until we have reliable gene therapy, which is still in testing stages, the only treatment is by regular injections of Vitamin K and clotting factor concentrate — screened for HIV, of course. A patient can inject himself at home, which the reverend did, or on demand in an emergency, which I did once."

The needle marks, I thought. And the quick trip to the clinic after Kenny bashed him with the tray.

"Are only the joints affected, Doctor?"

"No. Stress or heightened emotion affects blood pressure and the strength of blood-vessel walls. Capillaries break under stress, and the internal bleeding can damage organs. Most dangerously, a cerebral aneurysm — bleeding in the brain — can cause brain damage or a quick death."

"Was this, in your medical opinion, the cause of death?"

"Yes," Rashidi said. "The stress of an extremely busy week and the intense emotion of the occasion made him vulnerable. But something else caused the bleeding."

"What was that?"

"He had a severe reaction to a foreign substance in his blood."

Christ, have mercy, someone cried. I heard sobbing.

Here it comes, I thought. Dan was right.

"What was the substance?"

"There were three, which we have recorded in the toxicology report. First, we found a trace of warfarin. It is a blood-thinning anti-coagulant used in small doses to treat heart problems, and it is a substance usually found in rodenticides."

"You mean rat poison?"

The crowd gasped. A woman fainted. I nearly did.

"Yes. A rodenticide works by rupturing small blood vessels and then inhibiting any clotting. Ingested over a period of days or weeks in small amounts, it can build to a fatal concentration in a human being. It causes weakness and bruising and swelling — symptoms that would be regarded as routine for a hemophiliac and left unnoticed. The effect of warfarin would be intensified by vitamin K, which, as I said, he was administering to himself."

"But this wasn't all you found?"

"No. He had been taking an over-the-counter decongestant and cough medicine for the relief of a cold."

I remembered the medicine cup on Ray's desk.

"That doesn't sound dangerous, Doctor."

"It isn't. Unless you are also taking a prescription medication which can react violently with its active ingredient, dextromethorphan."

"Was he prescribed such a medication?"

"No. I had prescribed no such thing for him. Still, his system tested positive for a prescribed antidepressant, and a somewhat unusual one. Something called an MAO Inhibitor."

My breath rushed from my lungs.

"And why might this medication pose a danger, Doctor Rashidi?"

"Normally, it helps to build up certain enzymes in the brain that ease depression. But it allows the build-up of another enzyme that affects blood pressure called tyramine, an enzyme found in many processed and fermented foods, such as cheese, chocolate, smoked meats —"

"Red wine?"

"Yes."

"The kind Detective Gordon just told us about?"

"Yes. Patients on MAOIs are on a highly restricted diet to avoid an adverse reaction."

"How does it react?"

"It causes a sudden and severe rise in blood pressure in the brain, producing a crippling headache or fainting, and in this case, combined with the dextromethorphan and warfarin, the bursting of blood vessels and a fatal hemorrhage."

My head pounded. *I'm about to suffer the same thing*, I told myself. My hands trembled like dead leaves in a March wind.

"When, do you estimate, were these substances introduced to his system in order to result in the fatal effect?"

"Over time, fairly recently — over a period of six to eight weeks prior to his death, I estimate."

"If you did not prescribe these three medications, Doctor, how did they get into his system?"

"He was taking the decongestant for a cold," Rashidi said. "As for the other two substances, that is for the police to answer."

The crowd, stirred to a feverish heat, ignited in a furor of prayers and profanities.

"Reed, what's wrong?" Casey whispered. "You're shaking so."

Lance Boyle cackled in the balcony. Estrella Esperanza cried out something in Spanish, fanning herself. The coroner thumped her book again.

"I will not tolerate another outburst," the coroner commanded. "Officer, see to that man." A cursing Mexican man was restrained and removed.

"*¡Son mentiras todas!*" he roared. "*Is all the lies! Lies!*"

"The rest of you, be seated," the coroner directed. "Immediately."

Once the tumult quieted to her satisfaction, she adjusted her glasses on the tip of her nose and read a formal dismissal to chambers: "Members of the jury, this testimony, along with the aforementioned documentation, constitutes the evidence available in this case. It will now be your duty to deliberate your findings and, if possible, arrive at a verdict as to the manner of Raymond Boudreau's death, whether you deem it to be accidental, suicidal, homicidal, by natural causes, or, if you cannot reach a verdict, you may rule the death as undetermined." She nodded to the foreman. The jurors stood and filed out.

Anderson called, "All rise" as the coroner exited. An excited chattering filled the room all the way up to the sky-blue thirty-foot ceiling. No one seemed to be gathering coats to leave.

"We can go, you know," Casey told me. "They'll take at least an hour in there. I think we know the outcome."

I'm afraid I did.

I held onto Casey's sleeve, my knees rubbery and my mind reeling. Fingers pointed at me, eyes accused me, mouths clucked behind knuckles, but I told myself it was because of Dan. Manny Garcia, the Gnostic EMT, glared at me and whispered to the leather-jacketed men beside him. He'd been right about the hemophilia, I thought. Once outside, I bent over, inhaled deeply, and tried not to vomit.

"Wait here, Reed," Casey said. "You'll be all right. I'll get the car."

"Fine," I croaked.

I kept my hands on my knees. Rain trickled down my neck. *Do you know what just happened in there?* I queried myself, head spinning. *I'll tell you what happened. You just became the chief suspect in a murder case, Reed Stubblefield.*

"Reed Stubblefield?" a man's voice said.

I felt a heavy hand on my shoulder.

I looked up.

Detective Gordon tipped his hat. "Would you come with me, please? I have a few questions for you."

CHAPTER 22

After Detective Gordon and I arrived at the police station, he left me alone in an apple-green, soundproof cinderblock room. I shivered, thinking about what I'd just heard at the inquest and dripping wet, sitting in a wooden chair pulled up to a plain table. A swivel chair with brown vinyl upholstery and a little white foam poking through a rip faced me on the other side. Gordon said I should make myself comfortable while he checked on some paperwork. Maybe he was fetching the rubber hose.

Rain drilled the wire-grilled window. A wall clock behind a catcher's-mask mesh stared at me like an unblinking eye. 8:23. A red second-hand swept across its ivory face like a rising blood-pressure dial.

The small mirror over the sink, I presumed, was two-way; he wanted to watch me sweat for a while. My pant cuffs were sopping, and I hoped I wouldn't wet myself otherwise. I adjusted my white-knuckled grip on Citizen Cane; he let me keep it, knowing I wasn't really dangerous. I guess.

8:24. Tick. 8:25.

The walls closed in, and I shifted my feet. The yellowed fluorescents buzzed like flies trapped in a window. I wondered where the microphone was hidden. I shrugged off my coat; I was going to be in here a while. Then I felt cold. So why was I sweating? *Don't wipe it; he'll see it.* I did anyway.

Was Casey waiting outside? She followed us, or so I thought. So maybe he's gone out to say, *He'll be out in a minute.* It wouldn't take this long. Would it? Maybe he was sending her away. *Check in the morning, Miss Malone. We'll probably hold him, print him, and wait until after the assistant D.A. has a talk with him; then I'll probably have a story for you around noon tomorrow, all right?*

I took a deep breath and hoped it didn't look obvious. Rashidi's voice echoed in my head: *His system tested positive for a prescribed anti-depressant, and a somewhat unusual one. Something called an MAO Inhibitor.*

How was that possible? Ray would never take such a thing; Rashidi didn't prescribe it. How the devil did it get into —

My stomach lurched. What if I was arrested? Wasn't I allowed a phone call? Who to call? Dan? Right, give Dan a heart attack on top of his other medical issues. Someone else. Who was that lawyer who talked to me about my testimony in the school shooting? Weinberg, Weinbaum, Weinstein, Wein-something — I forgot. How about Casey?

8:33.

A door slammed; I heard some clicking. Gordon walked in. Closed the door.

"Lousy weather, huh?" he said. He came to the table and set his ham-hock hands on it.

"Yes," I said.

"Ripping the flowers off the dogwoods and crabapple trees already. Want some coffee?" He jerked a thumb to the outside office.

"No. But thanks."

"Hey, thank you for coming in. This is a difficult time for you, hearing all that in the meeting just now, huh?"

Huh seemed to be his verbal tic.

"It wasn't easy," I said.

"Whazzat?"

"I said it wasn't easy."

He grinned. "Nope, never is. I know you were close to Father Ray, and it's gotta be hard to talk right now, huh? But I really wanna hear what your story is."

"My story?"

"Yeah, your story."

"About what?"

"About how Father Ray died. Because you know, Professor, I've gone over my files and I've talked to a lot of people and there's no doubt in my mind that you had something to do with this death, bud. No doubt at all."

"Are you going to arrest me?"

"No, no. I'm just after some information here, that's all. You know, while it's fresh in our minds."

"Don't you need to read me some rights or something?"

"Only if you did something I should arrest you for, Professor. Did you?"

"You think I did?"

"So did you?"

"No."

"What would you say to me if I said that we were told by some-body close to you that you killed Father Ray?"

"You're kidding."

"Who do you think would say that?"

"I don't know. I don't know many people here."

"OK, but why do you think they would say that?"

"I don't know. I haven't killed anyone."

"So do you know who killed Father Ray?"

"No."

"Who do you think would be capable of doing such a thing, Professor?"

"I don't know."

Gordon brushed his hair impatiently. "You know, Professor, I want to believe you're not a violent person. Not a criminal. I want to believe you're a tax-paying, regular guy a little down on his luck. You know what I'm talking about?"

"I guess."

"Do you know what I'm talking about here?"

"Maybe not."

"Don't lie to me. I don't appreciate being lied to."

"I'm not —"

"This can go easy, it can go hard, it can go however you want. You help me, I'll help you. It don't look too good right now, huh?"

"I know how it looks, but —"

"I got enough to hold you, bud. It can be the county jail, the state holding facility, or a place where big black men bad as hell will have their way with a gimpy white guy, you know what I mean?"

"Maybe I need a lawyer."

"Why? Is there something you got to hide?"

"No."

"There's no need for a lawyer unless you got something to hide. Are you hiding something, Professor? Huh?"

"It's just —"

"You want a lawyer to bargain this down from Murder One to Murder Two? That's only 25 years to life. Is that it?"

"No."

"So there's just something you don't want to tell me?"

"No."

"You know, you'd be better off in the future if you confess now. I mean, the prosecutor and the judge will be easier on you if you confess."

"I have nothing to confess."

"You don't?"

"No."

"You sure?"

"Yes."

"Really sure?"

I paused. He grinned.

"Tell me, Professor," he said, drumming his fingers, "you ever shop at the Value Mart in town?"

"Yes."

"You know what I'm talking about here?"

"Yes, I do."

"Well, you don't know this or maybe you do, but there's been lots of shoplifting there the last year or so and a robbery so they put up security cameras, OK? Is there any reason why, when we check the Value Mart security-camera tape, we would see you purchasing warfarin?"

"What?"

"Would there be any reason when we check the tape we would see you purchase rat poison?"

They had the tape. A receipt record, too, no doubt. "The pharmacist suggested it."

"That's a good one, Professor. 'Here's a good way to kill a hemophiliac, sir.' Is that what he said to you?"

"No. There were mice or something in my cabin walls."

"Were? You mean they're gone now?"

"Yes."

"You killed them?"

"I suppose."

"Is that a yes?"

"It's simple cause to effect."

"You killed them, yes or no?"

"The warfarin did."

"You wanted to test the warfarin, is that it? Make sure it could kill?"

"Wait a minute —"

"Did it work?"

"Yes, but —"

"But not fast enough for a man?"

"No."

"So you needed something else? The MAOIs?"

"No, I mean — no, not either one. Someone else had to get these into his system."

"Oh, sure. Right." Gordon stroked his chin with his palms, a sarcastic smile curling his mouth. "*I been framed, officer.* Did you know, Professor, every guy in D.O.C. was framed?"

"D.O.C.?"

"Department of Corrections. Oh, yeah. All the real offenders go free. It's a shame. The pen is full of innocent men. They'll all tell you so." His cuffs jingled on his belt.

I tugged at my collar. I shouldn't have; it looked bad. It looked guilty.

"Look, I really want to understand this," Gordon said, his voice more sympathetic. "You knew Father Ray how long?"

"About six weeks. We were becoming friends."

"Get along fine?"

"Yes."

"Have a falling out?"

"No, not at all."

"You Catholic?"

"What's that got to do with it?"

"So you are?"

"No."

"But you went to his healing service anyway on — what date was that?"

"I don't recall."

"So you went?"

"Yes."

"You weren't healed?"

I wiggled the cane. "Guess not."

"So you were disappointed?"

"No."

"Mad, huh?"

"No, not mad —"

"Jealous, huh? Your brother gets healed, not you, your friendship goes to hell, and you didn't plan it this way."

"Now hold on —"

"Even your brother thinks he was killed."

Oh, Christ —

"You knew how the MAOIs would react to red wine, did you not?"

"Of course, but that doesn't mean —"

"And you were in the rectory for a visit the week before his death, were you not?"

"I was, to talk —"

"And you had opportunities over six weeks or so to doctor up his food or cold medicine, or both, did you not?" Gordon pressed, deadpan.

I hesitated.

"Just enough so it would kill him a day or two later, since the warfarin wasn't doing the trick by itself, huh? And everyone would think it was a goddam miracle."

My guts writhed. "That's not what happened."

"So what happened?"

"I don't know."

"Tell me."

"I don't know what to tell you."

"Sure you do. I have just one more question for you. OK? One more. Did you kill Father Ray Boudreau?"

"No. No, I didn't."

"OK, so let's change, change the question and say you didn't really mean to kill him, just make him suffer like you've had to suffer, huh? Make him bleed real good, and it went too far and it was an accident, huh? You didn't mean to kill him, for Chrissakes."

"I tell you, I didn't have anything to do with this."

"Nothing, huh?" Gordon glared and leaned close to my face. "Look, Professor, let's be realistic here, OK? You show up in town, you buy warfarin and fill an offbeat MAOI prescription here, and both show up about six weeks later in a dead priest you were visiting over that time, a bleeder who — some say — healed your brother but not you. And you expect me to believe that it was someone else who done it? I'd say we have motive, means, and opportunity here, huh? Don't you? Huh?"

Rainsnakes slithered down the windowpane.

Chills slithered down my spine.

He stood up straight. "I gotta go out for a second. I gotta make a phone call. I'll be right back."

He marched out and slammed the door shut.

I trembled. He's calling the assistant D.A., I thought. *Yeah, we caught him,* I imagined him saying. *Wanna get down here right away and authorize charges on this smartass egghead?*

Did he say that someone close to me said I killed Ray? Probably a lie, just to rattle me. Or not. He couldn't mean Dan, although he mentioned Dan. Could he? What did Dan tell him? *Ray was murdered; I could feel it.* Casey? She knew me better than that. Or it was that snake Lance Boyle looking for a way to discredit Ray and pin the blame on someone else. How would he know about my MAOIs? He has ways. Rashidi told him gladly. Rashidi, of course, knew. Sure. He could easily slip Ray some himself. Ray was ruining his clinic. Or wait: how about Estrella Esperanza, desperate to have Ray sainted, if not as a stigmatic, then as a martyr. My hip ached. My head ached. I need a Nardil badly, I thought, the drug they think I used to kill Ray. *My God, what will I do —*

The door opened.

"OK, I'm sorry to keep you waiting there, Professor. Now listen, I've gone over the files and I've talked to witnesses, and there's no doubt in my mind you had something to do with this. So listen. Are you listening?"

"Yes."

"What I'm about to say to you is real important. So please listen, huh? This is important. This is one of the most important things you're gonna hear in your whole life, OK? I don't think you're a bad guy. I talked with you before and you were straight with me, and Officer Anderson and I expected you to be straight with me now. But I tell you what. I know this: we got witnesses, we got evidence, OK? I can get a search warrant for your living quarters, check on your prescription, phone calls, the works. Huh?"

"I know."

"You know what, Professor?"

"That you can do that."

"You sure there's nothing you know and wanna tell me before you go?"

"No."

"You mean you're not sure?"

"I mean I have nothing to tell you."

"OK. You had a chance," Gordon said, rubbing his hands Pontius Pilate-style. "Looks like you got a ride waiting for you outside. Don't go far. You leave town, I'll find you. Then you'll really need that lawyer, bud. Got it?"

"I'm staying," I said. "My brother's still in the hospital. And I need to find out who did this."

"Right," he said. "You and O. J. Simpson."

I wobbled to Casey's Grand Am in the riddling rain, tremulous. I dropped into the passenger seat and pulled in Citizen Cane after me, gripping it firmly. I shut the door. The rain drummed the roof. The wipers murmured *gotcha gotcha gotcha.*

"Well?" Casey said, pulling out. "What did they want to know?"

"How long I knew Ray, how we got along, how I felt about him, you know."

"What did you tell them?"

"The truth."

"They trying to nail you for it?"

Nail me. An apt phrase. "They think I had something to do with it, yes. Hell, they think I did it."

"You're in trouble, aren't you?"

I nodded. "They say they have witnesses. Evidence."

"They have circumstantial evidence, that's all," Casey said.

"He said someone close to me said I did it."

"He was bullying you."

"He tried to make me confess."

"Geez, Reed, you shouldn't have said anything at all. They can twist what you say real easy. Probably recorded it."

No wonder Christ Himself was silent before his accusers, I thought.

"What I want to know is how MAOIs got into Ray's blood," I said.

"You missing any?"

"I don't think so."

"You don't *think* so, or you *know* so?"

"Now you sound like the cop," I snapped.

"OK, I'm sorry." She pinched her lips. Her eyes misted.

The wipers said *sorry sorry sorry*.

"No, I'm sorry," I said.

"So," she tried again, "so what do you think happened?"

"I don't know what to think right now."

"Me, either," she said dully, staring ahead.

"Say, you don't think I had anything to do with this, do you?"

"No," she said, eyes fixed on the road. Unsure. "No, I don't."

When we arrived at the campground, she helped me out of the car and up the step. I pushed the cabin door. It swung open.

"Funny," I said. "I thought I locked it."

"You were upset. You just forgot."

"I never forget that."

The desk drawers were pulled out unevenly, paper clips, pens and index cards heaped in a pile by the overturned chair. Logs lay strewn on the hearthrug and books flopped open face-down as if thrown. Kitchen cabinets yawned. Towels, shaving cream, aspirins, and my prescription bottle lay on the bathroom tile. I picked it up. It was empty.

"God, what a mess," Casey called from the parlor.

"Who did this?" I said into the air.

"Maybe we should call the police."

"I don't need more attention from them than I've got," I said, a tremor in my voice.

"Maybe we shouldn't touch anything," Casey said, arms akimbo, leaning on the doorjamb. "Whoever did it is the one who killed Ray. You find the vandal, you find the killer too."

"*Non sequitur*," I said.

"Non what?"

"Latin. Means *it doesn't follow*. What makes you think they're connected?"

"Oh, you know," she said with a coy shrug. "Whoever put the rat poison and MAOIs in his food wanted to pin it on you, so he came while you were out to get the evidence to show the police."

"They'd arrest him for burglary."

"Or it was Boyle, to confirm a hunch. Or the Fan, to scare you away so you'd skip town and look even more guilty."

"Maybe you should write detective fiction instead of news."

"Maybe you should report the break-in and make a record of it before the evidence is compromised. They'll take prints, check for tire marks —"

"I don't know."

"Look at you. You're shaking. You just don't feel safe here right now. Come on. You can call from my place."

"I wouldn't want to be any trouble."

She sucked her index finger. "I'll make it worth your while."

I sucked in my breath.

"You need something to relax," she said, the peanut-butter eyes soft and demure. "Take your mind off things. C'mon."

"Casey, I can't."

She turned her mouth down in a sexy pout. "Don't worry. It's not like you're taking advantage of me. And it's not like you weren't expecting this."

She sighed and her breasts rose against the fuzzy cashmere sweater. She'd been married once, and was lonely, too, no doubt. And experienced. Not like Peggy and me on our wedding night, our first time — so nervous, so in love, so —

"So?" she said with a crooked smile. "I'm ready if you are."

Lying in bed with her that night, I said how frightened I was.

"No, it's going to be OK, Reed. Don't worry."

Caressing her downy thigh, kissing her neck. "I'm not so sure."

"Everything happened so fast," she whispered.

"It's hard to believe."

My hand under her gown, touching her. Her hair fanned on the pillows, her face turned toward me, eyes wide. "Everything's happening so fast," she said.

Bleeder

"Who would've thought?" I said. I found her mouth, kissed her lips softly, smiled, and said, "Goodnight, Peggy Lynn. I love you."

"Love you, too, studmuffin," Peggy said. "We'll get through this together." She curled into me, trembling.

CHAPTER 23

"Musta been them spics," Hadley Berger told me in the morning when I walked over to his trailer to report the incident.

"What makes you say so?" I asked, accepting a new padlock and key from his leathery hands.

"Well, you know."

"Not really."

"They all watch too much TV and wanna play detective, you know? Someone figured you done it and tried to get back at you somehow for hurtin' their padree."

"Why would they think I did it?"

"Maybe they saw you being drove off by Officer Gordon."

"You know about that?"

He flashed an aw-shucks grin. "Small town. You know: telephone, telegraph, tell a neighbor."

"So they think I hurt Ray and now they want revenge against me? That's why you think my place got redecorated?"

"Dunno for sure," he said, scratching his ear in thought. "But I *do* think lots of them will leave town, now that the excitement's over. Just as well, you know?" He smiled at the prospect.

I didn't think it was likely but I kept my peace. The padre was gone, but the jobs were still here.

"Kinda scary, someone breakin' in," Hadley said.

"Yes, it is."

"Nothin' stolen, though, far as you can tell?"

No reason to mention the pills. "Nope."

"Not even your laptop?"

"They missed it, looks like."

"Just tryin' to scare you out o' town, then. Will you be goin' or stayin'?"

I squared my shoulders. "Staying."

"Suit yourself. Call in a complaint to the sheriff yet?"

"No. I decided not to. Just some punks, probably."

He sighed through his lips, like a let-go balloon. "I guess I better call. It's really my place, after all. They won't send out anyone, though. Too many little break-ins and dope-deals since all them spics come here. Not worth the sheriff's time to come talk about it. They'll just file it with all the rest. I hear you can even file a complaint with a computer now over the inner-net. You still got the laptop, you said, right? So you could do it yourself."

"No," I replied. "That's all right. You go ahead."

"Okey-doke. You be careful, hear?" He swung on his heel and departed.

I might have told him that I'd had enough police interaction for one day, just as I told Casey before she left the cabin last night.

And what *was* that look on her face when I turned down her proposal? Something between bewilderment and bemusement.

Call me old-fashioned, I told her. *You're worth more than that to me.*

Wow, she said. *You're — different.*

I took it as a compliment.

But I knew I should phone her soon, to prevent any misunderstandings. I still wanted to see her. She wasn't Peggy. But who could ever be?

The phone rang.

The Princess phone, under the bed.

It chirruped again, cheerily, sending a chill down my back.

"Hi, Reed? Yeah, it's Ray. Long distance. *Really* long distance. Ha! Anyway, I've been praying for you, as I said I would. Look, it wasn't you, we all know that; it was Rashidi. He couldn't stand to be humiliated by a man of the cloth. He used some free samples he gets from the drug companies; no one keeps track of those. Just mixed the right amount into my vitamin K and plasma injection after Kenny hurt me, and I was a goner. What a cheap shot, a really cheap, cheap, cheap —"

Cheep cheep cheep

The phone. Under the bed. I hauled the darn thing by the cord, like pulling a rat out by a long tail. Something hairy flew out and startled me.

Dustball.

I lifted the receiver to my ear. "Hello?"

Nothing.

"Hello? Who's this?"

"You weel be dead, too."

Click.

The line went dead.

For customer service, account balances and billing questions, press or say one. To open a new account or to add a phone line, press or say two. For equipment sales and repair, press or say three. To report annoyance calls, press or say four. *Para español, oprima el cinco.* To hear this menu again, press or say six.

"Zero" is an invalid entry. For customer service and billing questions, press or say one. To open —

Thank you. Our customer-service representatives are currently occupied with other calls. Please hold, and your call will be answered in the order in which it was received. Your call is important to us. Calls may be monitored for quality assurance.

Thank you for holding.

Thank you for holding.

Thank you for —

Customer service, thank you for holding, Bernard speaking, may I have your phone number beginning with the area code please?

Don't you have caller ID at the phone company?

Sir, what is the number from which you are calling?

Casey, what's the number on this phone?

Thank you, sir. And who is your long-distance carrier?

I don't know. Look, I'm calling from a friend's phone. By the way, your cellular service is spotty.

Bleeder

Do you wish to change your long-distance carrier? We are currently offering very competitive packages for —

I had a question for someone who knows something about phones.

Are you currently satisfied with your long-distance carrier?

No, I want to ask —

Do you make international calls?

No, I just want to talk with a technician —

Our Family and Friends Program is featured this month with an introductory rate of —

Stop. Wait. I want to talk to a technician about how phones work.

I'll transfer you to equipment sales and repair. Please hold.

Thank you for holding.

Thank you for holding.

Thank you for h—

Our service representatives are currently occupied with other calls. Please hold, and your call will be answered in the order in which —

Equipment sales and repair, may I have your phone number beginning with the area code, please?

Thank you. And how may I direct your call?

I want to talk to a technician about how phones work.

Would you like to upgrade your home service with a wireless Home Telecom Center?

No, I just want to talk to someone who knows something about phones.

Are you currently satisfied with your home and local service?

Besides your cell signal being lousy, there's something funny about my landline phone, and I wanted to ask someone about it.

We currently have a thirty-day free trial offer for a home walkie-talkie system beginning at only —

Look, do I need to call your competitor to get a question answered?

I'll connect you with repair.

Thank you for holding.

Thank you for h—

186

Hello? For which department are you holding?

Repair.

One moment.

Thank you for holding.

Thank y—

Sales and repair, Caprice speaking.

Why did your parents give you a name that means impulsive and fickle? Just a thought. Yes, hello, I have a question about how phones work.

Is your phone not working, sir? What type of phone is it?

It's an old Princess phone, touch tone.

And what seems to be the problem?

I seem to be able to get calls coming in, but I can't make any calls out. Do you know what might cause such a thing?

You receive calls but cannot call out?

Right.

Do you have a dial tone when you pick up the handset?

No. It's dead.

It's probably a blockage.

A blockage? Like, a squirrel's nest in a pole is messing up the line somehow?

No, a blockage by us for non-payment. When was the last time you paid your phone bill, sir?

I don't know. The phone is really in my brother's cabin, and I'm visiting, and —

He probably hasn't paid the bill in quite some time, then, resulting in the blockage.

That's all it is?

Yes, sir.

Calls can come in but not go out?

Yes, sir. Would you care to re-activate the account at this time?

No. No, thanks. Another time.

I'll connect you.

That won't be necessary, I don't —

Thank you for calling Sinnissippi Communication Systems. Do you make international calls? Then our Global Partners Plan may be right for you.

Click.

"That's one mystery solved," I said.

"I thought you were going to report the crank call," Casey said.

"Nah. They'd just send a report to local law enforcement, and then try to sell me Caller ID and other helpful features." I made quote marks in the air with my fingers for "helpful."

"So tell the police. You won't be so much of a suspect, then. It's gotta be the real killer trying to scare you out of looking for him. At least they'll narrow it down to someone Hispanic."

"Hasty conclusion," I said. "The more logical reason for the threat is that people in the inquest saw me talking to Officer Gordon and they think I had something to do with this."

"Then you'd better be careful in public," Casey said. She bent over to restart the CD player, her hips tilted to full advantage. "And you're still sure you won't report the break-in, either?"

The speakers pulsed with a slippery tune and lots of steamy sax.

"They'll just ask lots of questions. I just don't want more attention from them. Besides, I think Hadley Berger called it in. He said he might."

"You don't know if he did, though, right? So you should report it, Reed. They let Kenny go. It might've been him."

"Let go? When did that happen?"

"Just before the inquest."

"Someone bailed him out?"

"Yes. Want a drink? Seltzer water?"

I nodded. "How do you know about Kenny?"

"I'm a reporter, remember?" She scratched me teasingly in the chest with her fingernail like a cat on her way to the bar. "Listen, about last night. I don't want you to think I'm, oh, you know —"

"Interested?" I filled in. "I'm flattered, honestly. Don't let it worry you. You have enough on your plate."

She cast me that quizzical look again. "Gee, you're so — nice," she said, mostly to herself. She poured two glasses of sparkling water.

"So tell me about Kenny," I said.

"They couldn't hold him with the bail paid. Besides, they had the information they needed to rule him out once they had the toxicology reports, so they released him. He had time to get over there and re-arrange your stuff."

I wiped my brow. "Why would Kenny do such a thing?"

"Because you confronted him at the fish fry? Protected my honor?" She dimpled her cheek.

"Why didn't he take the laptop?"

"Too easy to find and trace."

"Why take the pills?"

"Thought they'd get him high, I guess. He stole the wine, but no books, remember?"

"Well, he's probably in a ditch somewhere with the worst headache of his life," I said, hand to my brow.

"And how are you feeling?" she said, handing me the water glass. "Want some aspirin with that?"

"I'm OK," I said, removing my hand from my forehead. "Just thinking. There's another mystery here we haven't thought about in all the commotion."

"What's that?"

"Why Ray — or anyone in the Church — didn't reveal he was a hemophiliac."

"I already told you. They kept it a secret so people would keep coming and keep donating."

"That can't be it, Case," I said. *Case?* What was I thinking? *Boyfriends use familiar short forms. Case?*

"What other reason would they have?"

"There's one person who would know that for sure," I said.

I found Monsignor DeMarco tending roses on cross-shaped trellises by the patio. A seasonably mild May breeze rustled his black trousers, and a faint perfume of crabapple scented the air. Mexican gardeners snip-snipped at the ninebark and black chokeberry shrubs. He called to them in Spanish, and then noticed my approach.

"Ah, Mr. Stubblefield," he said. "How good to see you." He nodded toward the workers who were walking away. "They're not used to being told to do less work. But if they prune too much, the birds will not come to nest."

"You knew, didn't you?" I said.

He clipped a dead branch. "Of his illness?"

"His hemophilia."

"Yes."

"But no one was ever told."

"I would have thought you, Mr. Stubblefield, to be the most sensitive regarding such matters of medical privacy."

"Yes, but wasn't this unethical? Misleading the public? They came because they believed him to be —" I choked on the word. A bleeder.

"A stigmatic," DeMarco said.

A bleeder in more ways than one. "So: was he?"

"Wasn't he? And did God work healings in his ministry? You see, Mr. Stubblefield, such questions remain open — and separate — issues from his illness. We must sift through the pious ravings of the faithful to get at the truth."

"Wasn't keeping his hemophilia secret a kind of lie?" I pressed. "It gives the impression of a cover-up of some sort."

"One must also ask what evil might come if his condition were revealed," DeMarco said.

"How could evil result from knowing the truth?"

He considered me over his glasses. "Let me cite a similar example. His Eminence Terence Cardinal Cooke of New York received secret blood transfusions and chemotherapy for over ten years to treat his leukemia. He never told anyone he had cancer."

My stomach cramped. Did he emphasize the word *leukemia* for my benefit? But I had brought it up before, hadn't I? That was it. Had to be. I straightened. "What's that got to do with it?"

"Father Ray, like him, did not want to call attention to his suffering," DeMarco explained. "He said that sympathy, although well-intentioned, could feed a man's pride and self-pity. That is a greater evil than the suffering itself. One must be on guard carefully for such evil in the soul. Humility tells us that suffering, of itself, is an evil we expect to find in a fallen world."

We cannot learn without pain, Aristotle conceded.

"But the people who came to him suffered; they expected something."

"And what did they find, Mr. Stubblefield? They found a man like themselves who suffered terribly yet loved God all the more. In Father Ray, they saw someone who did not focus on himself in his pain, but on others, because he knew that Christ himself suffered in him, since Father Ray was joined to him and his sufferings, and Christ is greater in our hearts than suffering will ever be, and is always closest to us when we hurt."

I must have looked at him as though he was speaking Latin to me.

"I would think that you could understand this better than other people, Mr. Stubblefield. This is a radical departure from the Greeks, who saw suffering as the necessary collision of our lives with the blind machine of Fate. For Ray, and for those who knew him, it was an encounter with the Wounded Healer."

"But that's what I'm saying: they came expecting to be healed."

"Jesus had the same problem," DeMarco said. "In the beginning of the Gospel of Mark, he is mobbed — no, hounded — by the sick and those seeking a sensation, and it is a distraction from his calling. 'Let us move on to the next towns to preach,' he said, 'for that is why I came.'"

"So that explains why you moved Father Ray around a lot. But people still came to be healed, anyway."

"There are many kinds of healing, and most are unseen."

The irises, dressed in penitential purple, nodded in agreement.

"I don't mean to sound glib," DeMarco added, draping a vine on the cross of the trellis, careful not to prick his fingers on the thorns. "The truth is, we will not know the answer to the profound mystery of suffering in full until we come face-to-face with the God who has himself suffered and who grieves with us. As a loving Father, he knows what it is like to lose a son to death, and in the Son, he knows what it is like to be rejected, to be betrayed, to be hurt, to be afraid, to be lonely, and to die. And his suffering Mother has much to teach us about grace in sorrow. When we get to heaven and ask our Lord about suffering, he will, perhaps, merely embrace us with his own pierced hands."

"But you see, that's why people came to Ray. They saw the wounds."

"They saw what they thought were wounds," the monsignor corrected.

"Were they?"

"The matter is still under investigation," he answered, evasive.

"As is his death," I said.

"That is a police matter, since the inquest ruled it a homicide, not a suicide, nor accidental."

"Nor a miracle."

"No," he replied somberly. "That would be quite beyond their jurisdiction."

"Don't you think that someone who learned his condition was medical and not miraculous would feel betrayed and maybe kill him?"

He tugged off his gloves. "Well, you have successfully identified a logical reason for Ray's silence regarding his condition," DeMarco said with a broad smile. "It was for his own protection. Unless —"

"Unless what?"

He stroked his chin in thought. "The medication in his system was similar to what you had been prescribed, isn't it? Have you come to make a confession today, Mr. Stubblefield?"

I felt the color flood my cheeks. "No. No, of course not."

"You see, your medical privacy is as important to you as it was to Father Ray."

"Who told you about my meds?"

"Father Brian knows. Remember, your brother notified the rectory about your dietary restrictions prior to your visit."

"So you suspect me?"

"The police do."

"And you, too?"

"I see no motive."

"Who do you think had an interest in seeing Father Ray dead?"

"I don't know."

"Might it be the same people who wanted to see him sainted?"

"An intriguing theory. What makes you think so?"

"The postulator has raised funds and invested heavily in promoting the cause. The candidate must be dead."

"For anyone to deliberately hasten his death to *ensure* the cause by murder, thus making him a martyr is — well, quite mad."

"So you're saying that you don't suspect Ms. Esperanza?"

"I said no such thing. The focus of my investigation is not criminal," DeMarco said sharply. "That is for the temporal authorities. And their findings could affect my investigation for the legitimacy of his cause. Simply to be killed is not sufficient. A martyr — a witness — must be killed in heroic defense of the Holy Faith. To be killed for greed, or revenge, or envy — even to somehow guarantee his sainthood — would not qualify."

"What if he was killed upholding the truth of the Faith against heretics — like the Ascension?"

"There may be cause there. But the members of the Ascension would not kill him in order to see him sainted. They benefited by his reputation. As more people were drawn to St. Mary's for healing, more were easily misled aside into their cadre. They had more to gain by seeing him remain alive."

"As Aristotle says, 'With a true view, all the data harmonize, but with a false one, the facts soon clash.'"

"That is why I have promised to cooperate with the police in their investigation," DeMarco said, "and I'll cooperate with yours, as well. I hope you are still willing to cooperate with mine. After all, as

Aristotle also says, 'This is characteristic of grace, that we should serve in return one who has shown grace to us.' "

Father Brian called through the open screen door. "Father, the stew is ready to serve."

DeMarco thanked him, and then turned to me. "You're welcome to stay."

"You're kind, but I'm on the way to visit my brother."

"Fine. Please tell him to expect a call from me soon. As you might suspect, he's a key witness in my investigation."

The door squealed shut. Father Brian's dark shadow filled the frame, his arms folded.

CHAPTER 24

I doubted my own doubt. Why did I feel compelled to disbelieve rather than believe, based on the available facts? To be sure, academics are trained to be skeptical, to question. Perhaps my resistance was a matter of the will, not the intellect.

It is the mark of an educated mind to be able to entertain a thought without accepting it, Aristotle reminded me.

But why should a fixed, even dogmatic *uncertainty* be regarded as more virtuous than a humble certainty? Wasn't it better to be willing to be proven wrong, than to declare that nothing could ever be proven true?

A is not non-A, Aristotle declared.

When one thing is true, its opposite is not. Oedipus killed his father; Oedipus did not kill his father. Father Brian killed Ray; Father Brian did not kill Ray. Aristotle's law of non-contradiction states that two opposite propositions cannot be true at the same time and in the same way. He never cared much for the self-centered Sophists such as Protagoras who said, "Whatever you believe, is true." As Socrates replied wittily, "Then, my dear Protagoras, I believe you are wrong."

Aristotle might have added that the open-minded relativist who believes that every opinion is equally valid and true could never solve a mystery. That's why —

"Reed?"

"Yes?"

"You all right?"

"Sorry, Danny. I was just thinking. Father Brian looked awfully unhappy to see me chatting with DeMarco."

"Can you blame him? His dinner was getting cold."

"Father Brian knew about my meds, and Ray's condition, and his cough syrup, and he always prepares the food. He could be our man."

Dan scratched his head. The hair was growing back over the several bald circles where they had attached sensors for the MRI. The streak of gray at the forehead had widened and turned a wooly white. "What about the warfarin?"

"He worked in the Food Pantry and at the Lenten Fish Fry. I remember seeing rodent poison in the storage area — the same kind I used in the cabin."

"Big deal. So they had mice like you," he said. "Any place with food is gonna have a problem with that. I bet the hospital cafeteria does, too."

"The point is that he had access to it, and to the exact same kind that I did."

"So he stirs a little into his partner's food every Friday, and it builds up over the six weeks of Lent just in time to kill him on Good Friday? And he actually planned it to happen that way? Is that what you're saying?"

"I'm just saying."

"The real question is: Why?"

"The timing? So it looks like a miracle to others and distracts them from —"

"No, Reed. Why do it at all?"

I counted on my fingers: "He's jealous of a young priest who blusters into his church with new ideas, a spectacular gift, and a popular following. He resents the sudden increase in the workload at just the time he's about to retire."

"So he told you all this?"

"It's just a hypothesis," I said.

"You mean a *guess*."

"I guess so."

Dan tapped his temple. "You wanna know what I think?"

"Sure."

"That EMT guy did it — what's his name."

"Manny Garcia?" I said. "It crossed my mind, too."

"You're not the only one, Reed. Take a look at this."

Dan pulled a rolled-up newspaper from his bed stand's saddlebag. He tossed it to me. I unrolled it like a scroll, turned it. It was Lance Boyle's *Weekly Beacon*.

There it was, beneath *Magic Purse Never Runs Out of Money; Capital Dome Is a UFO;* and *Mount Rushmore Presidents' Heads Speak and Give Advice to White House.*

Stigmatic Priest Bleeds to Death on Good Friday.

"Notice who's in the photo," Dan said.

I flipped to the inside pages, thumbing past the horoscopes and love psychic ads. The story was printed opposite a full-page pin-up, a sleepy-eyed model with big hair and a big nose, past her prime and spilling from her bikini.

In the story photo, Manny Garcia leaned over Ray's body, his benign face turned upward in grief like the Hispanic waiter over Bobby Kennedy in the Biltmore kitchen.

"Go ahead, read it," Dan said. "You'll see what I mean."

It read:

A Catholic priest allegedly bearing the wounds of the crucified Christ and who drew hordes of the sick seeking his healing touch collapsed and bled to death at the altar — on Good Friday!

Father Raymond Boudreau of River Falls, Ill., was conducting the worship service as usual, but soon began to breathe rapidly, bleeding at the hands and perspiring while bruises appeared mystically on his head.

"He looked just like Jesus in his passion," said 12-year-old Jose Alonzo, an altar boy on duty. "It was awesome."

Then, after carrying a life-size cross for the veneration rite, the priest breathed his last and dropped to the floor, his arms outstretched as on a cross!

EMT Manny Garcia sprang immediately to his aid — or was he checking to make sure the cleric was dead?

"He ascended to a higher planetary existence," Garcia said later. "Just as Jesus healed others and died for others and ascended, so did Father Ray. So can we."

Garcia, who claims he is mastering the arts of healing far beyond his medical training through spirit-beings of light who speak to him, claims the priest knew the same secrets.

"I saw him speaking over a dead man after a crash once," Garcia said. "And the man was raised from the dead."

"No picture of you," I said.

"The Charge Nurse is built like a tank. She won't let no one up here we don't want."

Garcia denies that it is a traditional form of prayer.

"I just repeat what the angels say to me," Garcia said. "It is their language of light."

Doctors and nurses at the county hospital still can't explain the latter-day Lazarus. And they're still baffled by the rush of women returning their rented wheelchairs after spending time in the priest's presence, either in worship or the parish fish fry.

But explaining the priest's mysterious death — that's another story.

An autopsy and inquest ruled his death a homicide — by poison!

Physicians and attending church officials found rat poison and unprescribed antidepressants in his blood, reacting to his medical condition to cause massive bleeding in his joints and brain. What medical condition, you ask? He was a hemophiliac, not a stigmatic!

"They sure use a lot of exclamation points," I said.

"Don't correct the punctuation, you blockhead," Dan said.

Hemophilia is a genetic blood disease that causes visible and uncontrolled bleeding in the joints, head and neck areas.

"We thought he had the gift, the power," Garcia said. "We hoped he could show us the way. We are disappointed."

By "we" Garcia means The Ascension, an alternative health and healing movement with a growing number of

198

chapters based in churches and with "licensed practition-
ers" in many hospitals where their work is billable.

The group's spiritual foundress, "Mother Mary" — aka
Marilyn Queen of Four Acres, Ill. — defines the movement
as "a spiritual journey to align ourselves with the energies
of birth, death, and resurrection. We're trained to be open to
the flow of the universe's spirit of light, so we can awaken
others to their own dormant, divine DNA, waiting to be
activated."

Members of The Ascension will be glad to "awaken"
your sleeping godlike genes any number of ways: Angel En-
counters, Ascension Acceleration Sessions, Magnetic Field
Balancing and Re-alignment (this involves sex with Marilyn), and Intuitive Star Light Activations in 4 levels of ad-
vancing divinity — all for about $80 per half-hour, $150 per
hour, and covered by most insurance plans in the same way
acupuncture and chiropractic sessions are.

Gift certificates are available!

"We all want to accelerate our evolution," Mother Mary
says. "We all want to ascend to the stars where we may
take our promised place in the heavens."

"Unwitting and ill-informed Catholics confuse this easily
with the church's teaching on the Virgin Mother Mary," said
Rev. Brian O'Neal of St. Mary's Parish. "This talk by someone calling herself 'Mother Mary' and of ascending to the
stars is mixed into our teaching about Mary's Assumption
— that is, 'taking up' — into heaven and the picture of her
in the last book of the Bible wearing a crown of stars."

Pastor O'Neal added that the church's teaching is opposed to such groups "masquerading" as healing ministries.

"Father Ray met with them and asked them to disband,"
he said, "and he told them in no uncertain terms that they
couldn't meet on our premises. He knew the story Jesus told
about the enemy sowing weeds in the field at night when
the farmer was asleep. And he considered them to be such."

Garcia denies any such meeting, and says the group's
aim is the same as the Church: "Our aim is to help others
pass through death and ascend to their true destiny, to be

in union with the Light. As Jesus said, "So believe in the Light and you will become Children of Light.'"

Father Ray didn't believe. So maybe they accelerated his ascension, free of charge.

Stay tuned.

"Can he do that? Accuse them in print? Isn't that libel?"

"If they sue him, it'll be bad publicity," Dan said. "That's something they don't want."

"How would you know?"

"Estrella told me."

"I thought you said the floor nurse keeps unwanted people out."

"I asked her to come."

I hitched my breath. "Whatever for?"

"To understand."

"Understand what?"

"What happened to me."

I tried not to press my nails into my palms. "But Danny, what if she had something to do with this? She —"

"She's not one of them," he cut in. "She doesn't like those Ascension people any more than Ray did."

"But she's the advocate for his cause," I said, my voice tightening. "She needed him dead for the cause to proceed."

"She's not like that."

"What makes you so sure?"

"I feel it."

Oh, brother, I thought. That *feeling* business again. "Feelings can get in the way of good thinking, Danny," I said. "They're fogging up your judgment."

"Are your feelings for Casey fogging your judgment?" he shot back.

The words struck like a bullet.

"Estrella was Ray's cousin," Dan said. "You knew that? You do, I can tell by your look. I'm telling ya, Reed, she thinks the Ascension people saw Ray as a threat, muscling in on their territory, and so they killed him."

"We know Ray was against this group," I said. "Some bad blood there."

"The guy coulda poisoned Ray while he was here, after the accident. He had access."

"Makes sense," I agreed. "But the police think that I did it. In fact, somebody told them I did. That's what that cop told me. But who?"

"The EMT guy? No probability," Dan said. "But you know what, Reed? I don't think anybody told them that. They do that trick on the cop shows all the time. It gets suspects talking, making excuses, or making a confession. You need to watch more TV."

He glanced up at the wall-mounted monitor. Columbo, in a rumpled raincoat and his hair awry, was questioning a tweedy man in a library.

So did you know Mr. Stubblefield well? Was he religious? No? Did he ever tell you what he thought about religious people? No logic, you say? Well, then, thank you, I'll be going. Oh, oh, there was one more thing. As an academic, did he ever say people of faith could do harm? He did? When was that? When his wife was dying? OK, thank you. Thank you very much.

The first time Peggy and I visited the hospital for her chemo, I nearly had a heart attack.

The parking-garage sign blinked "Full." The unshaven attendant, whose half-lidded look suggested he'd slept all night in the little booth, told us with a nonchalant wave of his hand and a heavy Indian accent to find street parking instead.

I lowered the window and leaned toward his stubbly face. "We're here for a *chemo* treatment," I barked. Somehow I thought the seriousness of the visit would prompt him to reconsider, to check his list like a hotel desk clerk, and say, *Ah, yes, we have one small space in the back for such an occasion.* What if I slipped him a bill, and, like a discreet *maître d'*, he'd slide his finger over the reservation book and say in a feigned and dignified manner, *Ah, yes, here you are. My apologies. This way, please.*

"There are meters," the man said, unmoved, the hand circling. "All around."

I mumbled something unkind, and Peggy put her hand on my arm. "It's all right, hon," she said. "There's no hurry."

I tried to smile, threw the Volvo into reverse, and tore up the street. The metered parking spaces were full for five blocks in every direction with a two-hour limit at the farthest edge. Who knew how long it might take?

"What do I do here?" I asked her, trying to make a joke. "Find a park-and-ride lot in the suburbs?"

"Just drop me off and come find me, hon," she said. "I feel fine. I just have cancer."

So I drove up to the front door and pecked her on the cheek.

"You know where to find me," she said, pulling her coat closed. "I'll check myself into the unit. Don't worry, OK?"

I nodded, stiff-upper-lipped. I didn't tell her about the dream where this very thing happened, and when I ran back, there were no doors to get inside.

She slid out, shut the door, and marched bravely up the canopied walkway past someone waiting in a wheelchair. She said hello to the candy striper before proceeding through the automatic doors. She pivoted to give me a reassuring little wave and the smile that always slew me. Then the doors swallowed her.

I pulled away with a squeal of rubber to find a spot, fighting off the guilt over sending her in alone.

When I raced breathlessly into the antiseptic waiting room (crowded with the people who had taken all the parking spaces, no doubt), Big Nurse Ratched asked for more identification than the security people at O'Hare. She studied my driver's license long enough to memorize the number and finally motioned me through.

I may have been breathless from running, but the chemo room sucked all the oxygen from my lungs. Suddenly I was in a science-fiction film, in Dr. Frankenstein's lab, where rows of people were sitting passively, hooked up to sighing machines that pumped poison into their veins through translucent tubes. Nurses ran from one patient to another, equipment bleeping and complaining when a bag needed to be replaced or when a line clogged. *Where are you, Peggy?* I wanted to shout.

I scanned the patients; a few grimaced in pain, some wriggled in distress, most looked resigned. A gaggle of relatives clustered around an older fellow whose corny humor kept them in stitches. And beyond them sat my Peggy in a flowered hospital gown and her pink socks, pigeon-toed.

She tried to smile, but her eyes looked foggy. She had a needle the size of a baseball bat in her arm. I hated myself for not being there for the terrible moment it invaded her. It stank of rubbing alcohol. The skin was blotchy blue. Redheads bruise so easily.

I seized her other hand. Why did it feel like a dead fish? "I found a spot in Downers Grove," I said. "I took the train back."

She smiled, and my heart melted. "This won't take long," she said. "You'd better go get the car."

"I paid that garage guy to go get it," I said.

"Can he drive a foreign car?" she asked, grinning wanly.

That's what she asked me when I said I wanted a Volvo. Peggy didn't know a thing about cars then. She thought foreign cars operated differently from American ones. She'd been raised in the city and didn't get her license until she was 35.

"Did Dr. Kushman come by?" I asked.

"Yes," she replied. "And Dr. DiGeronimo. He said he's been following my charts, too."

She squeezed her eyes shut, and I knew not to say any more. I surveyed my strange new world. The regulars walked with a purposeful gait. Check in. Go downstairs for blood work. Go upstairs for chemo. *Hello, Dr. Walsh. How are the twins, Nurse Samuelson? Good to see you, Carla. Hey, does this wig make me look fat?*

They could tell I was a newbie, with my eyes popping like a freshman on the first day of high school, looking lost and small, not sure where anything is or who anyone is. But they weren't looking at me.

Why should they? They were there for their loved ones. Some were getting better. Some not.

Why? Why Peggy? Why anyone? No one deserves this. And no one deserves the vapid platitudes of well-meaning comforters who say, *God will not allow you to endure something you cannot handle.* Hallmark hooey. This is why, every Sunday, we pray: *and do not bring us to the time of testing, but deliver us from calamity.* "Testing" is the more accurate rendering of the word that others translate as "temptation," Pastor Stuart said once, and "calamity" was the evil people feared. Don't ask me how I remember that sermon. Well, the testing has come. The calamity has arrived big time. The temptation to doubt has come with it. God did not answer this prayer.

I didn't understand. Why did I need to understand, anyway? Did it matter if I understood it or not? Understanding wouldn't change a thing. Still, I thought there must be some answer, and I wanted to know it even if I didn't understand it. Aristotle said that the basic drive of human beings is to know, and I wanted to know. Maybe the answer was that there are some mysteries in the wide universe beyond our knowing or understanding. The science was straightforward — cells malfunction, rebel, no longer recognize you. It wasn't enough to know that.

A nurse scurried by and paused to check on Peggy's pump.

"You her husband?" she asked.

I nodded.

"Lucky gal," she said, and moved on.

Peggy opened her eyes sleepily. "Who was that?"

"Nobody," I said.

"Yeah, right, studmuffin. Another nurse checking you out."

"Yeah, right," I said. I studied the pump. "Peggy, do you ever think about why this has happened to us?"

"I think I'm going to be sick," she said.

CHAPTER 25

When my mail came, I wearily sorted through the latest round of hospital bills and insurance statements.

Explanation of Benefits (EOB). This is not a bill. Your 40% Coinsurance Amount. Amount You Owe Provider.

I rubbed my eyes. Yawned. Who could read these things, and why did the print have to be so small?

Deductions applied to Plan Deductible. Adverse Benefit Determination for Plans providing Disability Benefits. Review of Denied Claims. Denied.

Denied? Wait a sec. I peered more closely. How could that be? There was an explanation code in the footnotes requiring both a microscope and law degree to decipher. My breathing quickened, and I felt the panic getting a grip on my heart like a pitcher on a fastball. Breathe in, out. In. Out. Call the insurance agent. That's the logical thing. Get an explanation in person.

The receptionist at the Town and Country Life Assurance and Casualty Agency told me to come right away. I skipped taking a pill — no need to be woozy — and found my way there. The office occupied the street-side part of an old motel converted to business suites. After parking, I gathered my papers and my gumption before entering the office. A bilingual sign on the door read:

Muchas Necesidades, Un Solo Agente.
So Many Needs, Only One Agent.
Selena de la Cruz.

The cheerful door chime brought the receptionist to her feet. A smallish, sepia-skinned woman in her twenties with a black ponytail, hoop earrings, and a bright lipsticked smile, she stood to welcome me at the chest-high counter. It was a little high for her.

"May I help you?" Her embossed nametag read, "Rosita Alvarez."

A swarthy middle-aged man in a white T-shirt, jeans, and boots eyed me from a vinyl waiting-room chair and went back to reading a Spanish-language annuities brochure.

"I called earlier for an appointment with Ms. de la Cruz? About a disability claim?"

"I remember," she said. "May I see your card please?"

She took it and typed in some data. My attention was drawn to a three-panel oil painting on the far wall, set between award plaques and posters advertising the agency's services. It looked like a medieval triptych depicting the Annunciation.

"You like the painting?" Alvarez noticed.

"Is it an icon? How old is it?"

"Oh, a year."

I took another look at its gilding in disbelief.

"Miss de la Cruz makes it look that way," Alvarez said, returning my card.

Peggy tried some watercolors but never did anything like this.

"She is in our claims garage out to the back. Just walk around outside, that way, and at the end of the driveway you will find her there, inside."

"Think she's almost done? *Tengo prisa*," the man asked, tapping his foot, checking his watch, impatient.

"I do not know, *señor*," the secretary said. "It will not be long, I am sure."

"Do not make me wait longer," the man warned me as I reached for the doorknob.

"I'll wait my turn," I assured him. I thanked Alvarez and left. The man's hot gaze followed me out.

I strode past the other businesses — the Nail Parlor and a cell-phone store. Not my carrier. This is a bit unusual, I thought, accustomed as a city boy to insurance offices in office complexes. But how convenient to have a claims garage onsite for estimates. I crossed the driveway to the two-bay garage that probably once protected the motel owner's cars, snowblower, and mower. It looked remodeled as a drive-through with double-doors front and back. *Town and Country Claim Center* announced the stylish sign. *Enter here.* Two cars sat inside, one beneath a blue tarp and the other customer's late-model Buick with its doors open and hood yawning. No sign of the agent. I approached the Formica counter, where I might ring a bell to announce myself, but there was only a computer with green screen lettering, a phone, a stack of trays, and a pegboard on the wall cluttered with clipboards. A tinny radio somewhere was playing soft Latin *bachata.* I smelled oil and a hint of vinegar.

"Good afternoon?" I called over the music. "Hello?"

"Be with you in a minute, Mr. Rivera," a woman called from beneath the car. "I think I found *el problema.*"

"It's someone else."

"Oh. OK, hold on."

I circled the car, avoiding the grease stains in the gray concrete floor. Two legs in black jeans and cherry-red high heels poked from beneath the chassis. A tool clinked, two gloved hands gripped the door lip, and out slid Selena de la Cruz atop a rolling platform.

Her jet-black hair was pulled into a bun, but two errant strands fell across her oval face into her sienna eyes. She blew the tendrils away and smiled up at me. "So sorry. I thought you were somebody else."

"No trouble at all," I said, extending my hand. "Need a lift?"

"No, thanks." She levered up to her feet fluidly. She tugged off the gray work gloves and brushed away hair from her copper forehead. She rubbed off a grease stain on her high cheek and examined her knuckles. "I bet that made it worse," she apologized with a little laugh. "I must look a mess."

"Not at all," I said.

"Good." She unzipped the work jacket, smoothed her white blouse, and crossed to the counter, heels tik-tikking on the floor. "I'm going to call over to the office. Do you mind? I'll be with you in a moment."

"Go ahead."

De la Cruz punched an extension button on the phone. "Rosita? Send Mr. Rivera over. Tell him I found the problem. Uh-huh. *El taller arruinó el trabajo de soldadura. Si. Gracias.*"

She hung up and turned to me with a shrug. "Can you believe it? They installed the catalytic converter upside-down."

That explained the vinegar odor.

She rounded the car, shutting the doors. "The hard part will be to get them to redo it for free. I'll take that shop off the list for sure. Sometimes you try to do your people a favor and —" She caught herself, dropped the hood with a loud bang, and sighed. "And what can I do for you today, Mister —?"

"Stubblefield. Reed Stubblefield."

She tapped a finger to her glossy lip. "Stubblefield. Oh, yes. You called about a disability claim. Let's take a look at your account. We can do it right here." She returned to the counter, swung the computer screen up, and tapped at the keyboard. The fingernails were bitten down.

Mr. Rivera scuffed in. "Took long enough," he grumped. He squinted at me disapprovingly.

De la Cruz cleared her throat. "Mr. Rivera, I think I found the problem."

"You *think* so? I sure *hope* so."

I excused myself with a nod. The cool air refreshed my face. I wondered if the enclosed space and oily smell had made my head spin. But then I recognized that my stomach was twisting from the harrowing prospect of dealing with an insurance company again. Legal con artists. They made big promises, took your premiums, and then denied you coverage when needed. I recalled, with distaste, the adjusters' visits in my hospital room, inspecting me as though I was a car with crumpled fenders in a claims garage.

Mr. Rivera, after a few angry gestures and choice words in Spanish, dropped into his Buick and screeched out in a puff of foul-smelling smoke. De la Cruz faced away from the fumes, fanned away the odor with her hands, and then beckoned me back inside. She leaned close to the computer screen and traced a cheap plastic pen across the data while waiting for me to join her there. Her bronze face was flushed.

"I'm sorry Mr. Rivera was unhappy," I said.

She pinched her lips. "I offered to fix it myself for nothing after I finished my meeting with you. I'm customizing the exhaust system on my own car over there and have everything I'd need. He wasn't interested." She sighed and changed the subject. "You have car insurance with us, too, Mr. Stubblefield. Let's see: collision, medical, and protection against the uninsured. Life insurance as well, I notice. When was the last time you had a check-up?"

"Well, I was in the hospital for a good part of December, some in January. That's what I came to talk about."

"I meant a policy check-up. I'm looking at the life policy here. It's a universal cash value policy that is declining in worth. It looks like you stopped paying into it about — hmm — almost three years ago."

"Right. I had other expenses. I was told I could let it ride awhile."

"You could. But you may want to look at this again, before it's underfunded. Your cost of mortality is going up."

"My what?"

"With this kind of policy, your costs go up as your age does and the likelihood of — well, needing the policy."

"You mean my death."

"It's worth a look. The interest on the cash value isn't keeping up with the cost of keeping the policy funded at the current level of benefits. Maybe you and —" she checked the screen —"Margaret, your wife, can come in and discuss it."

"Peggy died two years ago."

She lowered her eyes. "I'm sorry. I didn't mean —"

"It's all right. It's why I stopped paying the premiums."

"Her name is still on the policy as the beneficiary."

"It is?"

She touched the pen to the screen. "Right there. We can update this later. Look, maybe I can save you some money by re-evaluating the policy altogether. Unless there are children — although I don't see any listed as beneficiaries."

"Let's just do the disability for now, shall we, Miss?" I said it too harshly. But I didn't need to be lured into buying something I didn't come for. I was in no mood for a bait-and-switch game.

"Sure. Sure, there's no hurry. Let's see what we have here."

"It's just that I received a notice saying my claim was denied, and I want to know why."

She tilted her head. Pointed at the screen. "Well, here's the reason. What they considered was your adaptive activity — the ability to do everyday things like cleaning, shopping, cooking, driving, caring for your own grooming and hygiene, using a post office, paying bills."

"I have bills to pay, let me tell you."

"They also considered social functioning such as your capacity to interact independently and on a sustained basis with others."

The heat rose in my belly. My chest tightened. "How can this be? I was — geez, I was shot, I couldn't walk, I —"

"I'm very sorry you were hurt, Mr. Stubblefield. But the very fact that you were able to drive here today, walk into the office, and have this conversation at all is the reason the adjustors left the claim unfulfilled."

I stabbed my cane into the floor. "I have to walk with *this*, for God's sake. Can't I appeal?"

"You'll need a lawyer. They're expensive. And you'd lose. I'm very sorry."

"I don't believe this," I fumed. "I just don't believe it." It took my all not to smash the cane into the computer. "What about Social Security? Will they tell me the same thing?"

"Their standards are even tougher. They require medical proof of 'total disability' with symptoms so severe that for at least twelve months no type of work is possible, not even sedentary work."

I clapped my hand to the top of my head — to keep it from blowing off. "This is unbelievable," I groaned. "What *else* can go wrong?"

De la Cruz furrowed her brow. "I'm afraid to tell you this," she began.

"No. No, there can't be anything else."

She planted her hands on her hips. "You saw Mr. Rivera chewing me out, didn't you? Do you really know why he was so mad at me? Because I was dealing with you."

"Why? Is it because I'm an Anglo?"

"Not that. He recognized you from that inquest. He says you had something to do with the death of Father Ray. So the rumor goes. Every *Latino* in town thinks so."

"That's crazy."

"It's true. I tutor basic literacy at the library and community college, and I've heard it myself."

"Do you believe it?"

She shook her head. "I'm inclined not to think so. But I think you had better be very careful in public. Otherwise, you're going to need that life-insurance policy. Care to talk about that now?"

"Hell, no," I said, and left.

"If I find out anything about the disability," she called after me, "I promise I'll come over to your place and go over the details with you in person."

"Don't bother!" I barked over my shoulder.

My stomach somersaulted as I accelerated away. I commanded my heart to slow down. A pill wasn't what I needed right now. My belly growled again, and I knew it needed something more substantial.

I steered into the drive-through lane of the Burger Palace just two blocks away. The early lunch crowd lined up in front of me. That would give me enough time to calm down a bit. Breathe in, two, three; breathe out, two, three. Don't blame the agent, I told myself. She's just the messenger. Not her fault. Maybe it was mine. Did I fill out the forms wrong? Did the college human-resources office mess up? I should call them. How could this all have gone so badly?

The car behind me honked me out of my reverie. I drove forward and ordered a fish sandwich and fries. Those were safe.

Once I pulled up to the pick-up window, the driver behind me honked again. Two times. Three. What was this guy's problem? The attendant, a young man with a bandana around his neck, leaned out the service window.

The honker leaned out his window and shouted, "¡No atienda a ese gringo!"

The attendant waved his hand. "¿Por qué?"

Honker pointed at me vigorously. "¡Eso es el hombre que herio al Padre Ray!"

I craned my neck to get a look at him in the mirror. It was Mr. Rivera, the fussy customer from the insurance office.

"Yeah, you," he said, noticing me trying to get a bead on him. "Move along! We don't want your kind here."

I turned to the service window. Four dark faces filled it, giving me the once-over.

"That's him," one of them said.

They vanished from the window.

I think I'll pass on lunch, I thought. I shifted the car into drive and tapped the gas.

Four young Latinos rushed into the driveway, blocking my exit. They folded their arms and scowled. I hit the brakes.

"Step aside!" I called.

They stepped forward. One of them, in a blood-stained chef's apron, held a kitchen knife.

I pressed the gas pedal.

They planted their palms on the hood.

"That's far enough," the knife-man hissed.

Some customers spilled from the restaurant to see what the fracas was. I had to brake. I waved them away and hastily glanced behind me at the thud of a door slam. Mr. Rivera was climbing out of his Buick, his face and fists tight.

Oh, Jesus —

That's when I heard the thunder.

It startled the four uniformed workers. They spun as a vintage '60s Dodge Charger prowled around the corner with a throaty growl, driving the wrong way on the pickup lane. The chili-pepper-red muscle car rumbled to a stop, its wide chrome grill gleaming like a set of dragon's teeth. The driver gunned the engine, and it roared.

The customers scattered, and the workers backed away, cursing. They clustered along the restaurant's brick wall, cracking their knuckles. Rivera retreated to his Buick.

Selena de la Cruz levered herself from the Charger. She tore off her sunglasses and drilled her dark eyes into the men.

"Don't you *hombres* have work to do?" she berated. "Or are you all on a break?"

"Don't you know who this is?" Rivera called out.

"It's one of my customers," Selena said.

"This isn't your business," the knife-man sneered.

"I take care of my customers," she retorted. "Now go and take care of yours."

"You have no right —"

"*¿Quizá usted prefiere escoger plátanos en Guatemala?*" Selena said, her black brows knitted. "*Puedo arreglar eso.*"

The men blanched. They muttered, squeezed their shadowed faces, and slinked back into the restaurant. Knife-man hawked and spat on the driveway before he disappeared through the door. Rivera, back in his Buick, glowered.

"You all right?" Selena asked me.

"Yes."

"Follow me."

She replaced the Ray-Ban shades, slipped back into the Charger, and shifted into reverse. The beast snarled back to the street.

I followed her for about a mile, taking two rights before entering a lot for a public park. There was little traffic to speak of, but certainly no danger of losing her — not in that bellowing monster that turned every head on the road.

She unfolded from her seat as I parked. She closed her door and leaned against it, buffing a spot with the heel of a black driving glove.

I got out, and she spoke up before I could thank her.

"I had a feeling this might happen," she said. "After you left, I could smell Mr. Rivera's car and knew he hadn't gone far. Probably waiting for you across the street. I was right."

"What did you tell those guys back there?" I asked.

She brushed back her midnight hair. "Let's just say I offered to find them new jobs overseas, and they didn't like the idea."

"Look, I really —"

"It's all right. I just don't want our people to get a bad reputation. The town isn't all that welcoming to begin with."

"So why are you here?"

"You go where the business takes you," she said, shrugging.

"I didn't get my lunch," I said. "Can I interest you in grabbing a bite somewhere to say thank you?"

"I need to get back to the office."

"Just coffee, then?"

She primped her mouth. "Look, Mr. Stubblefield, you're a nice enough fellow, and I don't mean to be rude, but to tell you the truth, it's not a good idea for me to be seen with you right now."

"I understand."

"I doubt it. Look: there's a saying in my culture: *Las desgracias nunca vienen solas.* Misfortunes never come alone. So watch your back. I probably won't be around the next time."

She slid into the Charger. It roared to life like an angry, awakened panther and pulled away in a swirl of dust.

CHAPTER 26

Once I returned to the cabin, I made a sandwich and popped a pill. Closed my eyes and considered my good luck that Selena de la Cruz had some sharp instincts. Still, the insurance glitch troubled me. I wondered whether the college hadn't sent the right paperwork. I could phone Human Resources myself but decided to ask my dean to check on it for me. He knew I wasn't good with administrative details, forms, and so on, and would look into it as a favor. At the same time, I'd ask about the next semester's schedule. I checked the time. He'd still be in the office. I punched the numbers and even remembered the right extension.

"Jamieson here."

"Hello? Mike? This is Reed Stubblefield calling."

"Reed. Hey, how are you? Glad you called. How are you feeling these days? How's the hip and all?"

"Much better. The time away is doing me good."

"And the book? You said you were going to write a book."

"Not doing as well. So, how are things at school?"

"Same old, same old. You know. Listen, Reed, I was going to call you to talk about coming back to teach in the Fall —"

"Good, that's one reason why I'm calling. My disability claim —"

"There might be a problem with you coming back, Reed."

"— didn't go through — excuse me?"

"I said there might be a problem with you starting in Fall."

"What do you mean? I thought everything was set. I got a proper medical leave of absence. What's going on?"

"Well, you see, the state articulation board sent its evaluation of the program review your department did last Fall."

"And?"

"They had some issues with the courses you teach."

"Issues? Like what? With what courses?"

"You know the topics courses that we entered into the regular rotation and put in the catalog a few years ago? They won't articulate anymore with four-year institutions as they are."

"Why not?"

"They say they're upper-level courses that we can't offer at a two-year institution."

"We have for years."

"Yes, since the last accreditation review. I'm talking about the new courses you've developed. You know — Ancient Rhetoric, Classical Mythology —"

"I know they're under-enrolled, but the comp courses make up for it financially, don't they?"

"That's not the issue. They don't look at that. They won't allow them to transfer, not even as English electives or humanities credits anymore."

"So I'll rewrite the course descriptions to fit their requirements."

"We have to take them out of the catalog."

"But, Mike, I've taught them for years."

"I know, I know. You can work in some of the ancient rhetoric and Aristotle content into Composition I or II, can't you?"

"A little. Not as much as I'd like to. Listen, can't we keep them into the Topics rotation?"

"It's too late for that, Reed. The paperwork is already in Springfield, and the Fall Schedule Book has already been printed and posted online. Your courses are not being offered."

"Then, in Spring?"

"Maybe not anymore."

"Not even as a topics elective? I understand it's too late for Fall but it's not too late to offer them in Spring."

"That's where the enrollment is an issue. Dr. Gilman told us deans that we can't average out class sizes anymore. All sections need sixteen seats minimum filled for full-timers' courses to 'make.' These courses have never come even close to that."

"So what will I be doing?"

"At this late date, I can bump some part-time adjuncts and offer you a schedule of five Comp One and Basic Writing sections."

"I haven't taught those since — I can't remember."

"Still want to come back, then?"

"What do you mean by that?"

"I mean I'll hold these slots open for you since you're tenured, but it's what your schedule will be from now on."

"But we decide that as a department. We always have."

"It's what the department has decided, Reed. Oh, did you hear Francine left?"

"What for? New job somewhere else?"

"Her elderly Mom needed her in Florida. I've been told not to fill the position and to cut one more if I can. Budget cuts."

"Hold it. Hold it right there. I hear where this is going. The college is hoping I won't come back, either, and these intro courses can then be staffed by part-time gypsy scholars willing to work for minimum wage without benefits."

"I didn't say that, Reed."

"Dr. Gilman did, then. Or the Board."

"You're the logician."

"It's a pretty simple deduction."

"Listen, Reed — I think it stinks. But it's happening all over the state. We're losing good people who are taking the state's offer of an early retirement and a generous severance buy-out —"

"Like Francine?"

"No, she's different. Like Artie Maxwell in Poli Sci, and Ann Marie Bergstrom in Econ, and — well, look, I'm hiring back some of them as part-timers, though, so you could —"

"Is that what you're asking me to do? Get out early, take a diminished pension, and make up for it somehow as a part-timer?"

"Don't make this harder than it already is, Reed. We've been colleagues a long time."

"You used to teach in our department, Mike. For God's sake —"

"Listen to me, Reed, listen to reason. I know you didn't expect this —"

"I still have hospital bills coming in. If I leave, the college will say they're no longer liable for the payments."

"That's not true, Reed."

"Are you calling me a liar?"

"No, not at all. The retirement system will still cover you if you have the traditional plan. Don't tell me you chose the self-managed plan instead when you enrolled?"

"No, I didn't."

"Good. Then the plan will kick in within ninety days. You've got nothing to worry about."

"I'm calling the union steward about this."

"He'll tell you to take the deal. That's what he told Artie and Ann Marie."

"You're joking."

"They got a good deal. You will, too."

"I'm not even 50."

"Calm down. I'm trying to help you here."

"Some help."

"You have enough service credits to get a good deal from the state, Reed. I think you'd better call them and get a statement of benefits. Then you can make a decision. And you've got other investments, too, right?"

"Not much. Not since Peggy — got sick."

"Right. I'm sorry. Listen, take a week or two to think it over. Will you think it over?"

"Sure."

"Good."

"Bye."

"You OK, Reed?"

"What do you think?"

I rang off.

This couldn't be happening. I felt like I was choking, and the college and insurance company both had their hands locked around my throat. I thought about taking another pill. So what if it knocked me out? How was I going to pay these bills? The radiologist had even contracted with a collection agency.

With the radiation-room schedule backed up, the waiting area filled with milling patients and their families. Visitors wore street clothes and half-moon smiles. Patients wore ill-fitting hospital gowns, hanging like draperies on the thin ones, hugging like sausage casings on the hefty. Some men kept their trousers on. The rest, Peggy included, wore the gown with socks and sneakers. A blue bandana covered her thinning hair, which kept combing out in clumps.

"If the blood work looks good, we can put off the next series of chemo until after Thanksgiving," Peggy said. "I said I want a real dinner and be able to keep it down."

"Sure," I said.

"It's going to be my last Thanksgiving, hon."

"We don't know that."

"I'm not afraid anymore."

My hand trembled.

"You'll marry again, won't you?" she said. "You promised."

"Do we have to talk about that now?"

"It's OK, Reed. I don't want you to be alone."

"I'll be fine."

"Sure. Who'll pay the bills? You? Mr. Counts-on-his-fingers?"

"I'll hire Pat in the math department."

"Listen, you: when I get to heaven, I'll be praying for you. I'll ask God to find another wife for you, and to send her to you."

"Peggy, please don't —"

"You'll meet someone. I know it."

My dream was shattered by the smashing of glass.

In the parlor, a thump.

A voice: *¡Andele!*

I jerked upright, flipped on a light, and shuffled to the braided rug. A chunk of limestone had skidded through the shards to the desk. A curtain fluttered by the splintered pane, and looking out into the plum-colored twilight, rain spitting into my face, I saw nothing but shadows.

Punks. The same ones who broke in? Or harassed me at the drive-through? Checking to see if I was here?

I rubbed my temples and noticed the elastic band on the rock. I tipped it over with Citizen Cane. A folded note.

You will be the victim, to.

CHAPTER 27

By habit, I reacted first to the improper spelling of *too*. Then I noted the awkward use of the definite article, a common error with ESL students.

That was easier than realizing I'd been given another death threat.

My hands were still shaking when I called Casey. "I hope I'm not bothering you."

"You sound upset, Reed. What's up?"

I told her about the rock.

"Omigod. Who would do that? The same one who trashed your place?"

"It's somebody Latino, it must be," I said. "I heard someone call out in Spanish just after it was thrown."

"So there was, there was more than one person outside," she said.

"Had to be," I said. I told her what de la Cruz said about the rumor circulating in the Spanish community, and described the showdown in the drive-through.

"That just made them madder, and now they know where you live," Casey said. "If you don't get out of there, they'll just bust inside next time."

"I can't leave town," I said. "Maybe I'll go to the hospital and see Dan."

"Visiting hours will be over, Reed," she said. "They won't let you in. Why not, like, come over to my place?"

"What'll that look like?"

"Normal," she said with a giggle. "No one cares about that anymore. I'll fix you a drink and get out the extra pillows. No problem."

"Well, at least a little while."

"As long as you like. I'll leave the door open. Just walk in. I'll probably be in the shower."

"You sure?"

"Look, you know you can't stay there. They might come back. Lock up and hurry up."

I said I'd be right over. I duct-taped a flattened cardboard box over the window hole, shaking the whole time. Was it about the threat, or staying at Casey's? Was this a good idea? Departing, I dropped the keys when padlocking the door behind me. Rain dripping into my eyes, I used the wrong key to open the Volvo door. *Steady,* I told myself, gripping the steering wheel. *Don't pass out.* The Nardil fogged my vision.

I pulled out, splashing in a pothole. I switched on the wipers. *You too, you too, you too.* I adjusted the rearview mirror when I reached the two-lane road.

Behind me, a pair of headlamps blinked on and, like a hungry cat's eyes on a sparrow, followed.

Just someone else in the campground, I thought. Some early-summer clientele. Dan said they start arriving around Memorial Day. Or someone was hoping I'd leave.

I took the right fork toward town, and the other car fell in behind me. At the state highway stop sign, I bore right again. The car waited until I reached the bridge before taking the turn.

What if they had cell phones and were working with others? *He's on the bridge. Block the other end, and we'll have him.* A pickup truck heading my way flashed its brights. A signal to the car behind me? No, I had my high beams on. The Silverado rushed past, honking indignantly, wetting my windshield.

I shouldn't endanger Casey, I thought. If I go straight to her place, they might try something there. I passed through the first intersection as the light turned amber. The car behind me ignored the red, driving straight through it. At the next stop sign, I wheeled sharply into Main Street.

The bars on the corner were open, but everything else was closed — except the Value Mart. The store's fluorescents cast a ghostly glow into the street. I angled Ollie Volvo to a stop. I launched myself out, limping to the door. Over my shoulder, I saw the other car, a battered Ford Montego, prowling toward me. I pressed through the door, shaking rain from my sleeve.

The pharmacist stood in the middle aisle, swishing a mop. "We're closing, sir," he called, glaring at me over his glasses. "Sorry."

"This can't wait," I said, as evenly as I could. "I need — I need my prescription filled."

The man grumped.

The door hissed open.

Estrella Esperanza, the Fan, stalked in. Her dark eyes glittered; her heels clicked on the tiles. She stopped an arm's length away and stabbed a menacing finger in my face.

"You must be very careful, Mr. Reed," she said.

"About what?" I asked.

"Already you ask too many questions. You do not want to get yourself killed."

"Why are you visiting my brother?"

"That is our business. He will tell you if he wants."

The pharmacist, Barnes, was upon us, his mop raised in both hands across his chest like a spear. "We're closing, ma'am. I'm afraid you'll have to leave. Now."

She glared at him, at his mop, and turned to me. "Watch out. I am telling you."

She swung on her heel and marched out.

The door clicked shut behind her. Barnes threw a deadbolt and flipped the "Closed" sign. "I don't like these crazies any more than you do," he said. "The town should stop selling liquor at eight instead of nine." He switched off a bank of lights and led the way to the pharmacy desk. "Come on back," he said. "I didn't balance the register yet."

"Appreciate it," I said.

"I remember you," he said. "You're the fellow with the MAOIs."

"There must be others who still use them around here," I said, fishing for a clue.

"If there were, I couldn't say who," he answered, not taking my bait. "Privacy laws. Doctor-patient privilege and all that."

"Would you tell the police?"

"I already did. And there aren't any others. Just you."

I clutched.

He stepped up behind the counter. "Stubblefield, is that right?" He tapped at the computer.

"That's right. Say, is there another way to get this medication?" I asked.

"You mean, like, by mail order or something? I suppose. There are legit mail-order companies. Anyone can get just about any drug over the Internet now. But I wouldn't trust them. You pay double and get sugar pills. You're better off sticking to a licensed pharmacist that you know."

"Is there a black market for these?"

"You're asking the wrong man. Sure, I guess so. The community is full of drug dealers, especially since — well, you know. The population has changed here. They sell whatever they can get."

"Are you missing any?"

"You mean, has there been a break-in here? No. We had a robbery a while ago, but all they wanted was money. Punks. I'm ready for them if they try it again, let me tell you."

"I'm sure. How about an employee sneaking some out?"

"I work alone behind the counter and keep things locked up," he retorted. "You sound like the police."

He turned to the shelves, returning with a bottle. "You know, the only other place to get these might be the hospital, or the clinic, from Dr. Rashidi. Physicians get samples from drug companies." He printed a label, affixed it. Adjusted his glasses. "Now, you're sticking to your diet, right?"

"Who else might know how these react to fermented foods like, say, sauerkraut, or red communion wine?"

"Anyone who can read a Merck Pharmaceuticals Manual in the public library," he said, perturbed. He shook his pencil at me. "And I see where you're going with this. Again, you're talking to the wrong man. I nearly went bankrupt in this little town before this priest showed up. Look at all the closed stores on this block. I thought I'd be next after thirty years in business. But my business was coming back because of people like you looking for a miracle. Why would I want him dead?"

"I never said it was you."

He frumped. "Why don't you talk to Dr. Rashidi? He's the one who was losing business because of this priest. Sinnissippi Health Systems, his HMO, was putting pressure on him to turn a profit or the clinic would be closed. Well, it's closing. How do you think he feels about that? And he knew the priest's condition and gave him injections when the guy couldn't do it himself. So there you go, Sam Spade. Motive, means, and opportunity." He adjusted his glasses again. "Now, will there be anything else?"

"No." I paid cash and tap-tapped my way to the door, feeling his eyes drilling into my back. I slid aside the bolt and stepped out into the rainy night.

A flash of light blinded me.

"Smile, Professor." Another flash.

"Boyle?" I shielded my eyes. "That you?"

"Coming back for more ammunition?" he said. "Let me guess: Nardil, 20 milligram tablets, thirty count?"

"You've got a lot of nerve."

"I have to in this business," he said.

"What are you after?"

"The truth," he answered, pointing at me, "and I'm getting close to it."

"You're wrong."

"I don't think so. I'm reeeaaal close to figuring this out."

"Those pictures don't mean a thing."

"I mean something else."

Behind me, Barnes locked the store door.

"My pills," I said. "You know what kind they are. So you took the pills from my cabin?"

"Heaven forbid. Someone burgle your love shack?"

"My what?"

"You and my competition," he said, making a kissy sound.

I pushed past him to the car. Stepped in a curbside puddle up to my socks. Grimaced. "That's none of your business. Leave her out of this."

"What? And spoil the whole story?"

I slammed the door, jerked the Volvo into reverse, and screeched away.

Casey met me at the door barefoot, smelling of steam and soap, wrapped in a terry robe and with a white towel turbaned on her glistening caramel hair.

"Reed, you sweetie, you look terrible."

"Sorry to bother you this way, Case."

"— come in and take a seat over here —"

"I may have been followed —"

"— here, give me your coat —"

"— when I stopped at the Value Mart —"

"After what happened to you? Whatever for?"

I dropped into the sofa. My shoe squished. My rain-soaked pants stuck to my leg, and it looked as though I'd wet myself. "Like I said, someone followed me out of the campground. I thought it was whoever threw the rock. So I stopped in town. The Value Mart was open."

Her forehead knotted. "Then what?"

"I went in. Estrella Esperanza followed me in and basically threatened me."

"How?"

"Said to lay off. Don't ask questions."

Her white teeth indented her full lower lip. "She feels threatened by you, don't you see? She's afraid you'll find out how she killed Ray."

I wiped my mouth. "The pharmacist booted her out before she said much."

226

"What'd he say?"

"Just told her to get out."

"That's all?"

"Yeah. No," I corrected. "She's visiting Dan, too. He's allowing it. I don't like it. She might be dangerous."

She put her hand on my knee and gave it a squeeze. "Sure you don't want tea or something? You look cold."

I was shaking. Was it from the scare, the rain, or her touch? "Yeah, OK," I said. "I'd like that."

She stroked my thigh. "Geez, your feet are soaked." She untied my shoes, pulled them off, peeled off my socks. Rubbed my feet. "That better?"

"Yeah. Thanks."

"Just relax." She stood erect, pulled away the head towel, and shook her hair out in wet tangles. "You'd better stay here tonight," she said, now on the way to the kitchen. "Things are getting nastier out there."

In reply, lightning flashed in the window and I thought of Boyle's camera.

"That Boyle guy was there, too," I called. "The jerk took my picture on the sidewalk and said he was close to figuring everything out."

She popped her head around the corner. "Really? What'd he say?"

"Not much." I decided not to tell her any more.

"Did he say why he happened to be at the pharmacy?"

"No."

"I don't like it," she said. She poured tap water into a kettle and set it on the stove. She came back in, ruffling her hair with the towel.

I rubbed the dented place where my wedding band once was. Casey, too, had removed hers a long time ago. I felt myself stirring.

"C'mon, Reed," she cooed in my ear. "Let's dry you off, get you out of these clothes, and into bed."

"Casey, please," I said. "I shouldn't do this."

She pouted. "Don't you like me?"

"Yes, but —"

"Don't you want me?"

"More than ever."

She traced her fingernail across my lips. "So what's it gonna be, handsome?"

The phone jangled us awake. Casey reached across the queen bed for the handset.

"Yeah? No, it's fine. What's up? Oh, no. Just now? OK. I'll get right up there."

She dropped the phone into its cradle. "Reed, are you up?"

"What is it?" I called drowsily from the living-room couch, an afghan tucked under me. The Nardil hadn't completely worn off yet.

"It's Lance Boyle."

"That creep again? What did he want?"

"They found his car in the river off the Sinnissippi Bluffs. He's dead."

CHAPTER 28

By the time we arrived at the riverside park, yellow crime-scene tape stretched tree-to-tree. A regular-beat black-and-white cruiser, its lights off, blocked the access road to the picturesque limestone bluffs overlooking the Sinnissippi River. A patrol sergeant stepped up to Casey's Grand Am window.

"Hey, Casey," he said, pulling off his metallic shades. "I can't let you go any farther than this."

"What have we got, Paul?" Casey asked. "Hold on. Let me get this on tape." She clicked on her digital recorder. "Go ahead."

"Aw, c'mon, Casey, you know I can't talk about it now. Say, is that your dad in the car?"

He leaned in and cocked his head. "Oh, sorry. You're Stubblefield, isn't that right?"

I nodded and kept my mouth shut. Why would he think I was Casey's father? Did I look that old? And who would Casey's father be — obviously still in town, if he thought I was he.

"The professor's helping me with the story, Paul," Casey said. "You can, too, for old times' sake. Or are you still sore I didn't go to the prom with you?"

He shrugged, aw-shucks, boyish. "That was a long time ago."

"We're old friends, Paul." She pressed the recorder up to her breasts. He noticed.

"Chevy Cavalier in the river," he said. "Driver found dead inside at the wheel. One shot in the head. Point blank. You knew him, eh? That fellow Boyle?"

"We met," she said. "You sure it was him?"

"We ran the plates. And the bloating didn't mess up the face yet. We could still tell from the driver's license photo in his wallet."

"So it was a mugging, it looks like," Casey said.

"Nope. Wallet was full of cash."

"Suicide?"

The officer shrugged. "Not for me to say. But if you ask me, it'd be hard to shoot yourself and then drive into the river. Why would you? Besides, there's no gun and no note. No powder on his hands, but then again, the river water coulda washed it away."

Down the road behind the patrol car, uniformed officers with a German shepherd checked the picnic shelter. Detective Gordon, Columbo-like in a brown raincoat, stood by a tow-truck, taking notes while technicians worked the dripping vehicle on the flatbed. Officer Paul glanced at him, nervous.

"I shouldn't say any more."

"Gang activity?" Casey persisted. "Maybe he stumbled on a drug deal — you know how they deal out here, Paul. And they popped him."

"No evidence to say so. No matches, roaches, nothin'. No casings from the bullets. Guess they picked them up. No witnesses, of course. Had to be someone he knew, to get him to drive out here and let him get so close."

I may have been the last one to see him alive, I thought. I'd be suspected of this too —

"No sign of a struggle?" Casey asked.

"Nope. Just his newspaper, all bunched up."

"Someone upset with the paper did him in, then," I chimed in.

The officer leaned down to give me a look. "Something you know that you want to tell me, sir?"

My guts cramped, and I knew I shouldn't have come. "He wrote stuff in his paper that made people angry," I suggested.

"That was how he made his living," Casey said.

"Yeah. Well, the coroner already took him to the morgue," the sergeant said. "She'll be able to tell us more. We'll send the recovered bullets to Springfield for ballistics tests so we can match them to the gun when we find it. That should take a few days. The tests, I mean.

Those lab guys are always backed up, you know." He was trying to impress her.

"How long was he in the water, Paul?" Casey asked, batting her eyelids.

"It was just a few hours tops, it looks like. Coroner guessed between nine o'clock and midnight maybe. Anything else you need to know for now?"

"That'll do," Casey said. "Thanks." She stopped the recorder and then pocketed it.

"Hey, you still doing that literacy training thing at the college?" he asked.

"No. I left."

"A hundred twenty days was enough, eh?"

"I didn't really like it," she said.

"What was that priest really like? He worked with you there, didn't he?"

"Yeah. He was OK."

"Pretty weird about him, eh, Mr. Stubblefield?"

Was he hoping for a promotion? *Gee whiz, Detective Gordon, I asked him one question, and he spilled his guts.* "Pretty weird," I echoed.

Detective Gordon called out, waving his note pad.

"Oh, cripes," Officer Paul said. "For God's sake, Casey, don't tell him I told you anythin', OK?"

Gordon advanced to the car, arms swinging like sledgehammers, a man in a hurry. He tipped his hat when he saw Casey.

"Mornin'," he said, eyes pinched. "This one looks fishy to me."

No one laughed.

"You know how they say the culprit always returns to the scene of the crime, huh?" he said, peering inside. "Have you ever heard that, Mr. Stubblefield? Huh?"

"I have."

"Where were you last night between, say, nine and midnight?"

"I was with her," I said. "At her place. All night."

"Oh, izzat so?" He leered. "Was he?"

Casey nodded. "I'll vouch for that."

"Look, it's not what you think," I said. "Someone — someone vandalized my place last night. I wanted to be with a friend."

"Sure you did." He pulled at his chin, remembering. "We got a call about that," he said. "From Hadley Berger, the owner. That was a while ago, huh?"

"It happened again," I said.

"What time?"

"Just before nine. I called her right away."

Casey nodded.

"Go there right away?"

"No," I admitted. "I was followed. It upset me. I thought it was maybe the guys who wrecked my place, and I went into the Value Mart. It was still open. Just before nine."

"Someone there to vouch for you?"

"The pharmacist. Barnes, his name is."

Gordon rolled his eyes. "Yes, we already know his name, huh, Casey?"

"Been here in town close to thirty years," she said. "Go on, Reed, tell him what happened next."

"Estrella Esperanza walked in. She was the one following me. She was peeved. Told me to stop talking to people."

"Why do you think she'd say a thing like that?" Gordon asked.

"It felt like a warning."

"About what?"

"Talking too much."

"About what?"

"Father Ray, I guess."

"Might incriminate yourself, huh?"

I was talking too much. "Barnes heard it. Ask him."

"I will."

The pharmacist, no doubt, had seen me with Boyle outside the door, too. I had to bring it up, and not appear to hide it. "When I left, Lance Boyle came up to me, taking pictures."

"The plot thickens, huh?" Gordon teased.

"He said he was getting close to figuring out who killed Father Ray."

Gordon tipped up his hat. "So you killed him, too? To cover up the first murder, huh?"

"I went straight to Casey's. Didn't I, Case?"

"What time did you arrive?" Gordon interjected.

"The exact time? I don't know. I didn't look. I was flustered. 9:30, probably."

He tilted his chiseled chin to Casey. "That right?"

"Yeah. About 9:30 to 9:45," she said. "Somewhere around there."

His eyes stared, calculating the time mentally. He'd drive it later, I was sure, to see if it was possible to drive from the Value Mart to Sinnissippi Bluff Park and back to Casey's in a half-hour or so, allowing time to dispatch Boyle. It probably was.

"We'll talk again, Professor." He spun away and jotted notes while walking.

"Let's go, Reed," Casey said. "I need to write this up and turn it in."

She waved at Paul, and then pulled a U-turn. I studied the side mirror. Detective Gordon had stopped to watch us depart.

"If Esperanza threatened me, she would also feel threatened by Boyle. She was standing right there. If she is the one who killed Ray, and she overheard that Boyle was close to the truth, she'd kill him too. Don't you think? Just maybe?"

"I'm not sure what to think any more," she said, her knuckles white on the wheel. She was driving too fast.

"Wait. You don't think that I knocked off Boyle, do you?"

"No. No, I don't." She sniffed. She smiled unconvincingly. "I really don't."

Silence.

"Want to get some breakfast?" I offered.

"No, I really need to file the story on Boyle," she answered with another weak smile. "I'll drop you off at the cabin, OK?"

"Sure," I said. "Whatever you want."

The car became as quiet as a cloister. If she didn't suspect me, then maybe she was worried I'd be the next victim, given Esperanza's warning. Maybe she was worried that she'd be next, since Boyle was a reporter, after all.

Or she thought I was a killer.

"Don't worry, Case," I said as we pulled into the campground. "I'm going to figure this out. When I do, you'll have a great story to write, OK?"

" 'K."

The quiver in her lower lip told me she wasn't convinced yet that I wasn't dangerous. I'd lose her if I couldn't prove otherwise.

I couldn't — I wouldn't — let that happen.

CHAPTER 29

The whole is more than the sum of its parts, Aristotle said.

But first, we must identify the parts, I said.

We must begin with what is known.

Very well, I said. Let us begin with the established facts of the inquest.

Father Ray was a hemophiliac. He suffered for years from excessive bleeding in his joints, and most recently in his internal organs, from a gradual and undetected ingestion of a blood thinner and anticoagulant called warfarin, an ingredient found in rodent poison. The condition was worsened by his injections of vitamin K. The direct cause of death, however, was a brain hemorrhage prompted by a severe and sudden rise in blood pressure, a chemical reaction of MAO Inhibitors (which he had clearly not been prescribed) with a decongestant, which he was taking for a cold, as well as with red communion wine.

Well begun is half-done, Aristotle congratulated me.

Fine. So the first questions to arise are: Who had access to warfarin? And knew its properties? And knew that Ray was a hemophiliac?

Anyone in town had access to the compound warfarin, since it was sold in the pharmacy.

Anyone in town could learn of its properties by the label, prior experience, or by consulting the pharmaceuticals manual in the public library.

That's right, officer, the librarian probably told Gordon, *I saw the professor reading the Merck Manual. No, he wasn't browsing; that's what he came to read.*

But only a few knew of Ray's condition for sure, even if rumored, and at the same time could know the potential bleeding hazard that warfarin posed, especially for him: Dr. Rashidi. His nurse. Anyone else medical? The pharmacist, Barnes. The EMTs, perhaps.

Sure: Manny Garcia of the Ascension. Ray had been whisked away from several parishes by ambulances in the past; word gets around. He could get warfarin from a hospital easily — if not in pill form, then from the cafeteria storage area where there might be a rodent problem. Hadn't he mentioned that Ray's hemophilia actually qualified him for "the gift," as he called it? Maybe Boyle's speculation wasn't so wacky after all. And since he was about to prove it, Garcia killed him. Wait, wait. Let's not get ahead of ourselves.

How about nonmedical people? Father Brian. Estrella Esperanza.

How was it ingested? Probably through his food. Who had regular access to his food? Father Brian. Anyone else? The process was already giving me a headache.

Thinking is sometimes injurious to health, Aristotle cautioned.

There was rodent poison at the Food Pantry. So again, anyone who attended regularly had access. Father Brian again. Was a pattern emerging?

One swallow does not make a summer.

Hasty conclusions are to be avoided, I agreed. Who else, then, in the Pantry? Esperanza? Kenny. A food preparer. One of those college "groupies." Even Casey. She served his food. Ray didn't want her to go through the trouble. Yet how could they know of his condition? Unless they thought his "condition" was spiritual, i.e., that he was stigmatic, and thought that warfarin would make him bleed to death the next time he manifested the wounds, probably on Good Friday. I shook my head. But neither Kenny nor Casey was a true believer. Esperanza was, and somewhat desperately. Garcia was, although perversely.

It is possible to fail in many ways, while to succeed is possible only in one way, Aristotle sighed.

So let's move on to the most troublesome factor: the MAOIs. Who had access to MAOIs? And knew their properties? And at the same time knew it had the potential to rupture blood vessels in the brain when reacting to over-the-counter medicines or fermented products? Rashidi. Barnes, the pharmacist. Manny Garcia, the EMT. Father Brian knew I was taking such a medication but did not have immediate access to it. Who might have seen me take them, or seen them in the cabin, and possibly taken some? Hadley and Beth Berger. And Casey, of course. Who was also regularly at the parish's Fish Fry Dinners? But did she know about the hemophilia for certain?

Piety requires us to honor the truth above our friends, Aristotle said.

It can't be her, I insisted. She's been trying to solve this mess with me. And there's no way she could get a hold of the MAOIs, was there? So let's move on to motive, I said. Who would have both motive and means with opportunity?

The least initial deviation from the truth is multiplied later a thousandfold, Aristotle lamented.

All the more reason to sort this out together slowly, I resolved. Because if I didn't sort it out, Detective Gordon would come calling again, this time with cuffs and a Miranda warning. Or whoever killed Boyle to silence him would come for me next.

This was no logic exercise in Rhetoric 101.

Or was it? I wrote everyone's name on an index card, spread them on the desk, leaned back, and knit my fingers behind my neck.

What was the most common problem in deductive logic? I quizzed myself.

A false premise.

Get the premise wrong, and everything else is wrong.

Fine. So what is possibly the faulty premise here?

I worked through the names. No one, it seemed, had the motive, means, and opportunity not only to dispose of Father Ray, but to frame me for it.

There it was.

No one. No *one*.

CHAPTER 30

"Candlelight?"

"This is special, Case," I said. "Here. Take a seat."

"This is nice." She pecked me on the cheek, unbuttoned her blazer, and sat down. "What's that music?"

"Pachelbel's *Canon in D Major.*"

"Wearing a jacket, too? Oh my God, how formal."

"I wanted to remember the first time we met," I said, pulling out the chair.

"Why not meet at the Firehouse, then?"

"I wanted it to be just the two of us in the cabin. It's a special occasion. As I said on the phone, I think I have this whole thing thought out."

"I'm dying to hear it."

"I've got Chicken Parmesan for us, just like our first time together. I didn't want it then, but I do now."

"You dear thing. And is this what I think it is?" She pointed to the wine bottle, a palm over her luscious mouth.

"Yes. The Barn Red. Sorry, I don't have any merlot."

"Oh, Reed. I know it's important to you. Because of Peggy."

"Please," I said. "I want to think about you — about us — tonight." I wiggled out the cork and poured us both a glass. I circled to my chair, propped Citizen Cane on the edge, sat, and raised my glass for a toast.

"To happy endings," I said.

"And beginnings," she said.

We clicked glasses, sipped. We began with the endive salads, topped by olive and cheese shavings, and a tangy balsamic vinaigrette.

"Tell me: what beginnings did you have in mind just now?" I asked.

She brightened, and her burnished hair shimmered. "I have an interview Monday with the *Chicago Tribune*," she said, nearly giggling.

"You do?"

"They saw my stories about — well, you know — and asked me to come talk to them about an internship. It's the big break I've been hoping for."

"How about that," I said cheerfully. "That's just great. It's what you've always wanted more than anything else."

"I knew you'd understand, Reed." She swirled the wine. "Or are you disappointed? You sound disappointed. Are you?"

"No, I understand completely."

"You do?"

"Oh, sure. I know you've had your heart set on this for a long time."

"I really, really have. You know, if the story you tell me tonight wraps it up, there's time to get it into the Sunday edition of the *Observer*. I can bring a clip, and that'll get me in for sure. Just look at it this way — when you move back to Chicago, we'll live a lot closer."

"Sure," I said.

She told me more about the job. I refilled her glass, and then dished out the entree from steamy glass-covered bowls.

"OK, the main course, at last," she said eagerly. "I'm starving. Now, the other main course: tell me what you think you know."

"You might want to record this," I said.

"Oh, sure. Good idea." She reached down to her handbag, extracted her pocket-size recorder, clicked it on, and pressed the record button. "Test," she said, and the needle jumped. She set it next to the wine bottle.

"It's running?"

"Yes. Shoot," she said.

An unfortunate word. I tried to ignore it. "First, let's not talk about the issue of whether or not Father Ray could heal or not, or had the stigmata or not. That's a mystery, to be sure, but it speaks only to the timing of the death, not the manner or motive."

"Fair enough."

"Let's also put aside the question of Kenny's theft of wine from the vestry. That petty crime appears to be tertiary."

"Reed, the average person is not going to know a word like that."

"Literally, third in importance. But I mean it's a sideshow. Your speculation about cyanide, given the almond odor, was proven false by the toxicologist's report. Cyanide had nothing to do with it. Neither did Kenny."

"What caused the smell?"

"I'm setting that aside completely for now. It's off-focus. Moreover, the theft of pills from my cabin may also be inconsequential, a red herring, despite your speculations there as well."

"But what if —"

"No, it doesn't have any direct bearing on the matter. Ray was dead already. Had the theft occurred before his death, we might have wondered whether the thief used the stolen pills to kill Ray or delivered them to the person who did. But it was after the fact, and therefore irrelevant, despite your insistence that it has something to do with the murder."

"Well, then, why would someone take the pills but nothing else?"

"Let's not be concerned about that for now. More wine?"

"Aren't you having more, too?"

"I don't want it to go to my head," I said, pouring. "Not while I'm talking. So, now we know what we are *not* talking about."

"Right," she said. "It's really *who* that counts. So who done it, as they say?"

"Our man — so to speak — had to fulfill three conditions: he had to have access to warfarin. He had to have access to MAOIs, the same as mine. And he had to have regular access to Ray's circulatory system, either by injections or by food. And he might have known Ray was a hemophiliac — although that may *not* have been necessary."

"Why not? How else would he know about the possible reaction?"

"The warfarin and the MAOI medication would have affected a normal person the same way, Casey. The killer did not need to know

Ray was a hemophiliac. He didn't have to believe he actually was a stigmatic, either. As long as the public believed it, there remained a 'mystical' explanation for the death to possibly cover up the real reason." I pushed food around on my plate with the fork, sorting it methodically. "So the killer didn't need to know he was a hemophiliac, and he didn't need to believe he was stigmatic, but might have. All he really needed was access to the chemicals and regular access to Ray's bloodstream or his food supply."

"Regular access?"

"Sure. Regular, sustained, and unnoticed — to have both the substances build up in a predictable way over time. It couldn't have been a one-time action." I pointed with the fork to emphasize the last point, saying, "More than all this, our man had to have a strong will to do it, poisoning the food over and over again, and having a compelling motive to do so. As Aristotle says, *Men do not know a thing until they have grasped the 'why' of it.*"

"So we start with who had access to the substances. That could be anyone."

"True," I said, "especially with warfarin, commonly found in hardware stores and pharmacies, either in tasteless powder form or honey-flavored blocks. But MAOIs are harder to get, even online, and harder yet on such short notice in order to frame the new guy in town who has a prescription for them. Using them would not occur to anyone until I arrived. So it was someone who knew I was using them."

"Well, that begs the question, who knew?"

"No, it doesn't *beg the question*," I said. "You mean raises the question. To *beg the question* in rhetorical argument means to assume a proposition to be true without proving it."

"Whatever," she said, her mouth prim. "*Raises* the question. Go on, smart guy. Who knew?"

"Rashidi knew, since he had my records and renewed the prescription. And —"

"And his nurse."

"She had no physical connection to Ray. Neither did Manny Garcia, the EMT fascinated by Ray. He might have been opposed by Ray, or he saw Ray as a competitor, but he had no regular opportunities to invade his system. Rashidi did. Plus, he gave Ray injections, and as a confirmed skeptic, he was mortified by Ray's apparent raising of my brother. Moreover, the healings were hurting his business."

"Well, there you go. Now, how to prove it?"

"I'm not through. He didn't have *regular* access. Ray was injecting himself at home. The plasma was tamper-proof. And since he wasn't a professional, he left a few marks. Doctors and nurses with good hypos, steady hands and the good sense to use an alcohol swab right away don't leave tracks on the arm."

"How would you know that?"

"I've been in hospitals a lot, Case. I've seen my share of needles."

"So you're eliminating Rashidi that easily?"

"Let me finish. Now, to continue, Father Brian knew of my medication —"

"He did?"

"My brother mentioned it to Ray before my first visit, and Brian knew it. He regularly prepared the food in the rectory. And he seemed to be jealous of Ray, the mystic upstart."

"Works for me. Book him."

"But it isn't Brian, either. He had no ready access to MAOIs."

"By mail. Cheap drugs from Canada."

"Not enough time. As I said, the reaction required a gradual build-up."

"Express Mail."

"I think the police would have traced that by now."

She ladled out more sauce. "You haven't talked about Estrella Esperanza. She wanted him dead most of all, to have him put on the fast track to sainthood. Don't you remember how she threatened you?"

"She was warning me, that's for sure. But she wasn't the threat herself. Rather, the one who killed Lance Boyle was the real threat, and she was telling me to be careful. She was concerned that whoever killed Ray was also going to kill me for getting too close to the truth. Instead, that person killed Boyle, right after he clearly said he was close to breaking the case."

"So the person who killed Ray is the same one who killed Boyle? That makes sense."

"No, Casey. They were two different people."

"Oh, I get it," she said, brightening. "Boyle killed Ray, and Estrella got Boyle out of revenge. Maybe a Mexican blood-vengeance thing. So the case is closed on Ray. We need to prove Estrella killed Boyle."

"No again," I said. "There were two different people but working together."

"What?"

"The one who killed Ray had to have access to warfarin and MAOIs but also have a good motive. The pharmacist, Barnes, obviously had access, but no reason to kill Ray, as he said. In addition, he had no access to his food. But he had a good reason to kill Boyle. With a gun he had purchased as a security measure after a robbery last year."

"Are you saying the pharmacist killed Lance Boyle? Whatever for?"

"To protect his daughter."

She looked me dead in the eye.

"Yes, Casey. You. You told me you were divorced and you never wanted to talk about it. One reason is that you've kept your married name. I figure it's because all your published articles have Malone on them, and to revert to Barnes would confuse your resume. You've wanted more than anything else to get away from this town and your past, Casey Barnes. You told me that you deserve the inside story as the hometown girl."

She flushed. Her breathing became more rapid. "You're crazy, Reed. My divorce has nothing to do with this."

"When Dan said Ray was murdered — and who knows how he knew — you panicked. You asked him 'How do you know?' in a way

244

that was not disbelieving. You honestly thought he knew supernaturally, and you were greatly relieved when he couldn't name a culprit. Later, when I first started thinking this through, and you tried to divert me with the Kenny theory, your nervousness activated your perfume. When I made a joke about the pharmacist, you were offended. And I took notice when Detective Gordon said you knew the pharmacist's name and that he'd been here thirty years and you changed the subject. Fact is, you were born just after he arrived and you were baptized here as Casey Barnes. I checked with Father Brian. Those are public records. That's how you knew about the pharmaceuticals handbook, too, isn't it? And no wonder the librarian knew you, but didn't recognize your name at first when I said I was waiting for Casey Malone. She knew you growing up as Casey Barnes."

"So what? That doesn't prove I had anything to do with this. You're just guessing."

"You know it's true. You got the warfarin from the pharmacy and slipped away MAOIs from your father. You made sure that you personally served Ray his food in the fish fry every week, and you knew precisely what dosage to mix so it would build up over six weeks of Lent and react fatally at the right time, Holy Week. And you knew that by pinning this on me you'd get a great story of murder and miracles to advance your career and move beyond your past. Your father had the means, and through him, you did, too. But you're the one with the motive and opportunity to kill Ray, and to cover it up using me."

"You professors all think you're soooo smart," she said in a low growl. "You don't know a thing."

"The thing I really don't know," I said, "is why you'd go so far as to kill a decent man like Father Ray just for a news story. The miracle angle should have been enough. Something happened between you and him during your 120-day community service probation in the literacy program where you met him. What made you hate him, Casey? A failed romance?"

She guffawed. "He was a freakin' saint. No action there."

"Then it was the pill abuse you were arrested for and put on probation for. Did you steal those from your dad, by the way?"

"How dare you."

"You did. That's what got you in trouble the first time. It's how you learned to pilfer the MAOIs later by inventory tampering or prescription fraud when I conveniently showed up. And when you met Ray, you were still on the pills, weren't you, in violation of your probation? And Father Ray noticed. Teachers like us do. He confronted you, didn't he, and asked you to go to confession and get help in rehab. Your college chum Ashleigh told me at the fish fry that Ray helped you deal with a pain-pill problem after your divorce sent you into a depression."

"He didn't help me a bit," she spat. "I just made him think so."

"He wanted to help too much, didn't he? He rather liked the role of being the savior of young people in trouble —"

"And I told him that if he reported me to probation, I'd say I *did* confess to him and he was violating his confessional vows. That shut him up."

"But you decided to shut him up for good. Why?"

"He kept *pushing* me," she snarled, her sharp white teeth showing. "Said he was gonna tell anyway. *Who are they going to believe, Casey?* he said. He made me do it."

"Lance Boyle almost exposed you, thinking it would also expose Ray as a hoax, didn't he? Boyle said within your dad's hearing that he was close to figuring out the whole scheme, and pointed at *him* when I first thought he was pointing at *me*. So your dad killed Boyle to protect you. That was him telling you so on the phone when I was there sleeping on your couch, wasn't it? You didn't get the news from a police scanner, like you usually do."

"You're dreaming."

"You want to protect him now, as he protected you. He knew what you'd done after the inquest, and decided to cover up for you. Like you, he decided I'd take the fall for this. You certainly weren't very eager to get me off the hook when Gordon questioned me about Boyle's death."

"Of course not, you dip. That can be pinned on you, too. You couldn't account for the time. And if you turned up dead next, it'd look like a suicide of a guilty man."

She swilled the wine. Pushed away from the table. Smoothed her skirt. Stood.

"You know, a suicide would be just the right ending to the story, don't you think?" she said.

I put down my fork and knife. It might be useful as a weapon, but I was no match for her. "What do you mean?" I asked. My knees shuddered. Maybe this wasn't such a good idea.

Casey reached across the table and snapped off the digital recorder. "Maybe you hoped I'd forget this was on," she said. "I'm not stupid."

She plucked the cane from the table's edge. She hefted it. Gripped it like a baseball bat.

"Now, wait a minute, Case, you don't want to do anything that will —"

She swung it against my hip. The brass tip crunched into bone. I screamed and toppled in agony to the floor. The chair tumbled behind me.

"Oh, dear," Casey said in mock dismay. "Look, everyone. He hit his hip and head in a fall after his meds took effect when he tried to overdose in remorse."

"Casey, you'd better think about this," I said between gritted teeth.

"I've already done that," she said coolly. "This will be rich. Just the story I wanted. A saint and a suicide, just like Christ and his pal Judas who felt cheated out of something he deserved. So he betrayed his friend, and then killed himself."

"The police will find out you were here," I said.

"Shut up," she said. She swung the cane in a high arc; it smashed into my hip again. Pain sizzled through my spine. I inhaled sharply.

"The whole damn town knows I come here," she said with a curl in her lip. "We're the talk of the taverns. Small-town girl with the older, mature professor from the city. One of those May-November romances. Trying to do you some good, now that you're in trouble. That's our Casey. This time, the gossip will be: it's a good thing you invited me here for dinner and I found you like this. Tried to save you. Too late. Called 911. Well, Casey, it looks like you solved the mystery, they'll tell me."

She raised the cane for another blow. The brass handle flashed.

"There's one mystery left," I said.

"What's that?"

"Why you led me on. Sought my company."

"To keep an eye on you," she said. "To make sure you and everyone else kept guessing the wrong thing. And you know the funny thing? I actually started to like you. I started to feel guilty for leading you on. I wanted to make it up to you somehow, and that offer last night was for real. But you rejected me, you dumb hunk. What s'ammata — can't get it up?" She tilted her head to laugh, and her knee buckled. She caught her balance. She steadied herself with the cane.

It was working.

She shook her head. "What the hell?"

"Was he for real, Casey? I've got to know."

"I don't feel so good," she said.

"Was he? Was he a stigmatic? Could he heal?"

"You bastard." She tried to step forward, but staggered back, her hand to her head, her breathing rapid and shallow. "You put some in my food," she said, wobbly. "Didn't you?"

"Yes, quite a bit. It won't kill you. It's reacting with the red wine, the salad dressing, the olives, the sauce, the cheese —"

"But you had some, too —"

"I took the antidote before you arrived. It's called ProCardin."

Casey stumbled against the table, grabbing the edge. She tottered back, dragging off her napkin with the fork and knife. They clanged on the floor. Her cheeks turned a hot red; her watery eyes blinked away the dizziness. "You still can't prove a thing," she huffed, shaking the cane at me. "You'll still be the one arrested, you paranoid, for trying to poison me, just like you poisoned Ray. This — this just proves your guilt. Sure. That's the story. I was about to expose you, and you — you tried to kill me by slipping your pills into my food, like you did with Ray. I still win, you idiot."

"They'll just have to take my word for it — by faith," I said.

Casey's knees gave way, and she crumpled unconscious to the planks with a dull thump. Citizen Cane clattered from her hand and struck my forearm. She lay immobile, her breathing slow and ragged.

I lifted my wristwatch to check the time. My hip screamed. It wasn't broken, but even with the cane, I wasn't going to get off the floor without help. I withdrew my cell phone from my jacket pocket. I took a deep breath. Then another. "This is Reed Stubblefield," I called aloud to re-activate the VoiceWare on the laptop. I hoped it had picked up everything else. My eyes pinched in pain. "Casey Barnes Malone has just passed out on the floor of my cabin, the effect of my medications reacting to her dinner. It is 8:22 p.m. She'll be fine, except for a God-awful headache. I'm calling the police now."

"No, you're not."

I opened my eyes.

She struggled up to all fours.

"I won't — let you," she growled.

She pulled a 9mm pistol from her jacket pocket.

"I hoped — I hoped I wouldn't need this," she hissed.

She took aim, the eyes glazed, the hand shaky.

I stared down the barrel. My breath rushed from my lungs. "Casey, no —"

She fired.

I threw my head back. The phone went flying.

She fell to one elbow. It crunched into the floor, and she cursed.

She regained her balance, shaking her head to clear it.

She lifted the gun again and stopped short once she saw Citizen Cane clutched in my raised fist.

"You wouldn't," she said.

I slammed it into her ear. The pistol barked and spun across the room. She twisted away, the golden hair fanning in an arc.

Her limp body sprawled, unmoving, on the braided rug.

I dropped the cane and fell back to my elbows, wincing, my neck soaked in sweat. I wiped it away. Looked at my hand.

It was covered in blood.

She hadn't missed.

My palm flew to my neck. It made a splat. Oh, no. No. My life was pumping out between my fingers, spurting with each heartbeat. I didn't feel it. Shock.

The phone.

Out of reach.

No way to get it — not with the bleeding, not with the hip. No one near to help. *No one —*

I'll be praying for you.

Peggy —

I'll ask God to send someone to you.

Peggy, help — Ray — Jesus, somebody.

The thunder answered.

Don't end like this. This is how it started. Don't pass out —

Don't —

Omigod!

She's got a gun!

Look out!

Bang.

Bang.

Mr. Stubblefield!

Are you OK?

Mr. Stubblefield!

¡Madre de Dios!

A bronze angel knelt beside me.

Stripped off her jacket.

"You're going to be all right," she said, pressing the folded cloth to my neck.

"You're —"

"Don't talk now," Selena de la Cruz said. She pulled a phone from her belt holster and thumbed 911.

"I —"

"Not now. Just lie still. We'll discuss your policy later."

CHAPTER 31

"In Aristotle's theory of drama," Father Ray said, "the audience experiences a restoration of order, a renewal of emotional equilibrium, a return to balance caused by the purging of extreme emotions. Thus, in the same way that a physician of Aristotle's day purged the ill 'humors' of a sick man through bleeding in order to restore the balance of fluids in the body and bring about healing physically, the dramatist seeks to drain an audience emotionally, to draw out their fears of death and misery, to exhaust their pity for a victim, and thereby be healed psychologically."

"So why don't I feel healed?" I asked, sliding the stapled papers back in the manila envelope.

Estrella Esperanza shook her indigo hair. "It is God alone who works the miracles of healing," she said. She turned to Dan, as though demonstrating Exhibit A. "But some are chosen as his vessels, and he does the work in the name of the servant who makes himself available."

"And Ray was one of them?" I asked.

"*Si, creo que si*, Mr. Reed. I believe it. But it is for His Excellency the bishop to say."

"And Father DeMarco."

"And the Congregation of the Saints in Rome," she said. "Even then, it is not forced upon anyone to believe. No one is made to say a miracle has happened — or has not. The miracle of faith itself, for most people, is enough. It is a deep mystery."

"At least some mysteries get solved," I said.

"What's the latest word from the police?" Dan asked.

I sighed one of those here-we-go-again sighs. "The gun belonged to Mr. Barnes, as I thought. He got it after the store robbery last year and used it to kill Boyle. Then he drove Boyle's car, with Boyle in it, to the river and walked back to town. He phoned Casey in the morning to tell her what happened. Casey then brought the gun to the cabin, intending to plant it somewhere as further evidence against me. Actually using it was an unplanned split-second act of desperation."

"She woulda wiped off her prints and put it in your hand, you know," Dan said, "to prove that the guilty guy shot himself. I've seen it on TV a lot."

I knew Dan was right, and I quaked. "Anyway, Detective Gordon wants another sworn statement from me so they can build their case. Casey may have confessed in the cabin, and the police have her words and the scuffle on a CD, thanks to the VoiceWare, but it might not hold up in court."

"You're just lucky she didn't turn off the laptop, too," Dan said.

"I never told her about the VoiceWare on it," I said. "She didn't even notice it. It was sitting on the desk as it always does."

"They pick up the pharmacist yet?" Dan inquired.

"Detained and cooperating, so they say. But he's on a suicide watch. A pharmacist knows a hundred ways to do himself in."

Bad men are full of repentance, Aristotle noted.

"Did they catch the punks who messed up the cabin?" Dan asked.

"I did," Estrella said, her dark eyes lowered. "I mean, I did not *do* it. But I catch the ones who trouble you. This is why I was following you that night, Mr. Reed. I learn of the trouble too late to stop them, but I want to say that night, to say to you, be careful for the ones who acted in anger and caused you the fright. They are very sorry. I said it displeased Father Ray very much to hurt his friend. I wanted to apologize to you for them, but that Mr. Barnes, he make me go out. Now we see why."

"Didn't you tell the police yet?" I asked.

"I cannot," she said, the creases in her eyes deepening. "They are not legal in the country. They will be sent away, deported, and it will be very bad for them and their families. So I cannot. This is why I asked you not to ask too many questions. You must not tell, for the love of God."

"Why did they take the pills?"

"*Mira*, medicines of any kind, they can be hard to get, expensive," she said. "They take now, decide if they are useful later. They are not."

"Why didn't they take my laptop?"

"Bianca, she has no use for it. Easy for the police to find, too." She sucked in her breath, squeezed her eyes. "Oh, do not tell anyone I said this," she beseeched me, her weathered hands knit prayerfully. "She meant good. She is only a child."

"You won't report this, will you, Reed?" Dan asked.

In most things, the error is made to achieve what appears to be a good when it is not, Aristotle said.

I let the indignation pass through me, and then shook it from my fingertips. "No, I won't tell."

"*Gracias,* Mr. Reed, thank you. You are a good man," Estrella said, crossing herself. "Father Ray, he is well pleased with you and will grant you a favor. I know he will, *señor.*"

I smiled, grateful, but unsure. Her kind intention assumed, of course, that Ray was still alive in some other state of being, and aware of our conversation and requests. If Ray was praying for me, I thought, then he surely had been interceding during my dinner showdown with Casey. It was, perhaps, the only logical explanation for why Selena de la Cruz showed up.

So — if Ray could hear me now, I only had one more favor, one more question to ask: was my Peggy all right? Did suffering count for anything in the end? If we merely decayed into oblivion, it did not. Is that all that becomes of our humanity, our personhood? *Hey, if there's no Easter, what's the point?*

I had to laugh at myself. I was starting to sound like Ray.

"Reed? You don't need to ask Ray for anything right now."

"Sorry, Dan," I said. I unfolded my hands.

"What about your insurance, little brother? Hear anything yet?"

"Ms. de la Cruz told me she'd found I had a supplemental health rider with the disability coverage, and she wanted me to know right away in person, as she promised."

"So — she saved your neck," Dan quipped.

I fingered my bandaged neck. It hadn't been as bad as first feared. "She did," I said. "So the money is on the way. But Rashidi said he'd pull some strings, too, if the adjustors needed more convincing about my condition. Oh, and speaking of Rashidi, Danny," I added, "he wants to keep you here and study your brain. He needs your consent."

"Don't kid me, Reed."

"It's God's truth," I said. "He wants to figure out what happened to you. It puzzles him to no end. He told me there's probably a paper in it for him that he can deliver at the next AMA convention. He'll make his HMO proud, even if they are closing his clinic."

"But I won't have to stay here in the hospital for that, will I?" Dan asked with his forehead furrowed.

"I doubt it," I said. "We can stay in the cabin for the summer."

He sighed, relieved.

"Unless," I added, "I take up Rashidi's suggestion to get a titanium hip replacement as Jack Nicklaus did. He said he'd do it himself."

"It won't improve your golf game, you know," Dan said with a smirk. "But with all the fuss over, you can use the recovery time to finish writing your book on what's his name — Aristotle."

"Good thinking. I will," I said.

This is the book, by the way.

"I gotta go, Danny-boy," I said, punching his shoulder. "Oh, and now that you're on the mend, please don't pick up any nurses; there's room for only the two of us in the cabin."

He blushed. Estrella covered her lipsticked mouth in a mock gesture of shock, but her eyes twinkled at the jest. She took Dan's hand, and their fingers intertwined. I decided not to comment. *Love is a mystery.*

"There is one more thing," I said at the door. "The smell of vanilla and almonds, when Ray died. They say it is the odor of sanctity. What was it?"

"The aroma of Christ that the blessed Paul speaks of, it is humility, gentleness, kindness, and mercy," Estrella said. "But it is a popular perfume with young *Latinas* these days."

I grinned. "God bless you," I said, and wondered where that came from. "See ya tomorrow, OK, Dan?" I pivoted and walked out.

At the end of the hall, I pressed the elevator button. It hummed to life. Dan and Estrella, I thought with an amused shake of my head. Who would've guessed? I thought of the first time I took Casey's hand, and the hope I had grasped with it. But perhaps Hesiod was right. In his *Theogony*, the story of human origins, Zeus invites all the gods and goddesses of the pantheon to construct a woman in order to punish men for stealing his fire. Haephestus gave her a gorgeous face and a feline figure, Aphrodite donated painful desire, the Seasons fashioned her golden hair, and Hermes put in her breast wheedling words and a cheating heart. Alluring on the outside, Pandora was worthless inside, assigned by the divinities to break men's hearts.

That was Casey, all right.

Even so, Hope remained — trapped under the box's lid, as it were. Selena de la Cruz was waiting downstairs for our dinner date to discuss my college contract buy-out and a rollover into one of her company's annuity plans. Who knew? Something else might come of it.

You'll meet someone, Peggy said. *I know it.*

A candy striper, pushing a wheelchaired woman with her leg elevated, rolled to the door. The woman was dressed to go home. And from the nearest room a child's high-pitched laughter broke the dialog of a daytime hospital television drama.

I took a breath. Once outside, I'd leave the odor of antiseptics and the whisper of oxygen tanks behind and instead smell honey locusts scenting the air, sprinkled by flecks of ivory petals blown by the first breeze of summer. I looked forward to it.

For the first time in a long while, I looked forward, period. What else could I do?

Only one thing is denied to God, Aristotle said: *the power to undo the past.*

Aristotle was wrong about women. He could be wrong about that, too.

The elevator doors shooshed open.

"Mr. Reed! Mr. Reed?"

Estrella called to me from down the hall, waving.

"Wait, Mr. Reed, *por favor*! You forget something!"

She jogged down the hallway, breathless.

I felt for my keys, my wallet, my phone. All there.

She stretched out her arm, beaming.

She handed me Citizen Cane.

Epilogomena

A bruised reed he shall not break,
And a smoldering wick he will not quench,
Until he establishes justice on the Earth.
— Isaiah 42:3, 4

ABOUT THE AUTHOR

A former producer with Wisconsin Public Radio, John teaches journalism and English at Kishwaukee College in northern Illinois. His first novel, *The Throne of Tara* (Crossway, 1990), was a Christianity Today Readers Choice Award nominee, and his second historical novel, *Relics* (Thomas Nelson, 1993, 2009) was a Doubleday Book Club Selection. *Bleeder* is his first mystery. His work has appeared in a wide variety of Christian and secular journals, ranging from *The Critic* to *Apocalypse* to the *Rockford Review*. In 1997, he took Honorable Mention in the Writers Digest Competition. He holds an MA in Media from Columbia University and an MA in Writing from Illinois State University. A member of The Academy of American Poets and Mystery Writers of America, he is listed in *Contemporary Authors, Who's Who in Entertainment,* and *Who's Who Among America's Teachers.*

John can be reached at jjdesjarlais@johndesjarlais.com or at www.johndesjarlais.com

Chisel & Cross books are works of popular fiction by contemporary (and sometimes first-time) Catholic authors. Among them are thrillers, mysteries, fantasies, historical novels, teen books, science fiction, and even romance novels. Each is a tale well told, and each has a strong Catholic sensibility.

By means of *Chisel & Cross Books*, we at Sophia Institute Press® seek to help rejuvenate Catholic literature in our day by giving voice to novice writers and a wide readership to veteran Catholic authors more practiced in their art.

Sophia Institute Press®

Sophia Institute® is a nonprofit institution that seeks to restore man's knowledge of eternal truth, including man's knowledge of his own nature, his relation to other persons, and his relation to God. Sophia Institute Press® serves this end in numerous ways: it publishes translations of foreign works to make them accessible for the first time to English-speaking readers; it brings out-of-print books back into print; and it publishes important new books that fulfill the ideals of Sophia Institute®. These books afford readers a rich source of the enduring wisdom of mankind.

For your free catalog, call:
Toll-free: 1-800-888-9344
or write:
Sophia Institute Press®
Box 5284, Manchester, NH 03108
or visit our website:
www.SophiaInstitute.com